In the wake of a devastating attack by a rogue coven of vampires, hunter-turned-werewolf Ileana returns to the ruins of her family home. Believing her sister, Tamara, survived the attack, Ileana seeks the help of Liviu, the werewolf who turned her, and Evdochia, a hauntingly powerful vampire descended from Vlad Țepeș himself.

The attack is the first strike in a looming war threatening the fragile truce between humans and mythical nightwalkers. With time slipping away and danger closing in from all sides, Ileana and her allies must race to find Ravenswatch, the ancient fortress where the vampire coven is preparing to strike again.

THE RIVERS WILL RUN RED

House of Drăculeşti, Book One

Keira North

A NineStar Press Publication
www.ninestarpress.com

The Rivers Will Run Red

© 2025 Keira North
Cover Art © 2025 Patricia Lan-Anh Duong
Edited by BJ Toth

First Edition, July 2025

ISBN: 978-1-64890-880-4
Also available in eBook, ISBN: 978-1-64890-879-8

CONTENT WARNING:
Depictions of alcoholism, anxiety/depression, abuse of family member, death of a child (off-page), death of a prominent character, graphic violence/gore, guns/gun violence, grief, hate groups/speech, incarceration, non-consent (kissing), past trauma, suicidal ideation, suicide attempt, and terminal illness.

To Dad

Names and Pronunciation Guide

Most of the names in this book are either Romanian or Hungarian. While Romanian is the official language in Romania, many ethnic Hungarians live in the country's central and western counties, along with Saxons, Serbs, Germans, and other peoples.

ARGHIRA
Pronounced *ar-GHEE-rah*.
Medieval Romanian name.

BISTRIȚA
Pronounced BEES-tri-tsa.
Town in north-eastern Transylvania, named for a river that runs through the region.

CRIN
Pronounced *CREEN* with a hard R.
Romanian name that means "lily flower."

DARIUS
Pronounced *DAH-ree-oos.*
Persian name that has been adopted by Romanian culture as well. Unlike the Anglicized pronunciation, Romanians say it with a flat *ah*, like in *bard.*

DEVA
Pronounced *DEH*-va, with a hard V.
Romanian town in the region of Ardeal, near Transylvania, famous for the ruins of a medieval citadel at the top of a hill overlooking the town.

EVDOCHIA
Pronounced *ev-DOH-kee-yah*, with an *e* as in "ever."
Old Romanian name that was popular in the Middle Ages. St. Evdochia the Martyr is celebrated in the Romanian Orthodox calendar every year on March 1st, which is also Mărţişor, a traditional celebration of spring.

GORUN
Pronounced *GOH-roon.*
Town in north-eastern Transylvania. The name means "sessile oak."

IANCU
Pronounced *YAN-koo.*
A Latin derivate of the name Ion (the Romanian variant of John). Several rulers and prominent figures in Romanian history share this name, among them Iancu de Hunedoara (also known as Ioannes Corvinus), a Transylvanian *voievod*, and Avram Iancu, a 19th century revolutionary.

ILEANA
Pronounced *Ee-LEE-ah-nah*.
Traditionally, fair maidens and princesses in Romanian folktales were named Ileana Cosânzeana, which means "Ileana with the golden hair."

JÓZSEF
Pronounced *YO-zhehf*.
This is a common name among ethnic Hungarians in Transylvania. The nickname *JÓSKA* is pronounced *YOSH-kah*.

LIVIU
Pronounced LEE-vee-uh. His full name, Liviu Lupu, translates as "Liviu the Wolf."
Lupu is a relatively common Romanian last name, as are other animal-inspired surnames: Vulpe ("the Fox"), Ursu ("the Bear"), etc.

ORĂŞTIE
Pronounced *o-RUSH-tee-ay*.
Small town in western Transylvania.

SPINI
Pronounced *SPEEN*, with a slight ñ sound at the end.
Village in western Transylvania.

TAMARA
Pronounced *Tah-MAH-rah*.
This Hebrew and Russian feminine name is also encountered in Romania. The popular folk-rock band Phoenix wrote a song called *Tamara* about a woman who waits for her lost love to return.

Chapter One

Girl Who Cried Wolf

"When the blood moon rises, beware of the pricolici."
— From the wisdom of werewolf hunters in Crişana-
Banat

"It's here, I swear," Luca said. "Just a little farther."

With a small nod, Ileana said, "Uh-huh."

Her companion couldn't see that, of course. He was already charging ahead through the underbrush, so she had no choice but to follow, pulling her ratty cardigan tighter around her bony shoulders. She was all of thirteen and outgrowing her old clothes faster than she could get new hand-me-downs. Whatever survived her nightly escapades usually found its way to her younger sister, Tamara, much to the latter's chagrin.

Luca didn't need to worry about the cold. He wore a thick, fur-padded coat that molded perfectly to his slim body. A boy of fifteen, more nimble than strong and taller than Ileana by a head, his hair was wheat-colored and unruly, and he had piercing blue eyes and thick brows that made him look like he was always frowning. Ileana felt a strange flutter in her stomach whenever he looked her way. She *wanted* him to look at her but also not, and she found the whole thing equal parts vexing and confusing.

Luca was already blooded too. On a family hunting trip to the southern reaches of Oltenia, he'd found and killed a *moroi*, a risen dead who'd been walking around for so long it was more bone than corpse. Luca talked about it like he'd offed the great Impaler himself. Still, his one kill trumped Ileana's none.

Despite the full moon crossing the night sky somewhere above, the jumble of branches overhead cast a dense shroud over the sodden, uneven ground. Where Luca moved with the sure step of a journeyman hunter, Ileana had to stop and feel her way around tree stumps and patches of half-melted snow, pushing her long bangs out of her face every other step. Her hair was a dark, muddy brown in the sunlight. Here, under the canopy, it was black, and thick, and *annoying*.

"C'mon!" Luca shouted from somewhere ahead.

She walked faster, or at least as fast as her skinny legs could carry her. Where Luca was growing like a weed, Ileana was more of the short persuasion. *For now,* she'd tell herself whenever she looked in the mirror, standing on tiptoe and tilting her chin up.

A soft patch of earth gave way under her foot. With a startled yell, she fell forward, arms flailing in search of something to stop her fall. She felt a sting across the back of her right hand when she scraped it against the rough bark of a tree, but at least she'd stopped herself before she tumbled forward and scraped her knees too. Tears prickled at the corners of her eyes, swiftly followed by shame. She sniffled and bit her lower lip. Cradling her injured hand with her good one, she scurried ahead.

Soon, the trees dwindled away and the ground sloped gently downward toward a small pond, its ragged edges obscured by a dense thicket of cattails and pickerel weeds. With nothing to blot it out, the moon shone bright, its light tracing sparkling ripples across the water.

Pretty, Ileana thought.

And then, stealing a glance at her companion, *He's pretty too.*

Luca was waiting for her by the water, toying with his hunting knife, his hair shimmering like threads of spun gold. He caught her eye and grinned wide, tossing the knife up in the air. He caught it by the tip, then tossed it again, catching it by the handle this time. The blade flashed in the moonlight. It looked like silver. *Good for werewolves and basilisks*, Ileana's mind supplied, a rote response. She had her own knife stashed away in her boot, but the blade was steel, not silver. She rarely parted with it these days. Like a *real* hunter.

"Over there," Luca said, turning away from her to wave his hand toward whatever they'd come here to find.

Ileana turned to follow the line of his finger to where he was pointing. She spotted a storm drain on the other side of the pond, an old, battered thing with bits of rebar poking through the crumbling concrete. She'd ventured inside a few times over the years. The way was barred by a sturdy metal grill some twenty paces in, but that hadn't stopped her from pretending she was descending deep into another realm in search of glimmering treasure and forbidden magick. That was all make-believe, though, and she was done with it now that she was well on her way to being a grown-up. Hunters didn't waste their time with make-believe. They found it, and they killed it.

"What's there?" she asked.

"It's a wolf," the boy said, "and I'm gonna kill it."

A gust of wind tickled them from the side, poking through Ileana's cardigan and the flimsy shirt underneath. She stuck her hands deep into her pockets, hissing as the wound on the back of her hand scraped against the rough fabric.

"*A* wolf?" she said, her eyes flicking back to the drain. "Just the one?"

"Maybe it got lost, I dunno."

"So how do you know it's a wolf?" Ileana pressed. "It could be just a stray dog or—"

"Because I saw it, all right? Earlier, when I was..." The boy's face twisted in a scowl that was more comical than angry.

"When you were, what?"

"Gramma sent me looking for frogs again." He shuffled his foot.

Ileana snorted a laugh. "So, the mighty hunter went out to whack some toads with a stick. How'd you fare on *that* perilous adventure?"

"They taste good, okay? And, and anyway, that's not—it doesn't *matter*. I *know* there's a wolf in there, and I'm gonna kill it and make something from its pelt."

"You're going to kill the wolf with a knife?" Ileana said, her left eyebrow quirking higher than the right one. "They're stronger than humans, y'know. Faster too."

"Don't be stupid, Leana. *This* is what I'm gonna kill it with." Speaking, Luca pulled aside his woolen coat enough to show her the revolver tucked into his waistband.

Ileana had seen that gun before, on an ornate plaque above

the mantelpiece in Luca's ancestral home on the other side of the hill. She'd asked one of her cousins to hold her up so she could look at it once, when she was smaller, and she remembered it clearly. The grip was silver with intricate bone inlays, a relic of a time when craftsmanship was still a thing. Luca's family could trace their lineage all the way back to Aron Vulpe—Aron the Fox— the famed hunter who'd driven the vampires of the Ţepeş clan from the hillsides of Crişana-Banat and into the far reaches of the Carpathian Mountains. Three hundred years later, their coffers still ran deep.

"Does your dad know you took that?" she asked, a hint of un- ease tinging her words. She'd seen the bruises on the boy's face and wrists more than once.

He flashed her another grin. "I'll have it back before he knows it's gone. And you're not gonna tell on me, yeah?"

"Maybe I won't, if you ask me nice." The thought hadn't even crossed her mind, but Luca didn't need to know that.

He pursed his lips. "If you're gonna be like that, you can go home already."

"But I already know," Ileana said smugly.

"Then I'll—I'll make you something nice from its pelt, how about that?"

"I'll kill my own," she said, sweet as it was to think about get- ting a gift from him. "Or maybe I'll kill a werewolf and take its pelt. And I won't do it with some rusty old gun."

He scoffed, looking her over. "Yeah, right. Maybe in a year or two."

Ileana bristled at that. Every night, when her family went to sleep, she snuck out into the woods behind her home, Nightshade Lodge, and hacked and slashed until her arms grew so tired she couldn't raise them anymore, practicing her knife throwing and fending off imaginary beasts. And she was getting good, she could tell.

That was where Luca had found her earlier tonight. "I wanna show you something," he'd told her, and she'd let him talk her into coming along. Mostly because there was something about him that made her want to punch him in his stupidly handsome face and then kiss it all better. Not that she'd ever kissed anyone before, but she'd read about it in a book, and it didn't sound all that bad.

The object of her secret thoughts snapped his fingers right under her nose, yanking her back into the present with a startled, "Huh?"

"I said, I'm going. You can stay here if you're scared."

"Pfft. I'm not scared. But," she said after a moment, "are you sure—"

"Good. Let's go." He started ahead without waiting to hear the rest of the objection.

They circled around the pond, squelching through the shallow mud. Cold water seeped into Ileana's right boot, which had a sizable crack snaking its way across the sole. She sniffed and stomped her foot a little harder. *You won't get the best of me, boot.*

The storm drain gaped ahead of them, gray concrete melting away into a pool of darkness that stretched well beyond where the eye could see. The ground in front of it was rocky and didn't carry any tracks, so Ileana couldn't tell what, if anything, had gone inside.

A shiver stole over her. That didn't mean there wasn't anything there.

Luca stopped a few steps away from the mouth of the drain and pulled the revolver from his waistband. She watched him open the cylinder to check that it was loaded. He nodded to himself and snapped the cylinder shut, then spun it for good measure.

He looked like he knew what he was doing. Still, Ileana asked, "Are those silver bullets?"

Luca gave her a genuinely puzzled look. "No, what for?"

He knew what he was doing...right?

The wind picked up again, nudging them from behind this time. Ileana pushed her bangs out of her face and shivered, clenching her jaw so her teeth wouldn't chatter. She almost started to say something—*This was a bad idea, Luca. Let's go back.*—when something stirred deep inside the concrete tunnel, and all thought of words vanished from her mind.

"What'd I tell you? There it is," Luca whispered, pointing with his revolver.

A deep growl rumbled from the darkness, bouncing off the concrete walls.

Ileana froze, an icy terror spreading from her core into her limbs.

"Luca," she whispered, pushing the name past the sudden dryness in her throat. "That didn't sound like a wolf."

"You don't know what you're talking about," the boy said, although he, too, looked a little paler in the moonlight. "Stay behind me, okay? If it tries to come at us, I'll just shoot it."

The growling continued, and with it came the sound of sharp claws scraping against the gravel. If this was a wolf, it must have been a big one. Was it just her own apprehension, or did it sound like it was getting closer?

"Gimme a rock. I'm gonna draw it out," Luca said. The barrel of his revolver trembled slightly, but his voice was steady.

"Luca, I don't think—"

"*Fine.* I'll do it." He bent down, groping around in the near-dark but never taking his eyes off the drain and whatever lurked in it.

Ileana took a step back. She chanced a look over her shoulder and saw that the moon was starting to dip below the jagged tree line. Soon, they wouldn't be able to see at all, let alone find their way back.

"There we go," Luca was mumbling as he straightened up, clutching something in his fist.

"Wait," Ileana said. "The moon—"

"Would you shut up!"

The moon was full and tainted red around the edges.

When the blood moon rises, beware of the pricolici. It was an old hunter saying, older than Ileana's father's father and passed on to him from hunters whose line stretched back hundreds of years. *Pricolici* was an old name that no one used anymore. These days, people called them werewolves.

Luca pulled his arm back, then flung the rock into the darkness with all his might. A sharp yelp answered him.

"That's right," he said, and then he licked his lips. He bent to look for another rock.

A monstrous figure exploded from the drain and barreled, howling, into him. Its fur was long and shaggy, it walked on two legs, and it was much, much bigger than a wolf.

The force of the impact sent Luca and the beast tumbling into the shallows in a tangle of fangs and limbs and fur. A single shot rang out, echoing across the water. The werewolf let out a guttural whimper but didn't relent, its snarls and growls mingling with the boy's desperate breaths.

"Leana!" Luca screamed, his voice fraying with terror.

Ileana stumbled back a step, one hand flying up to her chest, where her heart was threatening to burst out of her ribcage.

"Help me! *Leana!*"

She ran.

Behind her, a bloodcurdling shriek pierced the night, cut short by a crunch so raw she felt it in her teeth. She stumbled forward, catching herself on a branch that cut across the path, then ducked under it and bolted back to the relative safety of the forest.

The werewolf let out a deep, primal howl that seemed to reverberate all around her, squeezing the breath from her lungs. She whimpered and willed her feet to carry her faster. Her eyes blurred, but she wiped them with the back of her uninjured hand, banishing the tears for later, when she was safe. Her cardigan caught on a branch. She yanked at it but couldn't pull it free, so she shrugged it off and kept going, hugging herself against the biting wind. She stumbled and fell, got up and kept going. *Help me,* she thought, desperately. *Someone, please—*

Her boot caught on a sharp rock half-buried in the damp soil. She hit the ground hard this time, catching herself on her injured hand. The pain was a sharp, bright thing, screaming up her wrist.

Get up.

Her body wouldn't move.

"Get *up*," she told herself, grinding the words out through her teeth. Slowly, she pushed herself to one knee, taking long, purposeful breaths: in-one-two, out-one-two...

She knew these woods, she just had to get her bearings. The pond was behind her and the ground was at an angle, so she'd been running uphill; no wonder she was out of breath. Nightshade Lodge nestled halfway down the hill, but she couldn't go back that way. There was a road farther up, coiling its way around the hill toward the ruins of a medieval citadel. If she could get to the road, then maybe she could trace it one way or the other. Maybe the werewolf wasn't even chasing her anymore. Maybe—she bit back a sob, thinking, *Luca is dead, he's dead*—the beast would be content with just one kill.

With a stifled whimper, she clambered to her feet. She straightened up, wincing at the feel of cuts and bruises blossoming across her skin.

"It's okay," she whispered, hugging herself tightly. "It's okay."

Pain surged up her ankle the moment she put weight on it.

Black spots danced in the corners of her vision, and a wave of nausea swept over her, roiling her stomach and pushing bile up her throat. She took a deep breath through her nose, then swallowed hard. When she looked up again, she thought she saw a pair of headlights peeking through the trees.

The brittle snap of a twig pierced the stillness, trailed by the contended growl of a predator closing in on the kill.

Ileana lurched forward, one faltering step after another. Her body was a mess of throbbing aches: ankle, knees, hand, wrist. It wouldn't be long before her legs gave out from under her, and then the beast would catch up and there'd be nothing left of her to find come morning.

The road. Must get to it, she thought, tears streaking down her grimy face.

The werewolf's howl pierced the night, desperately close.

Ileana didn't think. She ran.

She made it half a dozen steps before the brush ahead of her rustled, then something darker than the night erupted at her. Faster than she could comprehend, she found herself pinned down and staring into the beast's maw, its white fangs gleaming below a pair of eyes that burned like molten amber. Pain crackled across the back of her skull, sharp and immediate. The beast was on top of her, its crushing weight bearing down. Claws dug into her shoulder as the werewolf tightened its grip, holding her in place. It threw back its head, keening its conquest.

Through the haze of panic clouding her thoughts, Ileana

remembered the knife.

She twisted her leg until she could just about touch the collar of her boot. The knife was still in its sheath just below it, flush against her calf. Her fingers brushed against the bone handle. *Just a little more...*

With a grunt, she pulled the knife free just as the werewolf shifted its grip, likely preparing for the kill. She thrust the blade upward and was rewarded with a sudden spray of something warm and sticky that stung her eyes and tasted coppery on her tongue. She slashed at the beast blindly, again and again, her lungs burning with every labored breath. She might have been screaming; she didn't know.

Teeth, too sharp and too long, clamped down on her wrist, piercing skin and flesh. The knife slipped from her suddenly numb fingers as the renewed onslaught of pain brought with it a chilling flash of clarity.

This is it. This is how I die.

She hoped it would be quick.

The sharp crack of a revolver promptly dissuaded her of that notion. At first she thought, stupidly, that Luca was coming back for her. But, no, that couldn't be right. Luca was dead.

The werewolf released her wrist to snap its teeth toward its unseen assailant. A second shot made the beast shudder and whine. Its weight shifted, then disappeared altogether.

Ileana curled up on her side, cradling her injured arm close to her chest as two more shots came in quick succession. The werewolf's fading yelps amidst a crash of brambles told her the beast was in full retreat, but her own ragged breathing was so loud it was hard to be sure. Her tears fell freely now, mingling with the damp soil beneath her cheek.

The rhythmic cadence of a heavy step shook the earth,

drawing steadily closer. A heavy hand fell on her shoulder. She squeezed her eyes shut, but the hand was soft, and the fingers ended in blunt nails rather than claws.

Ileana turned her head just enough to glimpse the face of her savior through her tear-misted lashes: a bear of a man, his face shrouded in darkness. He smelled faintly of stale cigarettes and moonshine and wore a leather jacket that creaked as he bent down to look at her.

"Shit," the man said under his breath.

His voice, gruff but unmistakably human, made her open her eyes fully to look at him. She wanted to ask if the werewolf was really gone, but her throat was tight and the words wouldn't come out.

The man's shoulders sagged a little, like the tension in them had relented all at once. "It's all right, kid," he said. "The thing's gone. I hit it with silver, so it ain't coming back." He spoke with the lilting, unhurried accent of someone from the upper reaches of the Carpathians, far to the north.

In a voice so brittle it was a wonder it held at all, Ileana said, "Thank you."

He blew a sigh through his teeth. "The hell are you doing out here anyway? Where's your parents?"

"H-Home." She hadn't even thought about her father until now. He would be furious.

The man reached inside his pocket and took out something flat and metallic, about the size of his palm—a flask, it looked like. "Where's home?" he asked as he straightened up and began to un-cork it.

"Nightshade Lodge," she said. "Down the hill. There's a road." Her thoughts moved slowly, like fish swimming upstream. She tried to catch them and they kept slipping away.

He grunted an acknowledgement and took a long swig from his flask.

Ileana squirmed a little, trying to sit up. The pains and aches were merging into a diffuse kind of agony that bore down on her with a weight almost too heavy to bear.

"Show me your arm," the man said.

She gave her arm without thinking, hissing as his fingers closed around her wrist. He turned it this way and that, then let go and brought the flask to his lips to take another pull.

Finally, he said, "You got bit."

*

A white werewolf had been sighted in the woods around the town of Deva.

József had been following the trail of whispers all the way from Abrud, on the other side of the mountains, where he'd first heard about the beast. Werewolves weren't that uncommon if you knew where to look, but he'd never heard of a white one until now. There were gray ones, sure, and mottled ones, and the odd one with spots or other one-off markings. A white werewolf pelt, now that could fetch a pretty penny, and József wasn't one to turn his nose up at money.

If he ever found the damn thing.

The werewolf he'd chased off earlier had been a timber one, common as they came. Smaller than the one he was looking for, too. Must've been the runt of the litter, which was good news for the kid and bad news for both of them. Werewolves were pack creatures; where there was one you could see, there were a dozen others you didn't see until they were right on top of you.

He looked down at the girl, weighing his options. Getting the hell out of the forest seemed like a solid start. And then he'd take her home, he wasn't a monster. (*Not anymore*, his mind whispered, and he drowned the taste of old, bitter guilt with another pull of *țuică* moonshine from his flask.) If the kid's family actually lived in these woods, they might have seen the werewolf he was looking for, even if they didn't know what it was.

"All right, kid," he said. "Let's get you home."

The rest of it wasn't his problem. Not until the girl turned, anyway.

"I hurt my ankle," she said. "I can't walk."

"That's fine. I'll carry you." He stuck his flask back in his pocket and rolled his shoulders, ignoring the cracking of his really-not-that-old bones. "Does it hurt anywhere else?"

Her throat worked soundlessly for a moment. "No."

"Don't lie to me."

"I'm not lying."

"'Course you're not," József muttered. "C'mon."

The poor thing was light as a feather when he picked her up. She was battered and bloody, too, and her hair was slick with mud. He'd barely taken a couple of steps with her in his arms when he felt her start to shiver.

Right. It was cold as balls out here, and the girl only had a rough linen shirt to keep her warm.

He set her down long enough to shrug off his coat, ignoring her shaky ask of "Why'd you stop?" The coat was made of stiff, cracked leather, and it smelled like wet dog—he had a soft spot for strays and mutts, so what?—but at least it would keep her warm until they got to his truck.

"What's your name?" he asked as he wrapped the coat around her small frame. *Talk about runts.*

"Ileana," she said as she wiggled her arms into the sleeves. The coat was too fucking big; she looked like she was swimming in it.

"You can call me Leana. That's what my—" She sniffed and wiped her face with the back of her hand. "That's—"

"Nice to meet you," József said as he hurried to pick her up again. "Leana. That's, uh. Nice name. I like it." The last thing he needed was to cross the woods with a crying, squirming kid in his arms and nightwalkers lurking in the shadows.

Like the last time, came a treacherous thought. He licked his chapped lips, wishing he'd kept the flask on him.

"What about you?"

"Huh?"

"Your name," the kid—Ileana—said.

Oh. "It's József. Friends call me Jóska."

After a beat, Ileana said, in a small voice, "Thank you, Mister József."

He made a vague sound of acknowledgement. Sure, he might have saved her from a quick, messy death, but the bite on her wrist had pretty much sealed her fate already. Maybe not tonight, maybe not tomorrow, but on the night of the next full moon, when she started to turn...

"The hell were you doing out here alone anyway?" he said, to take his mind off that train of thought more than anything. "Don't you know it's dangerous?"

She muttered something, then squirmed in his arms until she buried her face into his shoulder. He felt the wetness of her tears soaking through his shirt. A pang of pity stabbed at his heart.

"What was that?" he asked. The road was just ahead; he could see it through the trees.

Turning her head a little, she said, "I wasn't *alone*, but...he's dead. The werewolf got him."

József slowed his step, suddenly aware of his own breathing.

"How d'you know that was a werewolf?" he asked, knowing he

wouldn't like the answer. "Could've been just a wolf."

"My...family hunts them sometimes, up north." Her voice was faltering. "I'm not old enough to go yet, but I...know what they look like."

This just kept getting better and better.

Ordinary folk, he could maybe bullshit into giving the kid a few more weeks. Hunters, they'd know. And they'd be just as quick to put down one of their own as they did the things who weren't.

Not my problem, he told himself, but then the kid brought up her skinny arms to hug his neck, and his heart cracked in his chest.

*

Nightshade Lodge wasn't much to write home about: a two-story manor in the ass crack of nowhere, with an overgrown lawn and a covered veranda running along the front. The walls were gray stone, worn and weathered by time and neglect. A lone chimney jutted up from a dark, sloping roof, spewing gray smoke into the night. On the ground floor, a lone window scattered a faint, flickering light into the night.

A cobbled path cut straight through the lawn. József drove slowly, weaving around loose stones and waterlogged potholes and careful not to rattle his passenger too much. She'd dozed off in the front seat, still bundled up in his big coat. Poor thing probably thought she was safe, and here he was, leading her to the slaughter.

His heart gave another painful lurch.

Stop it. Get her home, find out if her family knows anything, then get the hell out. That's what you're here for. That's all you're here for.

He stopped at the entrance, put the truck in neutral, then pulled up the handbrake. When he turned the key in the ignition, the engine cut off with a shudder. József had driven his old Volkswagen Amarok up and down the country for more than six years now, and he'd never been bothered by all the little ways in which it didn't work quite right. This time, though, he winced and caught himself hoping that all that rattling hadn't woken up his charge. Not yet.

He waited another minute, then reached across the console to give the girl a gentle nudge. She stirred and nuzzled her face into the crook of her arm, letting out a soft whimper.

"Hey," he said, nudging her again. "Wake up. We're here."

With a sharp breath, Ileana's eyelids fluttered open. Her eyes were dark and wide like a cornered animal's. Did she know? Hell, she looked old enough to know. Kids had a habit of picking up on—

No. *Fuck*, he couldn't think about Stefánia. Not now.

"C'mon, Leana," he said, lacing his voice with as much fake cheer as he could muster. "Let's go say hi to your mum and dad."

"Just dad," she said, looking down at her hands. "Mum's not here."

"Where'd she go?"

"Away."

József wondered if "away" meant "dead." It wouldn't have surprised him. Most hunters didn't live long enough to die of old age.

The manor's front door sat perched at the top of three rectangular steps, each smaller than the one below it. The door was made of solid wood, with faded bas-reliefs and an old-fashioned brass knocker dangling in the middle. József carried Ileana up the steps, bracing against the wind when it buffeted them out of nowhere. He had to adjust his grip so he could reach out and knock, and she latched on to him again and held tight. The old brass knocker rattled against its plaque with a sharp, tinny sound that grated as much as the anticipation of what he was about to do.

Stop it, you old fool. He wanted to slap himself—or drink himself to oblivion, which was something he would *absolutely* do later tonight.

"What's your dad like?" he asked.

The bundle in his arms stirred a little, then said, "Angry."

The first peal of thunder rumbled in the clouds just as the door began to open.

*

Ileana couldn't tell what was real and what was a nightmare conjured up by her feverish mind. Sweat ran down her back in burning trickles, but she felt cold to the bone. The bite on her arm throbbed with an icy kind of pain, each tooth mark its own circle of hell. The voice of her rescuer rumbled in his chest as he spoke, but his words were jumbled as if they were coming from far, far away. Another voice answered, one she immediately recognized. It sent a different kind of chill down her spine. Her father was here.

She thought she heard József whisper, "Sorry, kid," but she might have imagined it. Then, she felt him lowering her to the ground.

It hurt to put weight on her ankle, but she gritted her teeth and bore it. Clutching József's coat tightly around her, she peered up through her matted bangs. Her father wasn't looking at her.

She sniffled, then said, "Daddy—"

"Give the man his coat." Her father's voice was level, but it held no warmth.

Ileana wriggled out of the coat, careful not to let it fall to the dusty floor, then held it out with her good hand and murmured her thanks. She kept her eyes cast downward the whole time lest she invoke more of her father's wrath later on.

"Go upstairs," she heard him say after the weight had left her hand.

She turned and went, biting down hard to cage any sounds of pain. At the foot of the stairs, she turned to look at her rescuer one last time. Their eyes met. He gave a slight shake of his head.

Don't go, she thought, a prayer and a plea.

He looked away.

Ileana's shoulders sagged as she began to climb, dragging herself up by the banister step after agonizing step. The pounding of her heart was a fierce drumbeat in her ears, drowning all sounds in its wake. At the top of the stairs, she paused to catch her breath, her hand trembling as she pushed the hair from her eyes. Glancing back down into the foyer, she saw that it was now empty.

*

Ileana's father didn't strike József as particularly angry, but he wasn't exactly friendly. He introduced himself as Sebastian, no last name, so József didn't give his either. From the foyer, they stepped into a small receiving room where József sank into a worn armchair and Sebastian poured a measure of liquor for them both.

The older hunter cut a nondescript figure in the dim light of the fireplace. He was a man of average height, with a harsh, angular face obscured by several days' worth of gray stubble. His features had a hardness to them that spoke of a life of perpetual wanting, which was a little odd for someone who lived in a big-ass manor and drank their liquor out of fancy crystal tumblers.

"Tell me," Sebastian said once they were both seated, crossing his arms and leaning back in his chair. The sleeves of his forest-green shirt were rolled up to the elbows, revealing a pair of sinewy forearms covered in thick, dark hair. A jagged scar ran along the outside of his left arm.

József downed his drink first, letting the burning liquid soothe his nerves on the way down. He cleared his throat, then wiped his mouth with the back of his hand. "Ain't much to tell. I found the girl out in the woods, with a werewolf on top of her. Shot the werewolf, brought her home. That's all there is to it."

"A *werewolf*," Sebastian said.

"Yeah. That."

Sebastian's eyes narrowed. "There are no werewolves in these woods. We drove them out years ago."

Well, I got news for you, buddy, József grumbled inwardly, but he kept that quip to himself. "Listen," he said, "we both know what *we* are, so don't insult me by pretending *they* ain't real. Now this one, it wasn't all that big, and I'm thinkin' it wasn't all that *smart* either. Probably a runt, or maybe a younger one wandered too far from its pack."

"It must have been a wolf or some other kind of animal," Sebastian cut in.

József sighed. "I suppose you haven't heard of a white werewolf lurking around these parts, then?" He could already guess the answer, but he had to give it a try just to say he'd done it.

"A white werewolf? No. In fact," Sebastian said, shifting to prop one elbow on the armrest, "I don't think I've ever heard of one. There was a pack of silvermanes up in Mureş county some years ago, but we hunted all of them."

"So, you kill 'em where you find 'em," József said. With a sudden sinking feeling in the pit of his gut, he reached for his flask.

Sebastian didn't comment on the breach of guest etiquette. "Same as you, I would assume. Like you said, we both know what we *are*—right?"

"Ileana got bit."

He hadn't meant to be so blunt, but the other guy was starting to get on his nerves. It didn't help that Sebastian's words had dug up some not-so-distant memories that József himself wasn't very proud of.

After a beat, Sebastian said, "I see."

His voice was no different than before, but when he got up and went to pour himself another drink, the hand that held the bottle shook a little. He downed it in one go, then filled it again. He didn't offer to refill József's.

"There's still a chance she won't turn," József said, swiveling around in his chair to follow the movement. "You won't know for sure until the next full moon. Meantime—"

"Thank you. For bringing her home." Tumbler still in hand, Sebastian turned to regard József with a cool glare. "When the time comes, I'll do what needs to be done. I'll make sure she's cared for until then."

"At least *make sure* you don't scare her any more than she already is. She just saw her friend die, she doesn't need to know…" József couldn't bring himself to say the rest of it out loud even as he told himself Sebastian was right. If the girl turned, there was only one way things could end, and nothing he said or did would make any difference.

A flicker of irritation broke through Sebastian's composure at last. "She was with someone?"

József drained the last of his flask in two quick swigs before answering. "That's what I gathered, yeah. She said the werewolf got him." And then, because he didn't care whether he'd make it to the end of the conversation before he got his ass thrown out the door, he said, "Might wanna make sure it wasn't another one of your kids."

"I had a son. He died," Sebastian said, his voice suddenly thick. "I only have my daughters. Their mother…"

And then, without warning, he crumbled.

He didn't drop to his knees, sobbing and wailing like a lesser man might have. He just leaned hard against the drinks cabinet, head bowed, and his tumbler slipped from his fingers and rolled on the floor at his feet, its contents staining the wood a deeper shade of burgundy.

József was no stranger to this kind of grief. Then, as now, there hadn't been anything to do but wait for the inevitable, let it come to pass, then try to find a way to live with it. The kindest thing he could do for a father soon to be bereaved, he knew, was to let him mourn in peace.

"Right," he muttered, pushing himself out of the chair in one swift movement. "I'll see myself out, then."

Sebastian made no attempt to stop him.

Outside, it was raining, a thick, pelting deluge that drenched József to the bone in less than it took him to cross the lawn and climb into his truck. He turned the key in the ignition, sluicing water from his face with the other hand. With one last look over his shoulder, he pulled away and drove into the night, carrying the memory of Sebastian's grief with him like a weight around his neck.

*

Ileana woke to the feeling of being carried once again. She nestled closer to the warmth, too tired to think about where she was being taken or why. It didn't matter. As long as she was home, she would be safe.

She floated in and out of a shallow sleep, cradled by the rhythmic sway of whoever had her in their arms. At one point, she thought the air got colder, but then the torpor took her and she knew no more.

When she stirred again from a dead, boneless sleep, the milky light of daybreak revealed a room she'd never seen before. The walls were bare wood, with none of the paintings and trophies that decorated other parts of Nightshade Lodge. The bed was narrow and unfamiliar, the sheets rough and carrying a faint, musty smell. A slow rain pattered on the windowpanes.

Something clinked at the foot of the bed when she sat up to have a better look around. She bent to push the covers aside, gritting her teeth against the throbbing aches battering her body all over. A shackle made of dull metal was clamped around her ankle over the tattered socks she still wore. The chain connecting it to the bedpost was as thick as her wrist.

She reached down to touch the shackle but withdrew her hand as soon as her fingers made contact, hissing through her teeth.

The metal burned.

Chapter Two

Blood on the Wind

Twenty Years Later

There were two kinds of werewolves in this world, as far as Liviu was concerned: those who embraced who and what they were, and those who didn't. The second kind were no better than mutts. They went through life with their tails tucked between their legs, hiding away when the moon was full and the beast blood took hold, an insult to those courageous few who were out and proud.

Well, as out and proud as it was sensible anyway. Being *out-out* cranked the odds of an untimely death almost all the way up. It wasn't worth it.

Still, Liviu made the most of his nature-given endowments as man and wolf alike. He lived on the edge of Deva, where houses and alleyways melded into the thick forests and rolling hills surrounding the small town. He was on the shorter side as far as humans went, but also broad-shouldered with strong, muscular limbs and a preternatural endurance that made him especially adept at physical work. He did the odd job here and there to keep up the human appearances and roamed the wilderness when he felt the call of the wolf, which was often.

When he was in town, Liviu split his time between a select few eateries and a watering hole called the King's Pub, where he went whenever he was in search of a mate for the night. With his chestnut-colored curls and green-bronze eyes, he didn't have to try very hard to woo anyone so long as he didn't talk too much. Most women found him attractive. Some men did, too, and some of those men interested him in turns. He rarely, if ever, struck out; lust carried its own scent, both sultry and sweet, so all he had to do was follow his nose.

Liviu had been out on the prowl tonight. King's Pub had just opened its back garden for the season, and there was no better time to kick back and savor a pint in the chilly spring air. The grass was freshly cut, the earth moist and fragrant, and the more offensive smells he typically associated with the place—most of which had to do with too many patrons and too much drink—had yet to manifest. His mood was, well, not walking-on-sunshine happy, but he was feeling agreeable toward the world tonight, so he could maybe picture himself bringing someone home later, or several someones; he wasn't picky. The folks around the bar were getting lively, and it was only eight or so. The fun crowd usually woke up around this time.

He'd have to put a pin in that, though, because his exquisitely tuned nose had just informed him that another werewolf had wandered onto his turf, the first one in...he couldn't remember how long. Local werewolves tended to gather elsewhere, places where Liviu hadn't been welcome in years. King's Pub, on the other hand, was *his* domain, and this newcomer would have to either explain themselves or find somewhere else to drink.

He followed their scent to a small, rickety table in the back, the kind that made one hold on to their pint so it wouldn't end up in their lap. Seated at the table was a woman of around thirty (he was being generous) wearing a faded leather jacket, jeans, and boots, and smelling of diesel fuel and the open road. Her dark hair was choppy and uneven, and her thick eyebrows were drawn together like she was trying to stare her pint into submission.

Liviu dropped into the seat across from her without bothering to ask, then said, "You're a long way from home."

"And you're about five seconds away from a broken nose." The woman looked up from her drink—her eyes were the color of weathered ink—and added, levelly, "Werewolf or not."

So, she'd smelled him too. The corners of his lips pulled up in a smirk.

"You know what I am, so let's cut the bullshit," he said, letting a little growl into his voice. "You're on my turf. I wanna know what for."

She gestured to her beer, raising her eyebrows as if the question puzzled her. "I was *hoping* to have a drink."

"Could've gone to the Bulb instead."

"Maybe I didn't want to go to the Bulb," she said.

Her nonchalance was just this side of believable. She didn't know what the Bulb was, and that meant she was really far from home.

Well, he wasn't about to be a dick to someone who didn't know anything about the local status quo. "Okay, have your drink. Oh, and," he said as he pushed back his chair and stood up, "watch out for hunters while you're in town. There's more of them than there is of us, and they won't bother to chitchat before they brain you." He turned and started back toward the bar.

"What do you know about the hunters?" she called after him.

"I know enough to stay the hell away from them," he tossed over his shoulder, and then he turned his attention back to the task of salvaging the evening and pushed her out of his mind.

To his surprise, she was at his elbow not a minute later, offering to buy him a drink.

"Sure, if that's how you wanna call it. I prefer gay. *Straight* to the point, yeah?" He chuckled at his own wit; then, when the joke fell flat, he cleared his throat, his mood souring a little. "What's your name? I'm Liviu. They call me the Cat."

"Ileana." She didn't comment on the nickname, else he might have told her it was because he always landed on his feet (and definitely not because he was shorter than most of the other werewolves in Deva, thank you very much).

True to her word, she bought a fresh pint of Timişoreana stout for him and a lager for herself. They returned to her table, where her previous drink still sat at half-mast.

"So," Ileana said as soon as they were seated. "The hunters?"

Liviu eyed her over the top of his glass. "Hunters," he said gravely, like he was about to start an incantation.

And wouldn't that be a riot. Say "hunters" three times in front of a mirror, and one of them shows up and pops you in the head.

"There's a whole mess of them living in an old house up the hill, so don't go wandering that way. If you wanna roam, there's good forests to the south, on the other side of the highway. It's easy to cross at night, just gotta watch out for the semis." He paused to take a pull from his beer. "While you're in town, try not to draw too much attention to yourself. We're s'pposed to have a truce, but that's never stopped them before." Another pull. "There's bad blood between us and them. Has been, for a long time."

Something flickered across her face, there and gone before he had time to decipher it. After a beat, she said, "I'm sorry."

He nodded and drowned the shame of just *where* that feud had started with more stout. "Nothing for you to feel sorry for, it is what it is. Lots of folks left this area because of it. Those who stuck around usually go to a place called the Cheap Shot when they're in town. If you wanna try it, lose the attitude."

Her eyes narrowed in a glare, but then she seemed to think better of it. "You also said something about a place called the Bulb."

"The Haunted Bulb, yeah." He couldn't *not* scoff at the name. "It's a nightclub for people like us. Owner's a right bastard, and his crew aren't much better, so I'd advise you to keep the fuck away. Might get your drink spiked, or worse."

"I won't be in town long enough to make friends, but thanks for the warning," she said. "I was just curious, that's all."

"So what brings you here, then?" Liviu asked. "Plenty of other, more exciting places you can go."

"My car broke down."

He snorted. "Try again."

She chuckled and ran a hand through her shaggy hair, but her eyes were guarded. "What's so outlandish about what I just said?"

He shrugged and drank some more, mulling the question over. "You're asking a whole lot of questions for someone who just happens to be passing through and, well. You know what they say about curiosity."

"I like to stay aware of my surroundings, yes. Have to, being—what I am." She polished off about a third of her beer in one go, but he'd picked up on the way her voice had caught just then, and her face had a pinched look she couldn't quite hide behind the bottle.

Liviu waited another second or two in case there was more. When it became obvious that there wasn't, he planted his elbows on the table and leaned forward. "I'm gonna go out on a limb here and say you're in Deva because you want to be in Deva. As for why that is, that's between you and whatever gods you believe in. But if you go around asking about hunters, one of them is gonna catch wind, and *you don't want that.*"

She huffed a breath. "I didn't know I was talking to the Second Coming of Commissioner Miclovan."

"Don't get killed." It came out a touch more passionate than he'd meant to, but fuck it. "There's few of us left as it is, so don't go giving those bastards another notch on their crossbows."

Ileana gave him a long look, then finished the rest of her beer. He debated saying more, but in the end, he didn't. Maybe she really was just passing through, and then he'd make himself look like an ass.

Finally, she said, "I don't plan on staying any longer than I have to, but thanks anyway. Good to know the lay of the land."

"If you change your mind," he said as she stood, one hand moving to steady his drink, "you know where to find me." He tried to wink but ended up blinking with both eyes instead.

He watched her leave with an odd feeling of unease coiling in his chest and wondered why that was. She wasn't one of his pack (he didn't have one), nor his mate (he didn't have one), not even someone he cared about (he counted those on the fingers of one hand).

He'd had enough of King's for tonight, he decided on a whim. He crossed the garden, then the pub, and then he stepped out into the street. Her scent was easier to tell apart out here, with fewer things to conceal it. He followed, careful not to make his sniffing too obvious in case a human might be watching.

After a few steps, he stopped and cursed under his breath.

Rather than head back into town, like he'd thought she might, Ileana had gone the other way, straight toward the hill, where he'd told her not to go.

*

Deva had changed a lot and also not at all, like an old acquaintance you still knew, even if their face was lined and their eyes had dimmed. Apartment buildings had sprouted up in clumps here and there, with carbon-copy cafés and vapid storefronts at street level and their upper floors lost to conformity. Under the modern veneer, the town was still as she remembered it. As she walked along a cobbled street toward the hill, her steps ringing out a brisk, steady cadence, she took in the once-familiar sights. The old houses, hidden among the oak and chestnut trees, had weathered and changed with time, of course, but many of them still bore the same glass mosaics of floral or geometric patterns which had so fascinated her as a child. The ones that had been repainted or rebuilt now sported bright blues and oranges that glimmered softly in the night.

Ileana knew this street; she'd walked it countless times as a child. She still had to watch her step around the tree roots popping out from between the cobblestones here and there. She recalled her old school, just a few streets away, and the nearby nursery where she would drop her sister off when their father had more important things to do. Farther down that way was the abandoned opera house where she'd spent a whole night searching for ghosts, armed with nothing but a flashlight and a wooden cross. She hadn't found any, but the memory still brought a quirk to her lips. Maybe she'd wander that way tonight, after—

No. She wasn't welcome here. That much hadn't changed. When she'd told the other werewolf, Liviu, that she'd only be in town for the night, she'd meant it. She had no time to waste on pointless reminiscing.

At the end of the street was a small park, little more than a few wooden benches arranged in a semicircle around a square marble fountain. A gaggle of teenagers in dark makeup and black band T-shirts had claimed the two benches closest to the fountain. They didn't pay Ileana any mind as she slumped down on the furthest bench, letting her head drop forward with a long, heavy sigh.

Tamara had asked to meet her at the top of the hour, so she still had some time left to kill before starting the short hike up to Nightshade Lodge. She allowed herself to dredge up the few things she remembered about her sister. The last memory she had of her outshone everything else, but that was no surprise; if Tamara hadn't been there that night, Ileana would have died by their father's hand. It was the first and bitterest axiom of her life: that bloodlines didn't matter where the hunters' code was involved.

But Tam had been too young to know any of that. With their mother gone, she had, predictably, bonded with her older sister, even as Ileana had gone to great lengths to avoid her. Tamara, with her gap-toothed smiles and her clumsy, lopsided gait, would go from room to room, asking anyone she bumped into where "Ilena" was, until the latter, equal parts weary and exasperated, would inevitably concede to playing together for a while.

Before last week, they hadn't spoken in twenty years. That Tamara had managed to track her down was puzzling enough. Her words, crackling across a landline from the other end of the country, had been warm and full of promise, but Ileana hadn't lived to be thirty-three by taking people at their word.

She wondered now what kind of woman Tamara had become. If she still couldn't say her Rs properly. If she'd kept her long, sandy braids, or cut her hair short like their grandmother used to do. If her life had been any harder once their father had realized just how it was that his older daughter had managed to flee.

The sticky-sweet scent of a lit-up marijuana stick wafted her way, emanating from the chattering group still congregating around the fountain. Ileana was briefly tempted to walk over and ask for a hit. Anything to numb the prickling restlessness that made her want to turn back and forget all about hope. The pints she'd had earlier could only do so much, and she'd sworn off the stronger stuff years ago. The last thing she wanted was to end up like József, whose daily mantra, for as long as she'd known him, had been "Don't think, drink."

She hadn't thought about her old mentor in years. Funny, that.

She checked the time again, then rose from the bench and crossed the park with long, purposeful strides. She couldn't out-run those memories, nor the simmer of anger that came with them, but maybe she could make some new memories tonight.

A packed-earth trail started at the back of the park and wound its way up, snaking between the trees and bursts of tangled shrub-bery just awakening to the spring. Ileana followed the trail until she reached the tagged-up remnants of a concrete wall that had always been there, though she was no closer now to discerning its purpose than she'd been twenty years ago. At the wall, she turned left. Her nimble feet discovered the narrow footpath she'd taken countless times. In another life, this had been the way home.

As her soles melded with the soft, yielding soil, Ileana felt the wolf inside her begin to stir, enticed by the shift in their surroundings. Gone was the human-made stench of the town below, choked up by car fumes and rotting garbage and gods knew what else. Up here, the night was alive with the musky scent of decay, fallen leaves mingling with the damp embrace of the earth and the new life sprouting up from below. Soon, she was running, her senses unfolding like a nocturnal bloom. The darkness gave her no trouble as she weaved around low-lying branches trying to bar her way. Her feet danced over stones and roots, finding solid purchase whenever they touched the ground. She felt lighter with every step, and stronger, and *faster*—

Ileana's steps faltered as she became aware of how deep and raspy her breaths had become, how taut her jacket was across her heaving chest. She balled her fists and hunched over, squeezing her eyes shut against the colors of the night.

Breathe, she told herself, and then she started to count: in-one-two, out-one-two... The world was a maelstrom of scents, each one blazing a trail across her senses, like a falling star on a moonless night.

The wolf was restless. It wanted to chase the stars.

With a growl that rumbled deep inside her chest, Ileana said, *"No."*

The sound, coarse and inhuman, pulled her back from the brink, the sheer weight of her shame enough to bury the wolf for now. She ran a trembling hand over her face, relieved to find smooth skin and sharp cheekbones and eyes that were slightly moist. She started moving forward again, slower this time. She didn't want to think about what had almost happened. If Tam had been closer, if she'd seen her like that, heard that *voice*.

She focused on her steps, telling herself it didn't matter. *Almost* didn't have to mean anything. This wasn't the first time she'd beaten back the wolf, and it wouldn't be the last.

Ileana almost didn't notice when she reached the clearing she'd been aiming for. It was small and almond-shaped, and at the heart of it stood an old chestnut tree. As a child, she'd taken to climbing it whenever she could, striving to reach higher each time. Tamara, too short and too clumsy to pull herself up to the first branch, could only cheer her on from below, flailing her little arms and shrieking in delight when Ileana waved back.

Her heartbeat picked up once again. It was entirely possible that Tamara was already waiting for her under that tree like they'd agreed. She couldn't smell anyone yet, but maybe—

The snap of a branch shattered the stillness of the woods.

Ileana startled and turned around, a low growl slipping past her lips before she could contain it. The noise had come from downwind; if something was stalking her from the shadows, she couldn't catch its scent. She listened for any other disturbances, but the night was quiet except for the hooting of birds and chittering of small creatures that had always been there. After another breath, she turned and stepped into the clearing. The prickling at the back of her neck persisted, as if something with smoldering amber eyes still watched her from the shadows, ready to pounce while her back was turned.

Tamara wasn't waiting for her like she'd hoped, but it was still early, so she didn't worry. She walked up to the chestnut tree, letting herself take in the familiar sight of its broad, crooked trunk, the limbs that stretched toward the sky like the fingers of a sleeping giant. She'd never made it farther than a third of the way up before her courage faltered. She wondered how high she could climb now.

As the minutes wove into one another, Ileana began to pace, crossing her arms against a chill that wasn't really there. This forest reminded her of the night she'd been turned. Being close to

Nightshade Lodge reminded her of what had come after. Neither memory was a happy one.

She'd lost track of the days she'd spent chained to the bed in that unfamiliar room. Her wounds were closing much quicker than she thought they should. She remembered clawing them back open so her father wouldn't notice, biting into the musty sheets so she wouldn't scream. And it must have worked, because Sebastian had started sending Tamara to bring her meals, and then—

The rustle of dead leaves startled her out of her thoughts just as the wind shifted. Footsteps, slower and heavier than Tamara's would have been, made Ileana reach for her knife, the same one she'd used to fight off the werewolf all those years ago.

"Show yourself!" she called out, and this time she wasn't ashamed to punctuate her sentence with a snarl.

A man stepped out of the shadows, his hands buried deep inside the pockets of his ratty denim jacket. He looked human, but Ileana immediately knew better.

"What the hell are you doing here?" she demanded, feeling her hackles rise. "Were you following me?" If Tamara happened to come *now*—

Liviu didn't seem too impressed by her reaction. "Wanted to make sure you didn't start shit I'd have to finish. But, uh." He sniffed loudly, then shrugged and said, "Smells like shit's already started without either of us."

She started to say, "What do you..."

And then, she smelled it, too: a tangy, coppery scent that tapered off into a sickening sweetness at the back of her throat. If she hadn't caught on to it before, it was only because she'd locked herself so deeply from her other side after what had almost happened earlier that her mind refused to acknowledge what the other senses were telling it.

She felt Liviu's hand on her arm and realized her feet had started carrying her toward Nightshade Lodge without her even knowing it.

"Slow down," she heard him say through the pounding in her ears. "Let's take a second to think before we get ourselves mixed up in whatever happened there."

The word hit her like a punch to the gut, knocking the breath out of her in a strangled gasp. *Whatever happened... happened...*

If it was already over, if she'd spent all this time waiting, and Tam—

She wrenched her arm free and ran forward, oblivious to everything but the scent of blood on the wind.

Chapter Three

What Goes Around

There was death in the air. A lot of it.

Liviu was no stranger to death. He'd lived in its shadow for as long as he could remember, inflicted it on others, and come close to it too. But this...

The closer he got to Nightshade Lodge, the more he caught the eye-watering stench of human blood, spilled and then left to rot. If it was this bad even from a distance, he didn't want to know what it would be like up close. But the woman he'd been following—Ilona or something?—had run toward the manor, not away from it, so Liviu couldn't just turn around and skedaddle back to Deva, much as he wanted to.

Okay, so maybe he felt *a* little responsible for her, if only because she was the first werewolf in—hell, in years who didn't tolerate his presence just because they had to. So he followed her, albeit much more cautiously, keeping his eyes and ears wide open for any sign of trouble. His nose was pretty much useless at this point; he couldn't smell anything other than blood.

As he made his way through the dwindling trees, the looming shape of Nightshade Lodge came into view. Up close, it certainly lived up to its reputation as the kind of place where nightwalkers went to die, if a little more desolate than he'd expected. Even the lawn was overgrown with thistles and dandelions.

Liviu had never ventured this close to Nightshade Lodge before. For all his bravado, he preferred to keep his pelt on his bones where it belonged. He fought an instinctive urge to shrink back and meld into the shadows before someone spotted his dumb ass and turned it into Swiss cheese. If he'd been in his true form, his fur might have stood on end.

The ground between the tree line and the manor offered no cover except for a crumbling gazebo midway through. He couldn't see Ilona (*wait, no, she'd said Ileana*), but he saw a door, and the door was open, so she'd probably gone inside like an idiot. If she hadn't smelled *or* heard Liviu following her through the forest, she had no chance against, say, a pissed-off hunter with a crossbow.

"Goddamn it," he hissed under his breath.

Liviu broke away from the safety of the trees and ran straight to the gazebo. He darted into the relative safety under its crumbling roof, his eyes scanning the tall, shadowed windows for any movement. With his hide blessedly unpierced by any treacherous bolts, he sprinted across the remaining terrain, every muscle and sinew in his weak human legs screaming with exertion. By the time he flung himself through the open door, his heart was hammering like he'd run a marathon.

At least there was no one in the darkened hallway to raise the alarm. Which wasn't to say there wasn't anyone there, but they weren't in any shape to raise anything anymore. Or rise, for that matter.

Liviu looked down at the dead boy and caught himself thinking, *Poor bastard.* Then he remembered where he was and crushed that thought with extreme prejudice. The boy was a hunter; Liviu was a werewolf. Neither of them could be anything more than they already were.

Still, he couldn't help a twinge of sympathy at the way the boy had died. Someone had slit his throat in one clean stroke, then left him to bleed out.

Although…

Liviu frowned as he bent to examine the body. The boy was still clutching a hunting knife in one fist, and judging by the way the blood had flown and settled, it looked like—well, it looked like he'd slit his own throat. But that didn't make any sense.

He stepped around the body and into a kitchen that reminded him of a low-budget horror flick. Plates lay shattered on the floor, crunching under his feet when he moved. A large pot had boiled over, and the charred remains of what might have been soup or stew had long since cooled off on the depleted stove. Another body was wedged in a doorway that led deeper into the manor. He looked like he'd been trying to run out of the kitchen when something had gotten him from behind.

This one was much, much older, with a bald head and bony fingers that still clutched an old-fashioned bayonet. Liviu couldn't hold back a sneer as he stepped around the tip of the blade. How many nightwalkers had this man killed? Dozens? Hundreds?

And here you are, you old bastard, lying dead in a pool of your own—

Wait.

There *wasn't* that much blood, actually. The man had been old, sure. Even so, his corpse looked as dry as a raisin. Almost like...

"Fucking shit."

The swear exploded out of him in a hiss. He blew out a breath, long and tormented, then bent and inhaled deeply, trying to tease some other scent from underneath the reek of dead old bastard. He gagged almost immediately. The dead old bastard had apparently shat himself before departing this world.

Liviu coughed, then turned to the side and hacked a glob of spit onto the tarnished floor. This wasn't fucking worth it. He'd have to confirm his suspicions another way.

Ileana's scent was vibrant and alive, so he followed that. The more he saw, the more he wondered. Something had swept through the manor, killing everything in its wake. Some hunters had tried to put up a fight, but most of them looked like they'd been roused from their sleep and died before they'd had a chance to get their bearings. It didn't take a genius police commissioner to divine what had happened here: gather many hunters in one place, give them enough hubris to think themselves untouchable and, well. What goes around comes around.

On the upper floor, Liviu found the corpse of a young woman, pale and shriveled, with two small, round holes on the side of her neck. His eyes lingered on the wounds before the proverbial wheels in his brain started turning again. Fighting a wave of nausea that had nothing to do with his overtaxed senses, he straightened and broke into a sprint.

He found Ileana kneeling next to another corpse at the end of a short hallway—a man, older and haggard-looking. She didn't notice his approach until he was right on top of her, and when he cleared his throat, she straightened quickly and glowered at him. She was clutching a dagger with an elaborate filigree handguard and a long, thin blade that was caked in day-old blood. She must've pulled it from one of the corpses.

"Easy there," he said. "It's just me."

She nodded shakily and looked down at the dead man.

"We gotta go," Liviu said. Something nebulous but persistent was tugging at the fringes of his awareness, a sense that something wasn't quite right about the whole tableau.

She gave no indication that she'd heard him.

"Listen—"

"Vampires," she said, still not looking at him. "It wouldn't have taken more than a handful of them to overpower everyone." She fingered the blade absently as she spoke, peeling off flecks of drying blood. "But I don't understand…"

She wasn't going to tell him *what* she didn't understand, he realized after an uncomfortable bout of stilted silence. She didn't budge either. The way she was looking at the dead fellow, it almost seemed like—

"Is there a vampire coven nearby?" she asked abruptly, her head snapping up to pin him with a stare that was almost feverish.

"There a reason you wanna know?"

"That's none of your concern."

Liviu felt a twinge of annoyance prickling beneath his skin, like ants marching in formation. "What's your deal, huh? Did you know this guy?" He kicked at the corpse as he said it, and he could have sworn he saw her flinch.

She let out a breath, then tried to school her face into something impassive. It didn't quite work. "He was my father."

*

The last time Ileana had walked up these stairs to the room she shared with her younger sister had been twenty years ago, but her feet still remembered the way like it was yesterday. The bodies were just a distraction. None of her family had seen fit to intervene on her behalf when she'd been condemned. She had no pity for them now.

Until she found her father, struck down in front of the room she was searching for, and the reality of what she was seeing crashed into her all at once.

She dropped down on one knee, forcing herself to see him, *really* see him. When she tried to dredge up some kind of sentiment for the man, all she found was lukewarm pity, quickly buried under a slab of nothing. She'd spent years of her life hating him when the truth was he deserved even less than that.

Her father's clothes were torn and bloody. A deep gash across his forehead had bled into his eyes, likely blinding him in the fight that had become his last. He looked almost peaceful in death, certainly more so than when she'd known him alive. His eyes were open and unseeing, turned toward the heavens like there was anyone up there who gave a damn.

With a steady hand, she plucked out the dagger still sticking out of her father's chest. *Guess I got to outlive you after all, you murderous bastard.*

She didn't realize Liviu had come up behind her until she heard him clear his throat, and then she blurted out the truth to him like it was nothing. She hadn't meant to. She was just distracted, was all.

Liviu's eyes bugged out as soon as she told him. "He's—*wait*, you mean—you're a hunter?"

"I'm a *werewolf*. What do you think?"

His gaze darted to the body at their feet, then back to her. "I dunno. You tell me."

She let out a sharp breath. "I said this has nothing to do with you, Liviu. You can go."

"That's a yes, then." He scoffed, shaking his head from side to side. "Should've figured you were one of them. D'you know how many of us these assholes fucking murdered?"

"And now they're all dead, so that's the end of it," she said, fighting to keep her voice level. "Blood for blood, right?"

A deep growl tore from the back of his throat.

"Not all of them," he said, and that was all the warning she had before he charged her head-on.

There were two, maybe three steps between them. Ileana dodged him easily, whirling around for a wicked slash with the dagger she was still holding as his momentum carried him forward. She landed a long gash across his bicep.

The scent of blood cut across the lingering stench of day-old decay like a falling star on a moonless night. She recoiled for a moment, but the wound had staggered him as well, so she recalled herself enough to follow through with a kick to the groin that had him crumpling like paper.

He stayed down, wheezing and sputtering, but she put some distance between them just in case. His blood oozed from the cut she'd inflicted, staining the bare wooden floor. The wolf inside her was growing restless, sensing there was wounded prey nearby.

Not prey, she thought forcefully. Just a trespasser, one who was pretty damn stupid at that.

She waited until Liviu gathered himself enough to push up to his hands and knees, then growled, "Get out of my house." For once, she didn't care that her voice was tainted by the wolf.

Liviu stabbed a baleful glare her way as he shakily got back to his feet. "They'll never let you be one of them, you know," he said, spitting the words out, "and you sure as hell aren't one of us."

I know, Ileana thought, feeling nothing.

She watched him stagger away until he disappeared down the stairs and his footsteps faded, then listened for a while longer. If he changed his mind and came around for another bout, he would find her more than ready.

Her eyes turned to her father's corpse as she waited. He wouldn't have let a nightwalker go, much less one who'd attacked him under his own roof. Knowing that brought her some measure of satisfaction with what she'd done. She remembered József telling her how there wasn't any room for mercy in what they did. "Mercy gets you dead," he'd slurred over a glass of whiskey one night. She'd proven him wrong, too, and not for the first time.

At last, Ileana turned to the door that led to Tamara's room. Behind it lay closure. Answers, at the very least. She didn't let herself dread what she was sure to find.

The door gave way as soon as she pushed it, creaking on old hinges that sounded like they'd been neglected for a decade. She stepped into the room beyond, her heart beating a little faster.

The acrid tang of medicine hung heavy in the air, mingling with the sour stench of sweat and vomit, a lingering smell of sickness that immediately made her gag. A vanity in the corner held a haphazard collection of pill bottles, some opened, some not. Beside it, a small basket overflowed with soiled and bloodied tissues. The bed was unmade, sheets rumpled and pillows strewn about. Everything was coated in a thin layer of dust.

Alive or not, Tamara wasn't here anymore.

Ileana walked over to the vanity and peered at some of the pill bottles. Oxycodone, midazolam, haloperidol... Some of the names were familiar, but her head was swimming with the cloying smells of the room. She couldn't grasp the meaning of what the pills were trying to tell her.

When her eyes fell on a picture frame, her chest spasmed with a sudden, visceral longing. The frame was chipped in one corner, likely from being knocked over at some point. Spidery cracks spread outward from the fracture, crisscrossing the glass like a web. The photograph was faded with age, but Ileana immediately recognized the two girls hugging each other on a gaudy purple chaise longue. Their faces were pressed close together, cheek to cheek. They wore matching smiles, bright and wide, speaking of a life untouched by loss and death just yet.

Ileana picked up the frame and wiped away the dust clinging to the glass with her thumb. She tried to remember when the photograph had been taken, but she couldn't conjure up the memory. She wished they...

No, there was no point in dwelling on any of it. The past was just a ghost.

She set the picture back down and cast her gaze around the room, trying to make some sense of what she was seeing. No one had lived here for a while; that much was obvious. Equally obvious was the fact that she'd been speaking with Tamara, or someone pretending to be her, not a day before, whereas these bodies had been lying for at least twice as long. If there was a chance, however slim, that her sister was still alive somewhere, then she had to understand what had happened here. Which was a tall order when her only chance of doing so had walked away from her with a grudge.

Chapter Four

Crossroads

Liviu had never thought he'd be glad to be back among humans, but when his feet traded the forest floor for the jagged cobblestones of Deva's outer borough, relief washed over him like a cool wave. He sank onto an old bench nestled beneath a giant chestnut tree and just sat there, feeling the rough texture of the wood against his palms. After a while, he let out a short bark of a laugh.

Holy shit.

And then, because thinking it didn't lend *nearly* enough gravitas to the moment, he said it again, out loud: "Holy *shit*."

He'd thrown down with a hunter and come out of it alive.

And, actually, what the *fuck* had that all been about anyway? She could have easily snuffed him out while he was writhing around clutching at his dangly bits. Instead, she'd just...let him go.

That didn't square with anything he thought he knew about hunters. Hunters were cruel, sadistic bastards who plastered their shitty parlors with the pelts and bones of *people*. This one—she'd just kicked his reckless, moronic ass, then told him to scram.

He didn't get it.

The smell of death lingered in his nose, making him gag whenever he took a deep breath, but a shower and a fresh change of clothes would get rid of all that. The cut across his forearm throbbed with a sharp pain even though he could already feel the flesh knitting back together. Come tomorrow, he'd be lucky if he had a scar to show for it. And then, it would be like none of it had ever happened.

Just like that.

He couldn't delude himself into thinking this was over though. Most of the dead he'd seen were either too young or too old to go hunting. When the rest of the clan came back to find their loved ones slaughtered like lambs at Easter, there would be hell to pay.

For a moment, Liviu pondered skipping town for good, settling down somewhere his reputation couldn't follow him. It wasn't like anyone would actually miss him. Hell, if he'd croaked back at the lodge, would anyone have even cared?

A long, drawn-out sigh escaped him, a sad reflection of his current state. He hoisted himself up from the bench, but not before he felt a splinter dig into the heel of his palm. He was so caught up in his wallowing it barely even registered.

So caught up, in fact, that he neither saw nor scented Ileana until he lifted his head and saw her standing pretty much within arm's reach.

Liviu's body tensed, caught somewhere between fight and freeze. He let out a deep, menacing growl, baring his human teeth.

"I'm not here to fight," Ileana said quickly, holding her hands up to show they were empty. "I just want to talk."

"We got nothing to talk about," he snapped back.

Eyes scrunching shut, she said, "I need your help."

Liviu's thoughts skipped like a scratched vinyl record. This had to be some sick, shitty joke.

"Please," Ileana said. "I don't have anyone else I can—"

"No. Nuh-uh. I don't think so. First you lie to me, then you stab me, and now you want me to *help you*?" He scoffed a laugh. "Fuck off."

Her lips twitched in a grimace. "I didn't stab you, asshole. You came at me, so I gave you a little cut. You'll be fine tomorrow."

"Same difference. You're one of them, so I got nothing to say to you." He crossed his arms for good measure and instantly regretted it when the cut pulled open again. "Fuck."

She groaned and ran her hand over her face. "I told you, damn it, I'm not—"

"You said the guy was your father, yeah?"

"*Was*. He turned on me as soon as he found out I got bit."

He clamped down on another venomous retort. Anger was easy. It kept him grounded and kept most people away. It also got him into the kind of shitty situations that ended with him on the wrong end of a weapon, something he didn't feel like going through twice in one night.

"How'd you get bit?" he asked. It was as much of a peace offering as he was willing to make.

"That's..." She drew in a ragged breath. "It's a long story."

"Make it short, then."

Ileana seemed to wrestle with herself for another beat, her eyebrows rising, then falling in a frown. "Okay," she said finally, taking a pointed step toward him. "Move over."

His ass stayed firmly planted where it was. "You can tell me from over there."

She shrugged and didn't stop, so he had no choice but to move out of the way. She sat down with a long breath and immediately moved toward the far end of the bench, rubbing her hands together like she wanted to warm them.

Liviu felt some of the tension leave his body, replaced by a whisper of curiosity. He'd never been this close to a hunter before. (Well, not one who wasn't trying to skewer him with silver anyway.)

"I was thirteen," Ileana began, her gaze drifting past him and toward the deserted street. "Too young to be blooded. Too stupid to understand what was out there. And then..."

*

It was the first time Ileana had let herself unearth the full memory of that night, but she found the words came easier once she started. A shroud of numbness had descended on her like a leaded cloak, smothering all feeling. It was a dangerous thing, this spoken journey, likely as not to take her down a path that ended in a bottle. Talking about the past was good, even so. It meant she didn't have to think about the present for a little while.

"How'd you know you'd started to turn?" Liviu asked when she got to the morning after.

"The cuff was made of silver, so when it started to burn, I knew." Her gaze dropped down to her ankle, where she still had a scar from when she'd toed off a sock in her sleep and burned herself with the silver.

"Your old man, didn't he at least try to—?"

"No."

Liviu snorted. "Father of the year, that one. What else'd he do, lock you up in a cage or something?"

She met his casual dismissal with a sideways glare. "A cage, really? What kind of people do you think we were?"

"Hunters," he answered with a light shrug.

"We were—normal," she said, gripped by an inexplicable urge to defend the shadow of a past long gone. "My sister and I went to school. Our parents had jobs in town when they weren't—" She caught herself halfway through *hunting* and bit down on the word.

"When they weren't killing us," Liviu said quietly. "That's what you were gonna say, right?"

Shame burrowed a jagged claw in her chest. Never mind that she hadn't had anything to do with any of it. "For what it's worth, I'm sorry."

He scoffed. "Yeah. 'Sorry.'"

Ileana couldn't blame him. It stung, even so.

After a beat, he said, "So, how many did you kill? Before or after, doesn't matter."

"I stopped counting after my fifth." Looking down at her hands, she added, "Three of those were human."

"Hunters?"

"Just one. The other two..." Shaking her head, she said, "They had it coming."

"Why? Because you say so?"

"And how many people did you kill, Liviu?" she shot back. "Don't tell me you've never had a taste."

He rose from the bench and stretched until his back popped, then turned to her, looming. A flickering streetlamp behind him cast a halo around his silhouette, obscuring his expression. She watched him closely, ready to spring up and fight if he tried anything.

"You talk a pretty talk," he said, hunching forward so he didn't have to raise his voice, "but how do I know you're not just telling me what I wanna hear?"

Lightly, she said, "If I were, as you put it, one of them, I'd be sizing you up for a rug about now."

His teeth flashed in a grin, impossibly white in the darkness. "Don't be so sure you'd've won that fight."

She stood up as well, careful to keep enough distance between them to forestall any immediate aggression. "I'm happy to give you a rematch once I settle my business in town. And for that I need your help."

She felt the intensity of his gaze even through the shadows and braced herself for the *no* she sensed was coming. There were other ways she could get to the truth of things, she knew. She would have preferred not to use them.

"Okay," he said. "Let's go."

By the time she realized he'd turned on his heel and started walking, he was already several steps ahead, so she had to sprint to catch up. Her calves were sore after hiking up and down the hill.

"Where are we—"

"I got people to talk to. You can tell me on the way."

"Does that mean you trust me?" she said.

"It means I'm giving you a chance." He turned halfway to jab a finger at her. "One chance. Don't fuck it up."

"But why won't you—"

"It also means no more questions. You said you wanted me to help you with something, so talk."

Ileana held back a sigh, focusing on putting one foot in front of the other without surrendering an ankle to the uneven cobblestones. "It's about my sister," she said, and then she told him what she'd found in Tamara's room.

"Wasn't that long ago she was still there, if you could smell her," Liviu said at the end. "Couple of days, a week if you stretch it, but—look, there's no delicate way to say it, so I'll just come out and say it. How d'you know she wasn't already dead when this happened?"

"I called her from the guest house. That was yesterday."

A garish red Dacia drove past with the windows rolled down, oozing bass music into the night. Across the street, a few patrons at an open-air terrace were braving the chill, laughing and chattering amongst themselves. Ileana's lip curled at the sight. They had no idea what lurked among them, almost close enough to touch.

Liviu scratched his stubble, then slowed down enough so he could turn to her. "What's it to you if she lives or dies? Way I see it, she didn't lift a finger when it was your head on the chopping block, so you might as well wash your hands of this whole thing."

"She was six, damn it, and you're wrong," Ileana said. "She was the one who stole the key and broke me free. Father was going to kill me when I turned. I owe her my *life.*"

She didn't tell him how she'd tricked her sister into stealing that key from their father's nightstand while he slept. She'd told Tamara she was going to find their mother and hadn't stopped to think about the repercussions until days later, when she'd found safety and the time to reflect. Since then, she'd wondered many times if their father, in a fit of rage, had hurt his one remaining child in retribution.

"Her family was *normal*, she says," Liviu grunted under his breath as they rounded a corner and stepped into the wide open square at the heart of Deva.

Ileana felt a dull shiver ripple through her. Deva's town square, much like her own life, bore the marks of change while preserving its essence in an uncanny symmetry. The small round planters dotting the square still sported an assortment of pansies, geraniums, and other colorful flowers only just starting to bloom. The wooden benches lining the sides were newly painted in the country's national colors: red, yellow, and blue.

Overlooking it all, an equestrian statue of Mihai Viteazul—Mihai the Brave—rose on a massive concrete pedestal. In her younger days, tales of the country's medieval history had captivated Ileana, chief among them the story of the pioneering *voievod* who had been the first to unite the Romanian principates. Once, she had boldly declared to her mother that she'd grow up to have her own statue for people to admire. She and Mihai could share the square, she'd conceded, so long as her statue was the bigger one. The memory conjured a thin smile, quickly banished.

Beneath the towering statue, a small figure leaned against the pedestal. Their hair cascaded in a shimmering silver hue, stark against the black clothing that covered them from neck to toe. As they turned toward Ileana and her companion, only the pallid contours of their face were visible, like a disembodied presence lurking in the night.

Ileana shifted her foot until she felt the hilt of her knife graze against her ankle. Whoever this was, they weren't human. Their scent told her as much, though she couldn't place it any more than she could catch a proper glimpse of their face.

She nudged Liviu with the tip of her elbow. "Friend of yours?"

"Something like that," he said, raising his hand to offer the vexing figure a casual wave.

*

"I wasn't expecting you to return until well into the small hours," the silver-haired figure said to Liviu.

"Yeah," Liviu answered, an explosion of a breath. "Shit happened."

At the same time, Ileana felt the faint stirrings of a foreign presence brushing against her mind. Before she could do much more than brace herself against the intrusion, the presence surged with sudden intensity, flooding her thoughts and arresting her body where she stood.

Liviu was talking about what he'd seen at Nightshade Lodge, unaware of what was happening right next to him. His voice twisted on itself in Ileana's ears, thundering one second, whisper-wind-quiet the next. She could neither speak nor move as the unwelcome presence rummaged through her thoughts. Flashes of the night played before her eyes like a collage out of a horror magazine: the lodge, Tamara's room, their childhood photo, the bodies, *the bodies,* **the bodies—**

The presence withdrew.

Ileana reeled back with the force of the release. Chest heaving, she drew in a greedy breath, then another. She felt like she'd been trapped underwater for minutes. When she looked up again, she found herself staring into piercing black eyes glistening like faceted diamonds in a face so impossibly smooth it looked to be made of marble.

"You brought me a hunter," the vampire said in a low, husky voice. They were talking to Liviu, but their eyes still held Ileana's.

"I'm not a hunter—" Ileana had to pause for another breath. "—but try that again and I'll put a stake through your heart either way."

"No one's staking anyone," Liviu interjected, his voice seeming to emerge from a hazy space somewhere to Ileana's right. She didn't trust her vertigo-addled body enough to turn her head and look, but she shook off his hand when she felt it land on her elbow.

The vampire's eyes flickered over to Liviu. "Never let it be said that you keep dull company. Though I must say, this feels like an unusual first."

"She ain't *company,*" Liviu said, his tone making it abundantly clear he found the notion offensive. "She's just looking for someone, that's all. I figured—"

"I know. I've seen." The vampire's gaze returned to Ileana. Even without the obfuscating charm they'd used earlier, their face gave away nothing.

They already knew about Tamara then. With a scowl, Ileana wondered what else the vampire had seen. "I'm not looking for revenge," she said, just in case it needed to be said. "I just want my sister, that's all. I can't abandon her. If she's still breathing—"

"And if she isn't?" the vampire asked, their voice taking on a studied kind of curiosity.

Ileana breathed a short sigh. "I'll bury her if she needs burying. If not, I'll leave her be."

She held their gaze, daring them to say anything else, even though she knew it wouldn't be wise to piss them off. This was an ancient, a kind of vampire who'd lived long enough to turn statue-smooth and hone their powers to a frightening edge. József had told her once that ancients read minds as easily as humans read the evening papers. Ileana hadn't believed it until tonight.

The vampire nodded, a grave, somber affair. They moved stiffly, like a corpse held up by invisible strings. Their face was almost featureless and could have belonged to a woman, a man, or neither. They were short of stature and lithe of body. The deathless curse had taken them at an uncertain age, neither young nor old but somewhere in-between, but their manner of speaking was centuries old.

"That is good enough," the vampire said at length, and then

they held out a delicate hand with short, pearly nails. "My name is Evdochia of the Drăculeşti. You might have known my father."

"I think everyone knows *about* your father," Ileana said, and then she offered her own name, grasping Evdochia's hand with more confidence than she felt. Their fingers were cold and dry, but the flesh was plump, with a soft give to it, so the vampire had fed recently.

Maybe they fed on one of the corpses at the manor.

The thought sank into Ileana's mind like a stone into a well. It made no sound on the way down.

"Liviu," Evdochia said. "You must go and tell the others what has happened. Start with Darius. If you hurry, you might still catch him at his club."

Liviu, whose face had darkened as soon as he'd heard the name, grunted and said, "You want *me* to go to the Bulb? Why can't—"

"Time matters more than whatever feud still lingers between you. When word of this spreads, it will be more than just hunters who descend upon this town. We must all be ready."

Liviu's breath hissed out through his front teeth. "If they find me dead in a gutter somewhere, I'm gonna haunt you just to say I fuckin' told you so." He turned and stalked off, back stiff, shoulders taut. Ileana thought she might have heard him say "fuckin' vampires" under his breath.

Evdochia paid no mind to the outburst, turning instead to Ileana. "My brother's coven likes to roost not far from here. They've long since spoken of making war against the hunters on the hill, so I doubt they're ignorant of what happened tonight. I will go speak with them. You can join me, if you wish."

A whole coven of them. Ileana considered her choices. Evdochia had given her no more reason to trust them than Liviu had, but at least she and Liviu were of the same species. It was painfully obvious that she couldn't hold her own against one ancient, let alone a whole coven of them.

Evdochia leaned in, their black eyes boring into hers. "Do you perhaps fear that they'll eat you?"

Death by dismemberment was closer to Ileana's original concern. Still, she nodded and said, "Something like that, yeah."

"You needn't worry about that. Werewolves taste awful. No self-respecting vampire would subject themselves to that." Their tone was entirely serious, which made the whole conversation verge on the comically absurd.

Ileana took a small breath. "You've seen my thoughts. You know what I am. Why are you helping me?"

"You may not be a hunter, but I've seen enough to know you are proficient in the art of killing. And I," Evdochia said, the glint of a streetlight catching on a sharp fang as they cracked a smile at last, "may have need of your services before this night is through."

Chapter Five

The Haunted Bulb

The Haunted Bulb had been a fixture of Deva's eclectic underground scene long before the supernatural takeover. Originally a home for punks, metalheads, and all kinds of misfits in the rebellious days of the mid-nineties, the Bulb had undergone a number of transformations since the last change in management some three or four years ago. The club's original theme had remained as a tongue-in-cheek tribute to the werewolves who now ran the place.

The Bulb operated in an old mansion that stood three stories tall on the corner of two boulevards close to the Deva's northernmost edge. It was a long walk from the town square, which gave Liviu ample time to turn around and go back the way he'd come. He didn't do it. For all his grumbling earlier, he had to concede that Evdochia was right. This was bigger than the bad blood between him and the Bulb's current owner, whose name was Darius, though Liviu usually thought of him as "that bastard" or "that prick."

By the time he spotted the whitewashed stone walls and tall windows interspersed with patinated bronze caryatides, Liviu had stewed in his own resentment for about three quarters of an hour. He stopped on the corner opposite from the Bulb and sniffed the air. The club's entrance was flanked by two plain columns plastered with more half-torn flyers than he remembered. The doors were thrown wide-open tonight. Fierce guitar riffs surged into the night from down below, mingling with guttural growls and a relentless drum beat. His lips pulled back in a snarl. Of all the nights to come back here, it just had to be a gig night: more noise, more booze, and more assholes off their rocker and looking to punch or bite something.

At least he knew the bouncer who was working the doors tonight. His name was Ciprian and he was a distant cousin or something. They'd never really kept in touch.

Liviu cracked his knuckles, then smoothed the collar of his denim jacket and blew out a breath. *Might as well get it over with.*

He crossed the street and walked up to the Bulb's entrance with a step that was purposefully carefree. Ciprian moved to block his way before he'd even reached the doors, and Liviu barely suppressed a grimace. *So that's how it's gonna be, huh.*

"I'm here to talk to the boss," Liviu said, glaring up at the bouncer with as much authority as he could muster. "He in tonight?"

"Tonight's invitation only," Ciprian said, sounding almost agreeable for once. "Unless you got one—"

"Yeah, yeah, I'm not on the guest list, too bad, so sad. I'm here with a message. It's, uh." Liviu was going to say "life and death" but stopped himself at the last second. "It's important. He's gonna wanna hear it ASAP."

Ciprian's eyes narrowed in calculated appraisal. "What's it about?"

"That's need to know."

The bouncer leaned in closer, teeth bared in a grin that held very little menace in it. "C'mon, little cousin. You know how my missus loves herself some goss. Scratch my back, I'll scratch yours, eh?"

The fact that this guy even had a "missus" was news to Liviu, but he went with it anyway. "Y'know the hunters on the hill?" he said, lowering his voice to a conspiratorial whisper. He waited until Ciprian gave an uncertain nod, then said, "They're dead."

Ciprian frowned and drew back a little. "Dead?"

"Not breathing, not moving, *dead*."

The other werewolf guffawed suddenly, slapping him on the back so hard Liviu felt his bones rattle. "Good one!" he bellowed. "You know, I almost—" He paused long enough to dab at his eyes with the back of his hand. "—almost believed you."

"It's true," Liviu said with a lazy shrug because it was true.

"Yeah, yeah." Ciprian moved out of the way but held up a hand when Liviu started forward. "Just so you know, the boss is in a shitty mood tonight. Try not to piss him off, yeah?"

"Yeah," Liviu muttered as he walked past, thinking, *As if*. That ship had sailed some seventeen years ago. These days, he probably pissed Darius off just by virtue of existing.

The dance floor, bar, and a rickety stage were all in the basement, so Liviu went down. The stairs were bare stone, worn smooth by too many pairs of combat boots. He cautiously stepped around a puddle of waste that might have been someone's dinner and, pressing a hand against his nose and mouth, he took the steps one at a time. The stench of sweat, vomit, and other bodily fluids wafting up from the crowd was enough to overpower his nose even in his human form. How the hell could any werewolf stand to be down here?

With a cautious sigh and wary not to breathe in any more of the offensive odors, Liviu waded into the frenzy of bodies headbanging in time with the beat. He didn't know the band who was playing tonight, but he immediately knew they weren't human, if only because the guitarist was hanging upside-down from a beam some two meters above the stage as he shredded his instrument. His eyes glinted gold with each flash of the strobe lights.

Liviu shoved away a rocker with wild eyes and wilder hair who stumbled into him, then made his way forward. The bar, whose ghastly decorations—light-up ghouls, skeletal hands, and a "ghost" that looked to be made of a garden variety bedsheet—floated above the dance floor like an unholy beacon. His throat felt parched, but he knew better than to saunter up to the bar and ask for a beer. If he walked out of here with the same number of limbs he'd come in with, he'd thank his lucky stars and get drunk for a week. There was no need to push his luck.

He still had to walk past the bar to get to the door behind it that led to Darius's inner sanctum, and therein lay his next problem: the door was guarded by another bouncer, and Liviu didn't recognize this one.

The bouncer was big in every sense of the word, the kind of guy who could just stand in a door and nothing would have room to squeeze past. Nothing would *want* to squeeze past, either; he looked like he'd happily bite off the face of anything who tried. A long scar bisected his right eyebrow and disappeared into his hairline. The other eyebrow was pierced by a round metal ring. He rolled a coin over his knuckles idly as his eyes traveled over the moshers writhing in the pit.

Liviu spied an unattended bottle of beer on the bar counter and swiped it almost without thinking, then chugged down a third of it in a few large gulps. The beer was lukewarm, but it did the trick. Before he could talk himself out of it, he stepped around the bar and walked up to the bouncer.

Up close, Liviu realized he did know this one, though he'd never actually learned the guy's name. He'd been there the only other time Liviu had come to the Bulb, but there hadn't been much time for pleasantries on that occasion.

"I thought I smelled dog," the bouncer said, his deep voice cutting through the surrounding racket with ease. He caught his coin without looking and flipped it again. "What do you want?"

"Message for Darius," Liviu said. He was still clutching the bottle and debated whether it would be worth trying to knock out the bouncer with it. It probably wouldn't work.

The bouncer looked him up and down, flipped his coin again, then shrugged and said, "You sure?"

Whatever he meant by that, Liviu didn't like it. Still, he mirrored the shrug and said, "Guess so."

"It's your funeral," the bouncer said, lumbering out of the way.

*

The coven Evdochia had spoken of turned out to be a mundane two-story house a few minutes' walk from the square. It rose, rectangular and pragmatic, behind a wrought iron fence and an unassuming gate, its smooth walls betraying no sign that there was anything unholy going on inside. The air around it, though, carried faint wisps of copper and ash: blood, spilled not so long ago, and vampires.

Evdochia walked up to the gate and ran their fingers over the lock, murmuring a cantrip. Their fingertips glowed with a faint silver light, and a dull crimson luminosity answered their touch, skittering over the lock and flowing in through the keyhole. The gate swung open.

Evdochia stepped through. Ileana hesitated, lingering by the gate. A knot of something akin to apprehension twisted in her stomach. Beyond this, there would be no more chances to turn back.

Her fists clenched at her sides. *I'm doing this for Tam.*

She followed the vampire.

The front door posed no more of a challenge than the gate. Evdochia wielded the old magick effortlessly, a testament to their heritage, perhaps. The House of Drăculeşti drew their line from Vlad III, better known as the Impaler, whose legendary cruelty had seen him immortalized in the global entertainment pantheon even as his remains were said to rot underneath Snagov Monastery. His offspring had clearly inherited some of the old voievod's power along with his curse.

Evdochia led her into a darkened foyer, walking with the sure step of someone who knew their way around the place. They didn't talk, so Ileana didn't either. The air inside was thick and stale; Ileana's preternatural vision revealed dusty countertops and a mirror caked in a thin layer of grime. She strained her hearing to catch a sound, but aside from the occasional car passing outside, all was still. If it weren't for the smells, stronger here than outside, she would have thought the house had been abandoned long ago. The deep, unmoving shadows at the corners of each room they crossed made her want to glance over her shoulder every few steps. She couldn't help feeling like they were being watched.

Ileana followed Evdochia to the back of the house, where

another door led to a narrow pantry whose shelves stood barren aside from a few rusted pans and empty jars. She hovered by the door as Evdochia entered, equal parts curious and wary. *What's in there?* she wanted to ask, but disturbing the silence for such a mundane question felt unwise, so she held her tongue.

An errant thought stole into her mind: *I could kill them now, while their back is turned.* Funny how some old habits found ways to resurface at the worst of times. She hadn't killed a nightwalker solely on account of what they were since she'd parted ways with József. Then again, she'd rarely entrusted her life to one either.

Evdochia laid their palm flat against the back wall. A tingling sensation filled the air as thin tendrils of silver magick spread from their touch in all directions, arranging themselves into the shape of a door. The runes glowed softly, illuminating Evdochia's pale face with a ghostly light.

Ileana watched, transfixed, as the surrounding shelves dissolved into nothing and the magick shape coalesced into a real door with a real, solid knob that Evdochia reached for and pushed. The door swung inward, revealing a narrow stone passage and stairs leading down.

An underground coven, Ileana thought with a shiver of anticipation. Vampires were notoriously fond of hidden passages and secluded chambers. Those were usually barred from the outside world by powerful magicks that most humans could never hope to breach. Remembering that brought with it a disturbing realization: if the door vanished while she was still in there, she'd have no way to open it on her own.

"Are you not coming?"

Ileana startled and said, "Of course." Her hands were trembling a little as she wiped her sweaty palms on her shirt and followed.

The passage was barely wide enough for her to squeeze through, flanked by stone on one side and packed earth on the other. Light came from some twenty steps below, faint and flickering. The air was laden with a dry, earthy smell. The deeper they descended, the harder it was to breathe, which did nothing to soothe Ileana's growing unease. The silence was graveyard thick.

At the foot of the stairs, they emerged into a vast underground chamber that looked like someone had taken what was fashionable from every era since the 1400s, then ran it through a hurricane and scattered the remnants all over the place. Wooden benches of an older world stood side by side with a lavish crimson divan and a fuzzy bean bag that begged the question of how it had ended up in such distinguished company. Across from them, a decadent settee embroidered in gold thread presided over a table where a chessboard had been abandoned in the middle of a game. Floor-to-ceiling bookcases stretched along the walls, filled with all sorts of books, from leather-bound tomes with gilded spines to glossy hardcovers and humble paperbacks. More books and games lay scattered about. At the back corner of the room, two doors met at a sharp angle, their frames almost touching. One was closed, the other ajar.

Evdochia took a few gliding steps toward the middle of the room, stepping around a bright red ottoman. "I know you're here," they snapped. "*Come out!*"

The leftmost door, the one that was slightly open, began to move on hinges that were in desperate need of oiling. Ileana steeled herself to face whatever monster came crawling out of the depths of the lair. Instead, a boy who looked no older than seven or so strode into the parlor, blinking owlishly at them from underneath a choppy, mahogany-colored fringe. He wore a high-collared leather tunic, and his skin was ivory with the faintest glimmer of pink underneath.

"Your Highness," the child-vampire said with an exaggerated bow. His voice was silky smooth, lilting with an innocence that belied his true nature. "We weren't expecting you this century."

"Radu," Evdochia said, advancing. "I need to speak with my brother. Is he here?"

"No-o," Radu said in a singsong voice, drawing out the word. "No one's here. Just me."

"Where did they go?"

Radu tapped his chin with the tip of a manicured finger. "If I tell you, will you get me another human? The one they left for me tastes so bad."

*

Liviu smelled fear as soon as he stepped into the private area of the Haunted Bulb. It hung in the air, a cocktail of sweat, pheromones, and an undercurrent of rust that hinted at the presence of blood.

He'd entered an antechamber with a plush carpet and a crescent-shaped divan covered in dark velvet. At the other end was another door, closed and unguarded, which must have led to the backroom. Three girls in heavy makeup and various states of undress huddled by the door, whispering low among themselves. They looked like they were part of the club's usual clientele.

As Liviu approached, one of them raised her voice enough for him to catch the end of her sentence:

"But if we don't do anything, he's going to kill him!"

Liviu wondered if they were talking about him before he realized they hadn't even noticed him yet. He cleared his throat. "Who's killing who?"

Three pairs of eyes turned his way, and Liviu had a nasty

feeling of déjà vu. Two of the girls were werewolves; he'd seen them both the last time he'd been at the Bulb. Judging by her scowl, at least one of them, a slim blonde with a crescent tattoo stretching across her bare shoulder, had clocked him too.

"Darius," the third girl said. The tip of a fang peeked out when she bit her lower lip. *Vampire.*

"Is he in there with someone?" Liviu asked.

A sudden crash from the other side of the door was answer enough. It sounded like Darius had already found another warm body to take his mood out on.

"You have to do something," the vampire whispered, her hand springing to latch on to Liviu's arm. "This was all a misunderstanding, Crin didn't mean—"

"He won't do anything," the blonde interjected, throwing Liviu a venomous glare. "He's just a coward. Always has been."

The vampire looked from one to the other, aghast. Her hand still clutched Liviu's arm.

Liviu, who had never been one to embrace the virtues of purely rational thought—a fault he could trace many of his misfortunes back to—stared at her, mouth agape. He was many things, but *coward* was one step too far. His heart quickened as the wolf inside of him stirred.

A sharp yell sounded from the other side of the room, followed by another crash and the sound of splintering wood.

Liviu was walking backward before he knew it. When he judged there was enough distance between him and the door, he motioned for the women to scatter, crushing an expletive between his teeth. He allowed himself a quick breath to weigh the odds. *At least we'd be two against one.*

With his first running step, he thought, *Against him.*

By then, it was too late to stop.

He crashed into the door shoulder first, bracing for it to be locked. Instead, he all but tumbled into the Haunted Bulb's backroom.

This room extended just a touch wider than the antechamber, but the vast majority of the space was taken up by a monstrous couch draped in the same shimmering velvet as the divan in the antechamber. In front of it was—well, had been a low table, which was now in pieces near the door. A patchwork of sticky puddles and pointed glass shards covered the gaudy carpet, remains of the drinks and glasses the table had previously held. An upturned air purifier still thrummed in a corner, oblivious to all the chaos.

Liviu had a few seconds to absorb his surroundings before his eyes fell on the two protagonists of the unfolding drama. Darius, he already knew. He looked older than Liviu remembered; his short, black hair was graying at the temples, and the interceding years since he'd last seen him had etched deep lines into a face that had always held a strong aura of "don't fuck with me."

The other one, who looked to be in his mid-twenties, was thin and wispy like a runt, where Darius was two meters tall and built like a brick house. He sported a bloody lip and a string of bruises around his neck. The buttons of his torn white shirt were undone nearly to the waist, revealing pale skin marred by four parallel gashes that bled sluggishly into the fabric. They looked like claw marks, though Darius was presently in his human form. Maybe Liviu's sudden arrival had startled him into some semblance of propriety. It probably wouldn't last.

Taking advantage of the momentary distraction, the runt promptly scurried out the door, but not before his brown eyes met Liviu's. They were slightly glazed over and shimmering with un-shed tears. Liviu thought he saw a flicker of gratitude in them, which made him feel some sort of way before he realized that with the runt gone he was suddenly alone with Darius.

The door behind him was still open. For a moment, he contemplated going the runt's way. A chorus of sighs and half-whispered questions on the other side told him that the women were still hovering. *Like goddamn buzzards*, he thought.

Darius lumbered forward, not bothering to hide his bloodied knuckles.

Liviu had time to say, "Wait! The truce—"

A large hand wrapped around his throat and lifted him off his feet.

"The truce is *broken*," Liviu managed to squeeze out before a viselike grip tightened around his throat, cutting off his air altogether. The sudden lack of oxygen made black spots dance in front of his eyes as the world narrowed down to the sneering face in front of him. He clawed at the hand pinning him in place, but he might as well have tried to fight off a statue. Kicking blindly at the other werewolf's legs only earned him a tighter grip.

When Darius spoke, his voice was more snarl than words. "What did you *do*?"

"Nothing," Liviu choked out. "Vampires..."

Darius's eyes widened just a fraction. "What vampires?"

Liviu felt himself being lowered to the ground, slowly. He drew in a strangled breath as his feet found purchase and the grip around his throat eased a little. "Hunters...up the hill. Dead. *Killed*. All...all of them."

The grip vanished.

Liviu slumped back against the wall, gasping for breath. He felt the acrid taste of his own fear burning at the back of his throat. Through the spots still clouding his vision, he saw Darius turn around long enough to slam the door shut. The force of the impact rattled through the wall and into Liviu's back.

When Darius turned, the fury on his face had simmered to a deep, ugly scowl. "Start over," he demanded, but he didn't step into Liviu's space again.

Liviu's throat felt scratchy and raw when he spoke. "Y'know the big house on the hill?"

"Nightshade Lodge." The name made Darius frown even deeper.

"Vampires hit it." Liviu straightened up from the wall, holding back a wheeze. "I was up there earlier. Going by what I saw, it must've been at least two nights ago."

"And you're sure it was vampires?"

"Bite marks said as much. Must've been a whole damn coven. Hunters never had a chance." As he said it, Liviu flashed back to the dead boy he'd seen, and the memory made his stomach lurch.

Darius reached into the pocket of his jeans and pulled out a handkerchief. He started dabbing at his knuckles, though mostly he was just smearing the blood around.

"Who else knows about this?" Darius asked. The mean anger he'd shown before had been replaced by a colder, more calculated kind of fury.

"A few people. Evdochia wanted me to spread the word. They say we should all be ready when the humans come looking for blood."

Darius pinned him with a stare that held nothing good in it. "That truce was there for a reason. When the humans lost *one boy*, they went to war, and it almost took us all. What do you think they're going to do when they hear about this?"

Liviu shook his head. He didn't want to think about it. The war Darius spoke of still kept him up at night sometimes. Anyone who could fight, did fight. Liviu himself was barely old enough to shave back then, and he'd fought and killed plenty.

Likely sensing that Liviu wasn't going to indulge him, Darius let the now bloodied handkerchief fall from his grip and cracked his knuckles. "The humans can't know," he snapped, "so *I* need to know who else have you told."

"Why's it matter?" Liviu said, and his own voice sounded painfully resigned to his ears. "You can't bury something like this."

"Oh, I don't intend to *bury* anything," Darius said, a wicked grin spreading across his face. "I'm going to burn it to the ground."

*

Ileana felt her stomach give a violent lurch. *That's my sister you're talking about*, she thought, teeth baring in a snarl without her mind having much say-so in it.

Evdochia, meanwhile, rounded on Radu with lightning-quick movements and picked him up by the front of his tunic. "A monarch doesn't negotiate with the help," they said, raising him until their faces were inches apart. "Tell me what you know. If you don't, then maybe we'll get to see what *you* taste like."

Radu gave a startled yelp, but he had the dignity not to flail around too much. "Put me down!"

"We'll take the human," Ileana interjected. "Consider it a bonus," she added, doing her best to affect a false indifference.

Radu's eyes narrowed her way, his face twisting in a sneer that looked even more disturbing on a face so young. "North," he said after another beat, turning his now pleading eyes back to Evdochia. "He took the coven and went north, to Ravenswatch. That's all I know."

Ravenswatch. Ileana turned the name over in her mind. It wasn't any place she'd ever heard of. It didn't matter. Tamara was here; all she had to do was get her and get *out*. The vampires were free to settle their own business. It didn't concern her any more than whatever or wherever this Ravenswatch was.

Evdochia released their grip without warning, sending the boy tumbling to the floor in an unceremonious heap. "Why Ravenswatch?"

Radu stood up with ostentatious slowness, patting the dust from his black slacks. "That, I wouldn't know, Your Highness. After all, I'm just the help."

Once again, Ileana found herself speaking, "Why did they attack Nightshade Lodge?"

The boy threw her another venomous look. "You truly shouldn't allow your pet to speak when not spoken to," he said to Evdochia. "It's just poor manners."

Ileana's heart quickened. She felt the wolf straining to rip and tear, and for a moment, she contemplated giving in to that urge. Her fingers twitched, her body yearning for the savage release. *Not here*, she told herself, clenching her jaw so hard it hurt. *Not yet.*

"Take us to the human," Evdochia told the boy. "We will see to them for you." Their eyes sought and met Ileana's for a moment. "And do consider it a *bonus* for serving us so faithfully."

"Of course," Radu said, every syllable dripping with false deference. "Follow me."

They took the other door this time, which Radu unlocked with a small silver key he carried on a chain around his neck. Behind it, stone-paved catacombs branched out to the left and the right, both sides stretching well beyond the conceivable boundaries of the house upstairs. They must have predated the construction above by decades, if not centuries. Ileana had heard rumors about the catacombs running underneath Deva. She'd never seen them before.

They turned left and walked until they reached another flight of stairs that descended deeper into the bowels of the earth. These steps were paved with stone slabs; Ileana, who brought up the rear, saw dark blotches and faded palmprints marring each one. At the foot of the stairs was another door made of dark metal embellished with rows of pointy studs. Radu opened this one not with a key, but with magick, waving away the web of bright-red runes that bound the door shut. Ileana felt the tingle of it prickle her skin from where she stood several steps back. The child-vampire, it seemed, was powerful in his own right.

As soon as the door opened, the stench of stale blood and other bodily fluids exploded outward like noxious fumes from a sealed tomb. Wooden doors with narrow, grated windows lined a short corridor on one side. Chains and manacles dangled from the opposite wall. Ileana closed her eyes and swallowed back bile. This was where the coven kept their food.

The rasp of another door against the packed earth floor shook her from the momentary daze. Her heart beat in her throat. She hadn't seen Tamara in twenty years, but suddenly she dreaded what she was about to find.

She opened her eyes.

Radu stood in front of an open cell door, gesturing toward whoever was inside. Evdochia's expression had shifted minutely, though not in the way Ileana had expected.

"Oh look," a man rasped from inside the cell. "It brought friends."

The voice was a gruff baritone, distorted by the slight slurring of the words that came with a vampire bite. It was so different from the one Ileana had expected that she didn't recognize it at first. Her knees grew weak. *If she's not here, then—*

"Go on, you bastards, do what you came here to do," the man taunted. "I haven't got all day."

"Please, take him away," Radu said, turning back to Evdochia.

"His blood tastes like mud."

Something stirred in Ileana's distant memories. In a flash, she knew whom she'd find in the cell.

She moved as if trapped in a nightmare, her steps hobbled when all she wanted to do was spring forward. Her mind seemed to blank for an instant, and then, almost without realization, she was standing in the doorway of a stone-paved cell that couldn't have been more than two meters across. A barrel-chested man lay crumpled in one corner, his head pillowed on a thick, hairy arm. A tattoo of a wolf's head flag in the style of the ancient Dacians snaked around his wrist. The man's gray hair spilled over his face, and his overgrown beard spoke of the time he'd spent here. Days. Weeks, maybe.

Ileana's voice trembled when she called, "József?"

His eyes snapped up at that, focusing on her with some difficulty. Blinking a few times, he said, "Wha'?"

Ileana stood petrified. József was the last man she'd have expected to find down here.

József cleared his throat. It turned into a cough. "Ileana?" he asked, struggling to regain his breath. "That really you?"

"Yeah," she said. Her voice cracked on the word.

József regarded her for another moment, and then his eyes hardened. "So, you runnin' with vampires these days? Never woulda' thought."

Ileana found her words failing her. In her younger years, she and József had met their share of vampires across their travels. They'd burned or impaled most of them and let the sun take care of the ones who got away. If József still followed the hunter's path, he'd never understand the tenuous pact she'd made earlier tonight.

"What happened to the other humans you were keeping

here?" she asked, turning back to Radu. She could straighten things out with József when they were back above ground.

Radu looked up at her with something akin to pity. "That's the third time you've spoken out of turn, *meat*. Are you slow?"

Again, Ileana felt the wolf thrashing to get out. This time, she set it loose.

She was on the boy even before he'd finished delivering the jab, slamming him against the far wall with no concern for the integrity of his skull. She felt herself starting to turn, teeth growing into fangs, nails blackening and changing into claws, and let it happen. Hell, she'd never tasted vampire, but tonight was a night of firsts.

Radu's eyes flashed—in anger, she thought, but then she saw that something else was swirling in their gray depths and heard his voice reverberating inside her skull. "*Release me.*"

"No," she snarled, hoisting the boy higher to emphasize her statement. "Tell me."

Another presence, gentler but infinitely colder, nudged its way along the first. In her mind, Ileana heard Evdochia say, "*He is not yours to kill.*"

Radu, for his part, now regarded her with wide-eyed fear. That didn't temper his next words though. "I already did, you dumb beast. The coven went north. The thralls went with them. What else do you want?"

Slowly, Ileana lowered him to the ground. She didn't trust herself to be this close to him anymore, not when she felt a breath away from tearing out his throat with her bare teeth. She breathed deeply, counting. The wolf receded.

Again, she felt Evdochia's mind brushing against her own, a soothing whisper that tamed away the last stirrings of the beast. "*We will speak outside. You can bring your human, if you wish.*"

Chapter Six

Flame Purifies

Getting József up the stairs was painfully familiar. Ileana had done this countless times when he'd been drunk, hoisting and nudging and pushing until she'd get him close enough to a bed he could fall in to sleep it off. József was clearly exhausted; she didn't need to see the puncture wounds on his neck to know why. She braced herself to catch him every time he stumbled and thought bitterly, *Just like old times.*

She'd long since convinced herself that József was dead, either killed by a nightwalker or, more likely, by his own hand. Seeing him now, alive and walking? She didn't know what to do with that.

When they emerged into the damp, chilly air outside, József kept walking, brushing past Evdochia like they didn't even exist.

"Where are you going?" Ileana called after him.

"To find my truck," József shouted back. He neither turned nor slowed.

A cold, ghostly touch on her arm stopped Ileana before she could run after him.

"Did you know that man?" Evdochia asked, their eyes lingering on hers a fraction longer than necessary. A spark of curiosity danced in their obsidian depths.

"Yeah. He took me in, after I got turned." Before Evdochia had a chance to wander too far down that particular line of inquiry, Ileana said, "Ravenswatch. How do I find it?"

Evdochia's eyebrows arched up slightly. "I could tell you, but you would sooner ask the rivers to flow backwards than find your way into Ravenswatch alone. Even if you did, my brother's coven would rend you limb from limb."

"I'll find a way," Ileana said. She gave the air a long sniff almost despite herself. József's scent painted a vivid trail in the night, a strong odor of someone who'd been left to marinate in their own fluids for some time. It was easy enough to follow, but she had to move quickly. If he got to his truck before she could reach him, he'd be gone again, maybe forever.

"I'm not in the habit of sending people to their deaths," Evdochia said, "but the love you feel for your blood kin? That, I understand. It makes you do things that are unwise."

The quiet wistfulness in their voice made Ileana wonder if they were thinking of someone from their own past.

Love for a sibling. Was it really what this was about?

To Evdochia, she said, "Tamara was sick when they took her. I don't have the luxury to be wise."

"If it reassures you any, when the coven trouble themselves to take their humans all the way to Ravenswatch, they keep them alive for many days, sickness or not. We have ways."

"I don't doubt it," Ileana said, again choosing to avoid thinking too much about the implications. "So, when are we leaving?"

Evdochia tilted their head to the side a fraction, but otherwise they didn't look like they'd taken offense. "I will need a night to settle matters here, and then another to make the journey. We will meet in the town of Gorun, three days from now."

"Gorun?" Ileana asked. This name, too, felt foreign.

"It's half a day's journey north from Bistriţa. Look for a red house up the hill."

As Evdochia spoke, an image of a house flashed in Ileana's mind, with red brick walls and narrow windows obscured by thick velvet drapes. It looked, at a glance, perfectly ordinary. Ileana held on to the afterimage, burning it in her mind.

"Three days," Ileana said. "I'll be there."

"Bring Liviu with you as well," Evdochia said as Ileana turned, ready to sprint. "He knows where the house is. He also knows his way around the wards."

Ileana's eyebrows scrunched together at that, but she nodded anyway. With József's scent still lingering strong in her nose, she ran.

*

József didn't look back. Couldn't, to tell the truth of it.

He'd spent years torturing himself with thoughts of what-if. One minute he'd berate himself for abandoning Ileana, then he'd turn around and reason that she'd abandoned him first. Sometimes, when he was deep in his cups, he thought he saw her in a window or in the shadow of a passerby. When the vampires had snatched him and locked him up, he'd thought he'd reached the end of his days and told himself he deserved it. He'd never thought he'd see her alive again.

He felt lightheaded as he walked, but no more than he usually did after a night of drinking. As his steps chewed at the cobblestones, his mind gnawed at the problem of where the fuck to go from here. His truck was the obvious choice. He'd left it in a back alley next to a church, but when he looked up he only saw the rooftops of houses and, behind them, clusters of winking lights going up the hill. If there was a church somewhere up there, he couldn't spot it from where he was. All he could do was move around on foot and hope he got lucky.

He'd need some food before then, he decided, digging up some crumpled bills from the soiled back pocket of his jeans. Those turned out to be enough for a greasy convenience store sandwich and half a liter of orange juice in a plastic bottle. He also pilfered a pocket-sized vodka on his way out.

József spotted some concrete stairs leading up to a darkened building—a bank or a tax office or something—and crashed on a step about halfway up. First, he made quick work of the sandwich. That settled his stomach a little, but not enough; he'd need to find something more substantial before he skipped town. With the more pressing need taken care of, he turned to the other urge, the one he hadn't sated since the night he'd been taken. He popped the top of the orange juice, then, with some difficulty—his fingers were covered in grease and the damn thing was so fuckin' small—he opened the vodka. He then upended the smaller bottle into the bigger one, capped that one, gave it a few shakes, and finally raised it to his eyes and gave it a critical look.

Good enough.

With slow movements, almost like he was performing a rite, he uncapped the bottle again and brought it to his lips. For an empty moment, he wondered if he shouldn't. Detoxing in that God-forsaken cell had felt like death, but now he was pretty much clean.

Like all the other times I got "clean," he thought with a bitterness he'd long since grown familiar with. He tossed his head back and drained a third of the alcoholic mix in a few long, thirsty gulps.

That hit the spot, just as he knew it would. He could still taste the sharp alcohol underneath the tangy sweetness of the orange juice. It warmed him right up, sending a tingling all the way down to his fingers. It also dulled the pangs in his chest that had nothing to do with hunger or thirst.

A second sense, which he'd picked up over the years of living this life, made him look up as something shifted in the air. Sure enough, at the foot of the stairs, there she stood: Ileana, alive as you please and with the gall to look at him like he was the only one who'd fucked up.

Seconds rolled into one another. Neither of them spoke.

József pushed to his feet slowly. He had the high ground, but not much else. In his present state, half starved and weaponless, he felt all kinds of vulnerable, and that, in turn, pissed him off.

"Y'know, it's not like I thought we'd just hug and make up," Ileana said, her voice carrying easily upwards, "but I deserve a thank-you, at least."

"All right, *thank you,*" József said, waving the bottle her way. "There you go."

She looked over her shoulder for a second, then back at him. "Why'd you run off like that?"

"When'd you start hanging out with vampires?" He took a lazy swig while waiting for the answer. It gave his hands something to do.

She scowled at him. "What's it to you anyway? First you fuck off and leave me stranded in Bratislava, then you disappear for eighteen years, and *now* you suddenly give a f—"

"You left first," József cut in. He didn't shout. The words hurt like glass.

"I was *seventeen*, Jóska! Did you really think I'd gone for good? In Bratislava, where we didn't know anyone?"

His own heart was pounding in his chest; he could feel its reverberations up in his throat. That was the only damn reason his own voice shook when he said, "I came back to look for you, but you were gone. No one at the motel knew anything. The last they'd seen of you was—"

Damn it. There was no good way to finish that sentence. Whatever he chose to say, it still made him feel like scum.

"When I climbed into the dumpster to get my shit," Ileana finished for him. "At least you didn't leave it out in the street."

"I came back for you," he said again, refusing to let himself be cowed by the shame that rightfully tried to crawl its way up from his gut.

"That night was a full moon, you asshole. I couldn't just stick around and hope you'd sober up and realize you'd fucked up."

"The booze had nothing to do with anything. You had no right."

Her eyes scrunched shut. When she spoke next, the words were quiet, broken. "I was tired of being her ghost."

And, yeah, that shut him right up.

"Every time you called me her name," Ileana said. "Every time you looked at me and saw her. Every night I left you staring at her picture and went to bed wondering if I'd find you dead by morning. I couldn't be the daughter you lost, but I was *someone*, Jóska! Why couldn't you see that?"

József had heard some of it back in Bratislava, but the hurt had been too raw for him to listen back then. "You didn't deserve half the shit I put you through," he said, his voice thick with something he refused to call guilt. "That still doesn't excuse what you did."

"I'm sorry I tore up the picture," she said. Whisper-quiet, almost.

"I'm sorry too." It was as sincere as he could make it, but he didn't feel any lighter for having said it.

He'd tried to glue Stefánia's picture back together, but it was fractured, imperfect, like his memories of her were quickly becoming. He'd ended up burning it.

Ileana let out a breath. It sounded like one of those sighs that wait for years to get out. "You look like shit," she said, crossing her arms. "How long were you down there?"

He had to think about it; he'd lost track. "What day is it?"

"April fourth. Well," she amended, glancing at her watch, "it's the fifth as of two minutes ago."

József ran the numbers in his head and grimaced. He knew he'd lost time. He hadn't expected it to be this much time.

She was still talking. "I'm staying at a guest house not far from here. There's room enough for two, if you want to clean yourself up and sleep in a bed for once. Food's okay too."

I gotta leave. He almost said the words, but then he thought better of it. Another night wouldn't make much difference. He could think about Bear Lake and the people there—the people he'd failed, tomorrow—*'Cause that's what I do, I let people down.* A cold shower, a warm bed, and a pair of eyes to watch over him while he slept would probably do him good.

"Okay," he said, tucking the half-empty bottle in the back pocket of his jeans. "Lead the way."

*

From the top floor of an unfinished apartment building, Liviu watched Nightshade Lodge burn.

The flames had engulfed the place a short while ago, and now the humans were finally starting to catch on. Flickering lights wound their way up the hill toward the blaze: firefighters, most likely, though he spotted the red of an ambulance as well. He had to admire their optimism, pointless as it was.

It was the end of something, he told himself, and the beginning of something worse. Deva hadn't seen much bloodshed between hunters and nightwalkers for almost two decades now. A three-way truce, signed in the wake of months of bloody conflict, had seen to that. The killing, of course, went on in earnest elsewhere, but Deva had been a sanctuary, at least. And now, because of a few damn vampires, that peace had been shattered, and that was about to become everyone's problem.

All I wanted to do was eat, drink, and fuck my way into the afterlife, he thought, letting his head fall forward with a long sigh. Instead, a grisly death now loomed on the horizon, so pungent he could practically taste it. It smelled like blood, with a hint of smoke, stale booze, and—

Wait.

That wasn't just a fancy. He *could* taste blood and smoke, but it was cigarette smoke, not burning timber.

Liviu jumped to his feet, his gaze darting around as his pulse ticked up a notch. He was in a vast, empty room with the outer wall missing. He spotted a lithe silhouette in the empty doorway who drew back into the shadows when they realized they'd been spotted.

"I'm in no mood for this shit right now," Liviu called out, feeling his hackles rise. "Either come out or fuck off."

There was a slight shuffling sound, then the silhouette

reappeared. What Liviu had first mistaken for a ghostly gleam was, in fact, a white shirt, torn open and fluttering in the breeze. The skin peeking out from underneath was pale and streaked with red.

"Oh. It's you," Liviu said. "The fuck do you want?"

The runt who'd been consigned to Darius's punching bag earlier took another step forward, holding his shirt closed with one hand. He ran his other hand through his hair, which had been parted in a side quiff at some point—Liviu remembered it from the Bulb—but was thoroughly mussed now, falling around his face in a tangle of dark strands.

"I wanted to thank you," the runt said, smiling to reveal two bright rows of perfectly human teeth. "I didn't mean to intrude."

I wanted to thank you.

Again, Liviu felt some sort of way. It happened rarely enough that he didn't have a name for it, but it felt like a tingly warmth burrowing inside his chest, close to the sternum.

"Don't worry 'bout it," he said. "And, uh, maybe keep the fuck away from Darius if you know what's good for you. Asshole's got a long memory."

"That might be difficult, seeing as the asshole is my brother." The runt held out his hand. "I'm Crin. I don't think we've actually met."

"Liviu." He grasped the proffered hand and shook it. Crin's fingers were cold and slender, but their grip was firm.

"Oh," Crin said, or at least his lips formed the shape of an O. "You're Liviu the Cat, right? I heard my brother talk about you a few times."

Liviu pulled back his hand and stuck it into the pocket of his jeans, taking half a step back for good measure. Another day, he might have found it in him to drop some shitty line (*I'm afraid it's all true*, said with a grin and a wink). He wasn't in the mood to-night.

"You were the only one who stood up to him after the truce," Crin went on, either not taking the hint or not caring enough to stop himself. "You knew you couldn't win, but you still—"

"All right, that's enough," Liviu said, feeling the prickle of the old shame that came whenever someone brought that up. "This thing with you and Darius? I've seen shit like it enough times to know how it ends. Brother or not, one day he's gonna go too far, and then he'll either kill you, or he'll hurt you so bad you're gonna wish you were dead. Don't wait for that. Get the hell out."

"Everyone knows how he's—what he's doing to me." Crin's voice was quieter now. He stood statue still except for a faint tremor in his shoulders. "No one ever says anything, but you stood up for me, and you don't even know me. I'm—I need you to know how much that means to me."

And I'll pay for it with my hide, Liviu thought as he shrugged and said, "Sure, yeah. Don't mention it."

Suddenly, he was itching to get the hell away from here, get drunk, and forget that the thing at the Bulb had ever happened. He also wanted to stay and listen, and that vexed him to no end. *The fuck's wrong with me?*

Crin shimmied out of the way as he stomped past, a telltale flinch preceding the movement. Liviu had seen that too. Hell, he'd *been* that once or twice, when fate and/or his own subpar deci-sion-making had seen him trapped in the kind of relationships that ended with broken bones.

"Take care of yourself," Liviu said over his shoulder, "and think about what I said. I won't be around next time."

As he reached the stairs, he heard Crin's whisper drifting on the breeze, so quiet he thought he might have imagined it. "But...

I have nowhere else to go..."

He walked faster, ignoring the way Crin's words prickled at his skin.

Chapter Seven

Night of Many

Ileana's body slumbered through the day. Her mind stitched together a quilt of dreams where past and present blurred together and reality frayed at the edges, where József turned into a vampire while, at his side, Tamara, gaunt and pale and all of six years old, withered away into a husk. Ileana saw her mother as she remembered her, youthful and laughing while her neck bled slowly from a bite mark underneath her jaw. Her father was there, too, threatening everyone with a dagger he'd pulled out of his own chest.

She woke at dusk and sat on the edge of her bed for a while, letting the nightmarish images fall from her mind one by one. *Fuck dreams.*

József was still sleeping, so she left him undisturbed, and

bundling up his clothes under her arm, she went downstairs to look for a washing machine, her mind turning all the while. "Bring Liviu with you," Evdochia had told her, as if she could just snap her fingers and have him follow her like a lost pup. She didn't even know where to find him. All she had was two names—the Haunted Bulb and the King's Pub—and a vague recollection of what he smelled like. He'd mentioned one other place, the Cheap Shot, but that one wasn't on any maps that she could find.

And then, she thought as she attacked a plate of cold leftovers a short while later, there was the matter of getting to Gorun and to the red house. Ileana had hitchhiked to Deva, walking the last five kilometers when the car she'd caught a ride in had gasped its last mechanical breath in a puff of black diesel smoke. She might have asked József for a ride, but she doubted he'd welcome Liviu in the mix. At times, he'd barely tolerated Ileana, knowing what she was.

If it weren't for the wards Evdochia had also mentioned, Ileana would've happily left Liviu behind, but old magick was something to be ignored at one's own peril. She'd seen a victim of a nightwalker's wards once, a hapless hunter who'd charged into a hag's lair armed with nothing but a stake, a vial of holy water, and negative common sense. She still remembered the bone white of his skull peeking through the ruins of his face.

She watched József's clothes spin in the dryer as the hands of the wall clock above it crawled their way toward the top of the hour. Her foot bounced up and down, the rubber sole of her boot squeaking against the linoleum floor. When the clock hit ten past, she stood and went to find the host. Some mild flattery and a well-placed bribe saw to it that József's laundry would find its way back to their room as soon as it was ready.

"Heard about the fire?" the host asked her as she turned to leave.

Ileana paused. "What fire?"

"Big house on the hill burned down last night," the host said, sounding almost giddy to have such big news to share.

Ileana froze for a moment.

"I see," she said, then walked away.

Nightshade Lodge wasn't her home, just like the people who'd perished there hadn't been her family for twenty years. Still, it was like a gaping void had opened in her chest. It didn't hurt. It just felt empty.

József was still sleeping when she went back to their room, his form a quiet mound under the sheets that rose and fell with every deep, steady breath he took. A smile flickered across her lips, softening the harsh lines of her face. *He's okay.*

Moving carefully, Ileana made her bed, then scribbled a quick note and left it on her pillow along with a crisply folded bill. József didn't stir while she changed into fresh clothes: a washed-out pair of jeans that hugged her hips and a black, sleeveless shirt with slightly more cleavage than she usually wore. The Haunted Bulb was a nightclub, the kind of place where her usual attire would stick out like a sore thumb. Besides, she'd never been one to shy away from using her natural endowments to get what she wanted out of a conversation. She'd learned early on that most men, as well as some women, would answer questions far more readily when presented with a nice pair of tits.

Satisfied, she shrugged into her jacket, took one last look at József, who hadn't stirred, and tiptoed out. Had she lingered a little longer, she might have noticed that József's eyes were open as he watched her leave the room.

*

The King's Pub was closer, so Ileana went there first. When she found no trace of Liviu and no one at the bar could tell her whether they'd seen him tonight, she moved on to the Haunted Bulb.

Liviu had warned her about the Bulb, but there was nothing sinister about the place as far as she could tell, at least from the outside. Clumps of patrons loitered on the sidewalk, their smoke and idle chatter wafting in the air. Ileana had never understood the casual camaraderie of strangers, so she kept moving. A line was starting to form at the entrance, but it was a short one. Too early, she guessed.

She walked up to the bouncer, a bald, mean-looking guy towering over most everybody. He had to tilt his chin down to get a good look at her. When he also gave the air around her a good sniff, Ileana immediately knew him for what he was.

"We ain't opening until half past," the bouncer said, sounding like he'd parroted the same line at least a dozen times tonight.

"I'm looking for someone," Ileana said. "Goes by Liviu the Cat."

"You won't find him here." The bouncer lowered his voice and added. "'Specially not after last night."

Ileana knew enough to recognize a gossip when she saw one. She leaned forward and whispered, "What happened last night?"

"He got into a tiff with the boss. Can you believe it? He just went down there and kicked down the door outta nowhere."

"No way," Ileana said. Her shock wasn't just for show either. This was the guy Evdochia wanted her to travel with? *Fucking hell.*

The bouncer's eyes twinkled. "I saw it myself. The door, I mean. Darius was pissed. You should've seen him. He—"

"Is everything all right here, Ciprian?" a third voice interrupted. It was smooth and velvety with a barely there throaty quality to it.

The man who'd spoken had just walked out from the bowels of the Bulb. He was tall and slender, with dark hair parted down the middle and straight bangs framing his impossibly pale face. He wasn't a vampire, though, or at least he didn't smell like one. The garish red shirt he wore also didn't peg him as one of the club's regulars, who seemed to prefer ripped jeans, platform boots, and various bits with skulls and spikes on them.

The bouncer, Ciprian, nodded Ileana's way. "She's looking for the guy who broke into the backroom last night. Catman. You know the one."

The third man's eyes turned to Ileana, wide and questioning for an instant before his expression went back to a mild disinterest. "That man is barred from the Haunted Bulb. You should go."

Ileana had gathered as much. She wasn't likely to get anything else out of these two, and insisting would only draw the wrong kind of attention. She turned and started back the way she'd come with no aim in mind. On the other side of the street, she kicked at a rock in passing and sent it plinking off a parked car nearby. *Now what?*

She made it to the next street corner before she suddenly felt a presence at her elbow. Turning, she found the man from the club, the one with the red shirt. This close, she saw that the shirt had sequins scattered all over it. *Sequins. Jesus Christ.*

"You said you were looking for Liviu," Red Shirt said. "What do you want with him?" His tone was guarded, but not enough to hide the warning behind the words.

"What's it to you?" Ileana asked.

"You have his scent. Are you his mate?"

Ileana blinked slowly. "No," she said, and she didn't miss the way his shoulders sagged minutely. "It's business. Not the bloody kind, but also not the kind you share with strangers."

The man pondered this for a moment, then held out his hand. "My name's Crin."

"Still a stranger," Ileana deadpanned as she took his hand and gave it a firm shake, introducing herself in turn.

"As are you," Crin said lightly. "I've never seen you before, so I'm guessing you aren't from Deva. And, going by your scent, you weren't born into the blood. A turned werewolf is a rare sight these days."

This conversation was starting to grate on her nerves. "Look, I need to find Liviu. I'm not here to start trouble. I just need to talk to him, then I'm gone."

Crin seemed to wrestle with himself for a moment, then finally relented. "Have you tried looking at the Cheap Shot?"

"I know the name. I don't know where it is."

"It's not far. I can take you there. Besides, I—" He cut himself off abruptly, then said, "Never mind. Let's go."

*

Liviu ran his finger along the rim of his pint and tried to focus on what the man in front of him was talking about.

He'd picked up (or rather, he'd let himself be picked up by) a cute guy, all blonde hair and dimpled cheeks and the kind of cocky smile that brought a lovely, discordant note to the ensemble. Another time, Liviu wouldn't have said no to a night of wild, no-strings-attached sex, and maybe a proper date later if the guy was worth it. Tonight, the Cheap Shot was buzzing with talk of the fire at Nightshade Lodge, and Liviu couldn't help overhearing most of it from where he was standing next to the bar. That only served to remind him how well and utterly fucked they all were.

I need to get the hell out of town, he thought, hiding behind a long pull of his pint.

The guy, who was apparently a big football fan, asked him whether he thought Politehnica Timişoara would win the championship again this year. Liviu mumbled something ambiguous enough to pass for both a yeah and a nah. Whatever Darius thought he'd accomplish by burning down Nightshade Lodge would backfire spectacularly the moment a hunter with more than two brain cells to rub together figured out that the fire had been set *after* the murders.

And then they'll come for us, he thought bitterly. *All of them.*

Belatedly, Liviu realized that the guy had stopped talking a minute ago. When he looked up from his pint, the guy wasn't exactly glaring, but he wasn't far from it either. With a jolt, Liviu realized he didn't even remember his name.

Shit.

"I'm sorry," Liviu said, raising the pint between them like the world's most half-assed shield. Condensation had made the glass so slippery he almost fumbled it. "It's just. You caught me at a bad time, is all." Speaking, his eyes fell on the entrance and the two people who'd just walked in, both of whom he recognized. Suddenly, the man in front of him was the least of his problems. *What the shit?*

The guy shrugged, his eyes already scanning the room behind Liviu as he pushed away from the bar. "Maybe next time, yeah?"

"Whatever," Liviu muttered as he watched him go.

Ileana was the one who clocked him first. She made a beeline toward him, walking with the kind of stride that said she wasn't here just to get pissed and look for company. Crin trailed half a step behind her, looking hotter than anyone had the right to be in a red, sequined shirt with a deep V-neck and a pair of black jeans so tight they outlined every delicious curve of his—

Stop, what the fuck. Liviu was down for a number of things that other, more sensible people would deem to be reckless, stupid, or both. Drooling over Darius's brother was on the other side of a thick, hard line.

Lucky for his sanity, Crin veered toward the other side of the bar at the last second, and only Ileana came up to meet him. She immediately pointed at a free table near the back. Liviu followed, salvaging his half-empty pint in passing, despite the urge to glance over his shoulder and see if Crin was—

Doesn't fucking matter, he groaned inwardly, keeping his eyes trained firmly forward.

They'd barely sat down when Ileana said, "Did you talk to Eva?"

"*Evdochia*. Don't shorten their name, they hate that," Liviu said. "I didn't talk to them, not yet. They didn't come home this morning."

"That happen often?" Ileana asked.

"They keep me around to mind the place, not to keep tabs on how often they sleep in their own bed."

She quirked a brow. "Not a coffin?"

"Don't be offensive," he deadpanned. "How'd it go with the coven anyway?"

He listened as Ileana recounted the events of the previous night, nodding every now and then to show he was paying attention. Halfway through, he got up to get another pint from the bar and got one for her too. He also saw that Crin was now talking to the blond guy Liviu had turned down earlier. Something knotted in his chest, a diffuse sense that something was off about the whole picture. Maybe it was the fact that they were standing a little too close to each other. Maybe it was how Crin's eyes unexpectedly met his, and then he had the audacity to wink while still pretending to listen to the blond.

Liviu walked back to the table and set the pints down with a little more force than necessary. His gaze wandered back to the bar several times before the end of Ileana's story, only to see that Crin and the blond were still engrossed in their conversation, like they were living in their own microcosm or something. Eventually, he pinned the table with a hard stare and didn't look back up until Ileana was done talking.

"Shame that you didn't find her," he said, talking to a point in the air that was about halfway between them to keep his eyes from wandering again. "At least you got a lead, though. Ravenswatch."

Ileana nodded. "Evdochia wanted you to come with me. They said the place where we're meeting is warded, but you know how to get us in."

"The red house, yeah. Been a while since we were up there." He chuckled despite himself, remembering the first time he'd walked into one of the wards. Thanks to his instincts, the flames had only singed his eyebrows and ruined a perfectly good coat.

"Will you come, then?" she asked.

"I'll take you to the village, yeah, and get you inside the house. But I'm not coming to Ravenswatch." His eyes cut towards the bar as he said it, and then he wished he hadn't looked. The blond's arm was now curled around Crin's slim waist, pulling him close.

It wasn't jealousy he was feeling, he realized with a start. Or, well, it wasn't *just* that. He felt an odd sense of guilt, too, knowing he'd be safer on the road than in Deva when shit hit the fan. *But what about him?* said a small, treacherous thought.

Ileana let out a long breath, then drank deeply. Liviu did the same.

"I'm staying at the Loafer," she said after a minute, wiping her mouth with the back of her hand. "We can meet there first thing tomorrow and be in Gorun by dusk."

"Make that *second* thing, and yeah. You got wheels?"

She paused. "I'll ask József tonight. He still has his truck."

"Right, József," he said. "Funny how he showed up right in the middle of all this. Almost like he was looking for trouble."

Ileana's voice hardened. "If you have something to ask, then ask."

"He a hunter? Like you used to be?"

He could see in the way she hesitated that she was trying to pick her words, and that was answer enough.

"We can take my car," he said as she opened her mouth to speak. "I'll see you at the Loafer tomorrow morning. Bring your own food."

He waited until he saw her nod, then got out of his chair and headed for the exit. He was dying for a smoke.

*

The Cheap Shot was cloistered at the far end of a small, walled-in courtyard. There was no sign to mark the entrance; someone either knew how to find the place or they didn't. There were no loiterers out front either. The last thing the Cheap Shot needed was to draw attention to itself.

Liviu paced the courtyard, his thoughts churning like the embers at the tip of his cigarette. He owed Evdochia more than just his life. If they wanted him to go north with Ileana, then north he'd go, no questions asked. What gnawed at him was the thought of what, or rather whom, he'd have to leave behind.

His cigarette had burned down to a stub, and he still didn't have his answers. He threw its remains in a puddle along the wall, where the embers died with a hiss, then plucked another one from the battered pack he'd been carrying around since the last time he'd "quit." His throat was still sore after last night. It burned every time he inhaled the smoke, making his eyes water. The bruises had faded, a testament to the rapid healing his beast blood gifted him with, and he could breathe properly again. At least when he wasn't gagging on smoke that tasted like toenail clippings and denial.

He let out a groan, blowing smoke through his nose. The wind promptly snatched it and blew it back into his face.

Somehow, the notion that Crin would be dead soon had planted itself in his mind and refused to be dislodged. Thinking about it made him sick. It wasn't because of some stupid, half-assed crush; hell, he'd known the guy for all of two days. It was because what he'd seen last night at the Bulb and later had struck far too close to home.

Liviu had challenged Darius once, shortly after the war, and he'd nearly paid for it with his life. He still remembered the agony of what he'd thought would be his final moments. He remembered looking at the circle of gawkers who'd gathered to see Darius fight and thinking, *Help me. I'm sorry. Help me.* No one had.

There was no doubt in Liviu's mind that Crin would suffer the same kind of fate if he didn't leave while he still could. Maybe not as bloody, definitely not as public, but it would happen. Assholes like Darius always, *always* took things too far in the end.

Last night, Crin had told him he had nowhere else to go. Well, north was *somewhere,* and where there was room enough for two, there could easily be room for three. That was all he could offer Crin right now other than his own fucked-up self. He could offer, and—

And Crin would say no. He could feel it in his bones.

Crin's pack, his life, were all here. Besides, the good ones always said no to whatever Liviu had to offer, so he'd stopped asking, stopped wanting long ago. Instead, he'd settled for things that were quick and messy and bad enough to bruise him inside and out. If anything, this was different. For once, he could see himself doing right by someone without waiting to be hurt in return.

He had to at least *try*.

His mind made up, Liviu threw the second cigarette after the first and walked back to the doors of the Cheap Shot. His hand was on the latch when the door swung open from the other side, and Crin almost walked into him.

He looked like he was running away, eyes wild and shirt hanging halfway open. When he saw Liviu, he let out a short, brittle laugh. "Good," he said, "I thought you'd—"

"I'm leaving Deva," Liviu blurted out.

Crin's eyes widened for just a moment with a flash of hurt that twisted a knife in Liviu's gut. "Let me come with you," he said before Liviu could even ask. "I can be useful. I've got my own money. Just for a while, I can't"—his voice cracked on the words, and Liviu's heart cracked too—"I can't stay here. You're right. He's going to kill me."

Liviu wanted to tell him so many things. That it was fine, and that he didn't care about the money. That he'd have strangled Darius with his bare hands if he could, if only he was strong enough. That he didn't deserve the trust Crin was giving him, much as he desperately wanted it.

All he said was, "Okay."

"Okay?" Crin echoed, more breath than word.

"That's what I said, didn't I? You know a place called the Loafer on Decebal Street?"

Crin nodded eagerly. "I'll find it."

"Good," Liviu said, grateful the courtyard was dark enough to hide the small smile tugging at the corners of his lips. "Meet me there tomorrow morning. We leave at first light."

*

Back at the Loafer, Ileana found an empty room.

József's bed was neatly made, a departure from how she'd known him back in the day. There was a folded piece of paper on the pillow. She unfolded it and read:

> *Have to leave for Bear's Lake. Life and death. If you*
> *still want to talk, meet me there. I'll wait two days.*

She read the note again, then crumpled it and flung it at the nearest wall.

She had three days before she met with Evdochia in Gorun, time enough to cross the country and give the old bastard a piece of her mind once and for all. After that, she wouldn't care if she never saw him again.

Chapter Eight

The Winds Keep on Howling

József drove through the night without stopping with the windows rolled all the way down. The rush of cold wind kept him awake. Breathing it felt like a blessing after the seventeen days he'd spent languishing in the fetid air of the coven dungeon.

Thinking of that made his palms break into a cold sweat as the taste of bile surged up his throat. Time and booze would dull some of it, sure. The scars would fade, the memories would blend with the rest of the horrors he'd lived through. But—and there was no dancing around it—he was getting old. There wasn't enough sand left in his hourglass to bury all of it.

He'd given his beard a trim, so he no longer looked like a hermit, at least. The hair could wait until he found a barber. For once, his thermos had freshly brewed coffee in it, and it was the straight stuff, not the Irish. It had been full when he left Deva. After more than a hundred kilometers through the winding plateaus at the foot of the Carpathians, it was nearly empty.

When he veered north toward the mountains, he plucked out a CD from the glove compartment, slid it into the player, and cranked up the volume as high as it could go. The wailing vocals of one Ozzy Osbourne, himself an undying fixture of both the heavy metal scene and József's decades on the road, kept him firmly anchored to the waking world for the rest of the journey.

Bear Lake was nestled in a valley high up in the mountains, where snow lingered from November until early May. József knew the merfolk who dwelled in the lake, and he'd gone up to visit them a fair few times over the years. Sometimes, he brought gifts. Other times, he brought stories. Most of them only knew the lake, the forest, and the nearby village of Three Rivers, where some spent their days living in human disguise.

Before he'd been waylaid and captured back in Deva, József had been on his way to deliver a warning. (If only he hadn't stopped for the night. If only he hadn't gone looking for a whore.)

He turned his thoughts away from the slippery slope of *my fault, this one's my fault, if they died, they died because of me.* He changed the track, belting out the words to Black Sabbath's "Crazy Train" over the CD. He couldn't carry a tune to save his life, but the shouting felt good.

By the time he drove into Three Rivers, the hour was so late it was almost early. The sky was a deep blue speckled with more stars than you'd ever see from the plains. He turned off the music but kept the windows down, letting the crisp mountain air fill the cabin. The faintest whisper of wood smoke from hearths long since banked for the night drifted on the breeze. The only sound was the soft crunch of gravel under the Amarok's tires as it rolled to a stop in the center of the village, where the single street widened into a small plaza with a tavern on one side and a guest house on the other. József cut the engine and sat there for a moment, listening to the silence. He welcomed the peace.

Then, he spotted a brown Dacia SUV parked half on, half off the sidewalk by the guest house, and his heart sank. He started the engine again and drove forward until he was close enough to see the horizontal crack running all the way across the Dacia's back bumper.

Too late, then.

He'd already known this was a possibility. Seeing the Dacia here, covered in mud and darker splotches that may have been something else, only cemented his suspicions. Cursing under his breath, he maneuvered his much bigger truck around it, then floored the gas pedal, speeding away in a screeching of tires. He didn't trust himself to linger, not until he knew exactly what had happened here.

The dirt path leading up to Bear Lake was little more than a steep, sinuous ribbon made of mud. It was barely wide enough for his truck to pass through, but the deep ruts in the soft earth told him he wasn't the first to intrude here lately. Leafless branches hung low over the path, grazing the truck's roof every now and then. The steering wheel fought him every time the tires strayed from their grooves as the old suspension creaked and groaned. He was sweating by the time he reached the lake.

Bear Lake was long and narrow, a wedge of stillness amid the calcareous peaks of the Western Carpathians. On a clear day, its waters were a deep, serene shade of blue. Tonight, they would be dotted with stars, a perfect mirror of the heavens.

He parked the truck under the low canopy and cut the engine, then the headlights. From the glove compartment, he retrieved a flashlight, his revolver, and a small bundle wrapped in a square of dark fabric. His fingers shook when he undid the string and pulled open the fabric to reveal the small object inside. At a glance, it looked like a gemstone, only as big as a thumbnail. One end was rounded, the other tapered towards a triangular point. The shoal-mother had gifted it to József the second time they'd met. It was a scale, plucked from her own tail and enchanted with her magick, that marked him as a friend to the lake mer.

Some friend, József thought, running a hand through his beard on a long exhale. He pocketed the scale, stuck the revolver in his waistband, and stepped into the night.

The lingering chill of the Carpathian spring immediately snapped him out of the heavy torpor of the trip. His shirt stuck to his back, and the coat he wore over it was too thin to keep him properly warm. The air was cold up here, smelling of moss and water and freshly upturned earth. Ahead of him, the lake waters rustled against the shore.

The ground was wet and uneven. There was no path to speak of, just a gentle slope that ended where the water began. József followed the curve of the slope, using the flashlight to avoid stepping in puddles or tripping over a rock. Close to the shore, the mud was churned and pockmarked with footprints. When he shone his flashlight straight down, he saw blood.

Before he knew it, his hand was already rummaging inside his pocket for a flask that wasn't there. He'd lost it back in Deva, along with the time he could have used to warn the mer this was coming. His fingers closed around the ruby scale instead; he felt its warmth this close to the cradle of its power and hoped against hope that there was someone below the surface still alive to sense its presence.

When a few minutes passed without so much as a ripple on

the water, József started walking down the shore, hugging himself to preserve whatever warmth his body hadn't relinquished yet. The mud sucked at his boots with every squelching step. After a while, his feet found rocks where the shore jutted a half meter or so above the lake, smooth and covered in moss. He'd made it a third of the way around the lake when his foot slipped into the water. With a shout of surprise, he drew back, flailing his arms to regain his balance. His foot was the only casualty of his carelessness, at least, soaking wet up to the knee.

He found a relatively flat spot on the ground and sat down heavily, then pulled off his boot, shaking the water out of it. His pant leg was soaked, as was his socked foot. His toes were already starting to go numb. *Fuckin' great.*

When he looked back at the lake, a face covered in translucent scales was peering back at him from the water.

*

The face disappeared as soon as they made eye contact, but the concentric ripples where the mer had been were proof enough that József hadn't imagined it. He hadn't gotten a good look at them, but he could tell they were young. A child, maybe.

If the shoal's hatchlings were free to wander up to the surface on their own, something had gone terribly wrong.

József crossed his arms and waited, tapping his foot to keep it warm. Time crept forward at a glacial pace. His damp knee was starting to throb. It was an old injury that had never healed quite right, and the cold wetness was making it worse. He shifted his weight from one leg to the other and again looked for the flask before remembering he didn't have it.

Finally, the waters rippled again, and a different face emerged from below.

This mer was slightly older, but not by much. He had a thin face and eyes the color of moonstone that were wide and faceted. The scales adorning his neck and shoulders were a deep shade of red, almost black in the moonlight. Brown tresses framed his pale face like kelp.

"You were her human," the mer said.

József bristled at that. Sure, he was a human, but being called someone's human made him think of the coven and what they'd done to him there.

"My name's József," he said, keeping his temper in check. "Don't think we met."

The mer didn't offer his name in turns. "The shoal mother spoke of you sometimes, but she never named you. If you came to see her, you came for nothing. She's gone." His voice was strangely muted, as though it was coming from the depths. Teeth, pearly white and pointed as a pike's, glinted faintly when he spoke.

József bowed his head, feeling like less than nothing. *This is my fault*, he wanted to say. *I should've come sooner. I shouldn't have stopped.*

Voice thick, he said, "I'm sorry for your loss."

He heard the gentle lapping of small waves and looked up to see that the mer had slithered closer to the shore. He stood a little straighter, revealing his slim shoulders and slender arms. A woven necklace dangled around his neck, adorned with bits of colored glass that glimmered whenever they caught a wayward ray of moonlight. One gem at the center was larger and ruby-colored, pulsating with its own light.

"They came in threes," the mer said. "One woman, two men. They must have followed us from the village. It was dark. We didn't see. I swam to the deep to bring help." His large eyes closed, then opened again. The water rippled around him, fracturing the reflection of the starry sky above. "I swam too slow."

Two guys and a woman. Yeah, that tracked.

"Is there..." József cleared his throat, then tried again, "Is there anything I can do for you? For the shoal?"

The mer hissed, long and low. "*Give us their blood.*"

The words hit József like a knife to the gut. These mer had been peaceful. Curious. Some of them had even lived among the humans, learned from them. "I'm sorry," he said, hanging his head. "I can't give you that."

"Then you can go." The mer spoke quietly, the hatred from before gone from his voice as suddenly as it had come. Somehow, it stung worse than if he'd cursed at him or wailed.

József reached into his pocket and closed his fingers around the ruby scale. It pulsated with a steady heat, warming his skin and sending a tingle up his arm. He pulled it out, holding it up in his palm. "I think you should have this back."

The mer regarded him for a long moment, his faceted eyes never moving, never blinking. "You were her human," he said again. "Keep it. It's yours."

I don't deserve it, József thought but, coward that he was, he didn't say it. He pocketed the scale, and when he found no other words he could offer, he turned and went without saying goodbye.

Chapter Nine

Freedom, Bound

Crin might have had the whole back seat to himself. Even so, Liviu's car—a nondescript sedan with an aging coat of blue paint and the smell of tar and takeaway clinging to the leather seats—felt too cramped.

His heart had nearly burst out of his chest when they'd left Deva a while ago, and the adrenaline hadn't fully subsided yet. He'd never traveled anywhere without Darius, *never*. He didn't want to feel like he'd committed some dire transgression, but several times he had to bite down hard so he wouldn't ask—no—beg Liviu to turn the car around.

Liviu's friend, Ileana, had been less than enthusiastic about Crin joining them, but she'd relented before long. She hadn't said much to him aside from telling him to behave. Crin had taken it with a smile even as his insides churned with worry. He didn't want to be discarded early in their trip because he'd broken some rule he didn't know existed. Still, he figured asking her what she meant by it wouldn't earn him any goodwill, so he didn't.

They'd taken the old road rather than get on the newly built highway that cut through the mountains. It was poorly maintained, more of a lane-and-a-half strip of tarmac than a proper two-way road, meandering through every settlement along the way. So far, they'd driven through a small town called Spini, then crossed into a bigger one called Orăştie, where they'd run into a street market they'd had to drive around. Crin knew both of these names from the map of the region that hung in Darius's office, but he hadn't seen either of them until now. He wanted to ask Liviu if they could stop a little. Again, he bit his lip and didn't say anything. He had no right to ask for anything more than what he was already being given.

With Orăştie behind them, Liviu turned down a country road that forked off toward the mountains rising in the distance. The jolt as the car's wheels transitioned from asphalt to packed, rocky dirt pulled a long, laborious curse from Liviu. In the back seat, Crin shrank a little like he always did when someone raised their voice around him. He took a deep breath, then let it out slowly, careful not to make any sound. This wasn't about him. Just the road.

"You okay back there?" Liviu asked suddenly, nearly causing Crin to jump out of his skin.

"Fine! *Fine*," Crin said a second time when the first try came out a little too high-pitched, enough for Liviu to glare at him in the rearview mirror.

"You drive like a lunatic," Ileana piped up from the front seat.

"'Ey," Liviu said, bristling. "If you got a problem with the driver, how about you hitchhike instead?"

He doesn't mean it, Crin thought. He'd heard Liviu and Ileana bicker a few times already, but at no point had Liviu actually pulled over and kicked her out.

Crin wanted to know how Liviu and Ileana had met. She struck him as someone who spent more time on the road than with a roof over their head. He caught himself staring at her through the gap between the front seats and looked away quickly. If she warmed up to him later, maybe he'd ask.

Soon, villages grew further apart and hills peppered with last year's rusts and browns rose to flank the road on both sides. Their slopes became sheer cliffs before long, with tree roots breaking through the porous rock surface here and there. A frothing river joined them for a while before it ducked under a bridge and veered away to their left. When the oaks and aspens started to give way to spruces, pines, and firs, Liviu pulled over into a small parking space on the side of the road. While he made for the trees at a brisk step, presumably to heed the basest of nature's calls, Crin spilled out of the car and trotted awkwardly the other way, trying to relieve the cramps in his legs.

The air was colder up here, thick with the sweet, refreshing scents of pine and damp earth. The road was narrow and wound between ancient trees with thick trunks and twisted limbs. Browning pine needles and half-rotten leaves blanketed its edges. The asphalt was cracked and uneven; even the white centerline had long since faded. Crin saw no road signs, nor any indication of how long it would take to reach the next settlement.

He didn't know where they were.

Something caught in his chest at that, as if a spectral hand had suddenly reached in to squeeze his heart. His vision narrowed, the winding asphalt and towering pines blurring into an indistinct smear. The world shrank around him, pressing in on all sides. His breaths came quick and shallow, each inhale a feeble attempt to capture oxygen that seemed to be in increasingly short supply. The scents he'd found refreshing until a minute ago now overwhelmed his faltering senses. A tremor started in his hands and rippled through the rest of his body. He heard someone calling his name, but it was faint, like it was coming from far, far away. An over-whelming sense of dread enveloped him, rooting him on the spot. The sun was too bright when he looked up, so he squeezed his eyes shut. He put his hands on his knees, trying to steady himself, to force air into his lungs, to assert *some* semblance of control over a body that didn't feel like his anymore.

A hand landed on his arm, featherlight. He still flinched away from it. "Sorry. I'm sorry," he said quickly, the words tripping over themselves in his rush to get them out. "I'm fine, I just—"

I think I'm dying, he thought. He was breathing too loudly, and he couldn't make it *stop*.

Ileana's voice cut through the roaring in his ears. It was soft, gentler than she'd ever spoken to him before. "You're okay, Crin. I'm right here with you. You're okay."

Her scent enveloped him, not quite human and not quite wolf. He let the feeling of her touch ground him, and with some diffi-culty, he managed to lift his eyes to meet hers. She didn't seem angry with him, just worried.

"Breathe with me, yeah?" she said when she saw she'd gotten his attention. "Deep breath in—" She inhaled slowly. "—and let it out." She exhaled with an audible sound so he could follow along.

It took a monumental effort, but Crin managed to draw in a deep, uneven breath, hold it for a few seconds, then let it out as slowly as he could.

She gave him a small nod and said, "Again."

Crin repeated the process, the claw in his chest gradually relenting to something that felt less like an impending heart attack. He dabbed at his eyes with a shaky hand. He wanted to disappear.

"I'm sorry," he said again, his voice somewhat steadier now. "I didn't mean to be trouble. I'm okay now. We can go."

Ileana gave his arm a reassuring squeeze. "We're not in a rush. Catch your breath if you need to."

"No, I'm okay," Crin said, straightening. When he looked to the car, he saw that Liviu had been watching them. He was standing too far for Crin to see his expression, but he must have noticed. He was probably upset, maybe enough to reconsider his answer from last night.

Crin started forward with as much of a spring in his step as he could muster. They'd already wasted enough time because of him.

When he got in the car, Liviu didn't say anything, a small kindness in the grand scheme of things. He apologized anyway, then huddled up in the back seat, sank back into the worn leather, and closed his eyes. Nobody said anything as the car began to move again, but the tremors in his hands took a long time to go away.

*

József woke late in the afternoon, feeling like a prick with a jackhammer drilling straight into his skull. His tongue was dry and scratchy in his mouth. A sharp crick in his neck made him curse out loud when he turned his head the wrong way. Last night, he'd snoozed in his truck until the hour was sensible, then walked up to the guest house and asked for a room. He hadn't bothered with breakfast, just drunk himself to sleep.

Once he concluded his first business of the day, József went to the tavern across the street and got himself a plate of scrambled eggs with bread and sausages. That and a mug of cold coffee were enough to get him halfway to being properly awake. A small pitcher of water dispelled the last of the previous night's hangover, and then he was lucid enough to think.

Truth be told, he didn't *want* to think. Thinking while sober usually meant reliving the long, long litany of his failures, his mind holding up the kind of mirror he'd have shot to pieces if it were real.

Can't shoot thoughts, he pondered wryly. Not that he hadn't come this close to putting a bullet through his brain more than once. No brain, no thoughts. *Boom*. Easy.

The tavern was mostly empty and looked like every other tavern on the road: drab, greasy, and smelling like boiled cabbage and moonshine. A few patrons who looked like they frequented this place more than they did their own homes were gathered at a long table near the bar. József knew the type: dirty clothes, sallow skin, deep bags under dead eyes. He wondered if this was what other people saw when they looked at him. He wasn't young anymore, and the kind of life he led certainly didn't do him any favors. He wasn't as fast or nimble as he'd been in his prime. He was strong, sure, but even his strength was sapped after the tender mercies of the vampires he'd been a *guest* of, and it would take weeks for it to recover, if not months.

Thinking of his captivity made him grit his teeth and claw at the wooden tabletop with his blunt nails. When his strength recovered enough, he'd go back and stake every last one of those fuckers, then burn down their coven on top of them.

First, though, he had another day and a half to kill in Three Rivers. He'd told Ileana he'd wait for her and wasn't about to break that promise. If she never showed, he wouldn't blame her for it.

He realized he was clenching the steak knife so hard the wooden handle was digging painfully into his palm and let it clatter back on his empty plate. He held up his hand, running a finger along the indentation the knife had left in the heel of his palm. Trying to tackle the day sober was proving to be a cursed endeavor. Clearly, he needed something to take the edge off before he went and did something else he'd regret.

József flagged the serving girl and asked for a tumbler of moonshine. He tossed it back as soon as he had it, feeling the familiar tingle of warmth go down and spread, and then immediately asked for a top-up. He made quick work of that one, too, and was debating whether to go for another when the door rattled open. A group of three walked in, two men and a woman. It took him a moment to recognize Ileana at the head of the group.

*

Ileana spotted József as soon as her eyes adjusted to the dim light inside the tavern. He was hunched over a table like a question mark, staring at the empty plate in front of him. When she spotted the tumblers, the corners of her mouth turned downward. *Business as usual, then.*

Crin and Liviu already knew why they were here, so she wasn't surprised to hear them peel away toward the bar with Liviu making some overly excited comment about what kinds of meat they'd find on the menu. Ileana drew a breath to steady herself, then navigated the sprawl of mostly empty tables and sat in front of József. It was, after all, what she'd come here to do.

József acknowledged her arrival with an indistinct noise, uttered but not invested. His eyes roamed past her to settle briefly on her companions. "That your pack?" he asked.

"Forget about them," Ileana said, letting a little growl into her voice. "You made me chase you halfway across the country just to have a damn conversation. Anything to say about that?"

"I left you a note, didn't I?" His tone was civil, but his frown told her patience would be in short supply today.

She scoffed. "A note that said 'life and death.' What was I supposed to get from that?"

József grunted and waved the server over. He asked for more moonshine, just as Ileana knew he would. She asked for a beer.

József tossed back his tumbler, draining it in one go, then smacked his lips and wiped his mouth with the back of his hand. "It was death in the end," he said. "I got here too late."

That took some of the self-righteous wind out of her sails. "I'm sorry. Who died?"

"What do you know about merfolk?"

Ileana took refuge in her beer as she tried to puzzle out where this was going. The drink was flat and lukewarm, very much in tune with the rest of this establishment. "Not much," she said. "Never seen one." She thought for a moment, then added, "They eat people, I think."

"Some do, but these ones didn't. They just went about their business, didn't hurt a soul. And then, the hunters found 'em."

Her answer came slow, measured in a halting rhythm. "I thought you were a hunter too."

"*Was*, damn it!" He slammed his fist down on the table hard enough to rattle the cutlery on his plate. "I don't do that shit anymore, just—" He caught himself and lowered his voice to a furious whisper, "Just killing the ones need killing, all right? And these ones *didn't*."

She didn't say anything, just stared.

"Don't you fuckin' look at me like that," he murmured, softer now. "People change."

"How did you even..." she began, her voice trailing into a murk of unfinished questions. *How did you know there were mer here?*

Why do you care if they're dead? Why couldn't you be like this back then?

He caught some of her meaning and sighed, running a hand down his face to tug at his beard. "It was...six, seven years ago, I think. I came up here on a hunt. Whispers said there was something nasty in the woods. Might've been a *strigă*, I thought. You know the kind."

"Old woman, big teeth," Ileana said automatically. She'd been terrified of them as a child.

"I stayed in the village for a week, searched the woods up and down. Worst thing I found was a she-bear, nothin' unholy about her. I was starting to feel pretty shitty, and the tavern was full, so I went up to the lake to drink in peace. Next thing I knew, I was feeling really shitty." His voice seemed to wither, curling in on itself. "And the lake was right there."

Ileana reached across the table and, after hovering for a breath, rested her hand on top of his. It was strong and warm, his knuckles covered by thick, wiry hair. Just as she remembered.

He looked down, then away. "The mer found me floating facedown in the water. They dragged me back to shore, even made sure I didn't freeze to death while I sobered up. Turns out they were decent creatures, even if they weren't human." He was picking out the breadcrumbs scattered around the table as he spoke, rolling them into a ball between his fingers. "So, on the way down, I thought about it. Really thought about it. Why all the killin'? Because, yeah, there's some fucked-up people out there, werebeasts, mer, humans, whatever. But that's not all of 'em, never was. So why can't we just..."

"Yeah," Ileana said quietly, staring at nothing. "Why can't we just."

She pulled back her hand to fidget with a stray napkin, tearing it into little pieces. This kind of thinking was naïve. Humans and nightwalkers had always been at odds and always would be. That was just how things were.

"So, that's why you left Deva?" she said. "You wanted to protect them?"

His laugh was barbed with self-loathing. "Yeah. That's where I was going before those fuckin' vampires jumped me."

"How'd you get caught?"

"I was stupid. Let my guard down when I shouldn't have." He shifted in his chair, looked ready to say something else, but then he shook his head and muttered, "Doesn't matter now. How'd you know I was down there?"

"I didn't," Ileana said. "I was looking for someone else."

"Yeah. Figured," he said, sounding more deflated than angry. "I heard other folks in those cells from time to time. Who were you looking for?"

"My sister, Tamara," Ileana said, the words punctuated by an anemic flutter of hope. "She was sick when they took her, so she might have sounded weak. Coughing, or, or, I don't know."

"Doesn't ring a bell. There was a woman, but she sounded old. Older than me." Sighing, he turned around to beckon the server back to their table.

Ileana thought, *Again?* She didn't say anything.

A fourth tumbler materialized next to the other three. She busied herself with the dregs of her beer, trying to ignore the scent of roasted meat wafting from behind her, where Crin and Liviu were tucking into a platter stacked high with various cuts and bits. Judging by the delighted sounds Liviu made, it was good meat.

"So, you went back to your family after Bratislava, huh?" József said after a pause. "How'd they take it?"

The question startled a weary chuckle out of her. "I didn't. They'd have killed me on the spot. I only came back two days ago, only because Tamara wanted to see me. Don't ask me how the hell she tracked me down."

Then she told him everything since she'd arrived in Deva. The more she talked, the more she felt something scratching at her throat, much like a sob trying to claw its way out. She asked for another beer to chase the first one down, but that only made her eyes water when she took a bigger gulp than she could manage. Her stomach gave a pitiful rumble in response. At some point, she heard the door open, then close. When she looked behind her, she saw the table her companions had occupied was now empty. She envied their uncomplicated lives. They were free to eat and hunt and frolic, and here she was, walking a path that straddled two worlds but belonging to neither.

Some of the other tables were filling up now that dusk had fallen outside the tavern. It would be dark soon. She kept talking, all the way through to the end.

"Shit," József said quietly when she was done. "I'm sorry for your loss."

She shook her head. "Don't be. They've been dead to me for a long time."

"But your sister ain't."

"Yeah." The breath seemed to go out of her with the word.

"Look," József said, "I know you prolly don't wanna hear my advice right now, but have you thought about this? This whole Ravenswatch business—"

"I know," she cut in. "But I have to try."

"You're bettin' on a vampire to see you through it."

Ileana knew where this was coming from, why vampires would never earn from József the same kind of goodwill that mer and others might get. She had nothing to gain by starting a fight over it.

She must have let the silence stretch a little too long, because József reached for her hand and said, "Let me come with."

Ileana almost said yes. There had been a time when she would have jumped at the offer. Hell, she'd have begged him to take her back.

She shook her head and said, "I'm sorry. I travel with my pack."

"They can come along. Truck's big enough for everyone."

"That's not how this works," she said, drawing back. "We can't just pick up where we left off."

"I'm not askin' for that, but you're about to walk into something dangerous. You're gonna need all the help you can—"

"I'm sorry, Jóska. The answer's no."

He let his head drop with a quiet, defeated breath. "Yeah," he said. "Okay." He looked up. "Just so you know, after you left—"

His eyes caught something behind Ileana and his face immediately twisted into a scowl. That was all the warning she had before an older woman waltzed into her peripheral vision, draping her arm across the back of Ileana's chair as if she had every right to be there.

"Jóska, *darling*," the woman said, drawing out the words. "I didn't think you'd come.

Chapter Ten

To Leash a Cerberus with a Piece of Twine

The air was alive up here, a myriad of organic threads coming together in a tapestry of scents and sounds. The sweet, resinous smell of the pine trees blended with the wetness of moss and the faint rot of dead leaves. Close to the forest floor, the patter of small game scampering in their burrows rose in tandem with the chirps and calls of nocturnal birds.

Liviu was running, and he was free.

He'd left his clothes in a tree hollow at the edge of the village. Werewolves didn't need clothes when they changed, and a careless shift could ruin a perfectly good pair of pants. Without their chafing constraint and presently wearing what he saw as his true, nature-given form, Liviu felt more alive than he had in a long time. He wasn't running toward or away from anything.

He was simply running to be.

As a werewolf, he stood over two meters tall, with long, muscular legs and strong arms that ended in curved black claws. His body was covered in brown fur, and his eyes were a feverish shade of amber, cutting through the darkness like the remnants of a fire. As his powerful legs propelled him up the mountain slope, night critters scattered ahead of him and branches quivered in his wake. Predators, too, gave him a wide berth. Tonight wasn't about hunting, but any creature that crossed paths with him would swiftly become second dinner.

Without warning, a smaller form tackled Liviu from the side. They rolled, and Liviu came up on top. The unexpected assailant craned his neck, trying to nip at his chest. Liviu growled in warning. The other werewolf whimpered and went still. They were smaller, with dappled white fur and brown, gold-flecked eyes that were more puppy than wolf, really. They smelled familiar too.

Liviu's maw parted in a wide grin. *Figured he'd catch up.* He jumped back to his feet and kicked into a run without looking back.

Sure enough, Crin followed, darting between the trees like an apparition. Liviu, who'd let himself be pursued until now, was suddenly the one chasing. Crin was quick, surprisingly so. He wasn't just running away but inviting pursuit, ducking around the trees and zigzagging through the foliage, always leaving just enough of a trail to be followed. Liviu's heart pounded in a different rhythm now, alive with the thrill of something more than just a mock hunt. This was a game to Crin, and Liviu found himself enchanted. He barely noticed when he reached a road and darted across, but he didn't worry. The locals had no reason to drive up to the lake in the dark.

On the other side of the road, the scent trail gradually became too tangled with the other smells of the forest for Liviu to follow. He skidded to a halt, sniffing the air and tasting its nuances. Crin's scent was there, but it was faint. Liviu couldn't tell where he'd gone. He looked around, but all he saw were trees, their branches shifting in the breeze.

He was about to resume his chase when a sharp *thwack* punctured the night and a searing pain lanced through his shoulder. He let out a guttural howl, clutching at the wound. His fingers found the shaft of a metal bolt, and he howled again as soon as he touched it. It burned. It *burned.*

Another *thwack* sounded, and a fresh wave of agony shot through his leg, buckling his knees. As Liviu fell, the sound of footsteps crashing through the underbrush filled the air.

Crin, he thought as he bared his fangs in a snarl, clawing uselessly at the ground.

Run.

*

Crin stopped when he realized he could no longer hear his companion. He sniffed the air, swaying on his feet. Maybe he'd run too far, too fast, but Liviu would catch up if he waited.

Unexpectedly, he smelled humans.

A pained howl pierced the night not a breath later, and all other thoughts fell from Crin's mind. *Liviu was hurt.*

He turned and bounded back the way he'd come. It wasn't long before he scented blood, darker and richer than a human's, and also motor oil and human sweat. The hunters were too intent on their catch to sense his approach until he was already on top of them. One of them raised a crossbow and fired. Crin dove to the side as the bolt whistled past him. He lunged forward and fell on the human before they had time to reload. They didn't have time to scream, either, before his claws raked across their throat.

The rapid cadence of footfalls behind him told him that the second human was running. He turned his head that way, sniffing the air. Liviu was whimpering on the ground, in pain but alive. He'd come back for him once he'd dealt with the remaining hunter and made sure they were safe. The stench of the human's fear was so thick it was almost palpable.

Crin darted after the whimpering human and easily caught up with them. He fell upon them like the scythe of the reaper, his claws piercing their back, and they both toppled to the ground.

Before Crin could aim a killing blow, the hunter turned, faster than he'd been expecting, and slashed at him with a blade. He howled as the cut burned, stunning him long enough for the hunter to scramble back to their feet and keep running.

Crin paused, his body taut as a bowstring. He wanted to give chase, the scent of the human's blood mingling with his own plucking at his senses like a harp. But he couldn't abandon Liviu.

A flash of headlights ahead told him he'd hesitated so long that the decision had been made for him. He let out a frustrated growl, then hurried back to Liviu.

Even from a distance, even before he let the beast recede enough to shift back to his human form, he could tell it was bad.

Liviu was lying on the ground, breathing heavily and whimpering from time to time. Two bolts protruded from his body; one had pierced his thigh, the other was embedded in his shoulder. It looked like he'd tried to pry that one out, but werewolf claws were made to rend and maim, not to grab small, fiddly things. He couldn't shift back to his human form, either, not until the bolts were out. The damage would be considerable and, even with how quickly werewolves healed, it could be—

Crin fought back a rising tide of panic. He could help. He *would* help. They'd make it out of this. Together.

Liviu snarled at him when he saw him approaching, but Crin kept moving toward him, holding his hands ahead of him in a placating gesture. His naked human body would likely give away his fear, he knew. There was nothing he could do about that.

"It's okay," he said, kneeling beside the injured werewolf. "Let me see."

With Darius, this would have earned him a bite or a scratch. Liviu snapped his teeth only once, then went still. His breathing was loud and ragged, tongue lolling out to one side.

Crin didn't stop to think. He wrapped his long fingers around the bolt lodged in Liviu's shoulder, gripped tightly, and pulled.

He couldn't help the startled yell it tore out of him, not when it felt like he'd stuck his hand in a flaming brazier. The bolt was coated in silver. He'd expected it to hurt, but not this much. He took a deep breath and went at it again. The shaft was slick with blood, which made it even harder to get a firm grip on it. With every failed tug and pull, Liviu whimpered and growled.

"I know. I *know*," Crin whispered, his own voice strained, "but you have to let me do this. *Please*. Otherwise, you'll..."

Die, he meant to say, but he didn't want to speak misfortune into being. Biting his lip to keep himself from crying out again, he renewed his efforts. Tears prickled at the corners of his eyes. He tasted his own blood when a sharp tooth that wasn't quite human anymore sliced his lip open. Little by little, the bolt came loose until, finally, Crin pulled it out completely. He let it slip from his numb fingers and cradled his injured hand close to his chest. By the gods, it hurt.

Can't stop. He had to deal with the other bolt too.

"Okay," he whispered. He breathed deeply, once, twice.

"Okay," he said again, louder. "I'll take out the other one now. Hold still."

Cold fear rippled through him. Liviu *was* still, save for the labored rising and falling of his chest. His eyes were glassy, unfocused. With renewed determination, Crin wrapped his uninjured hand around the remaining bolt, the one in Liviu's thigh. He thought he'd steeled himself for the pain, but it tore through him in a flash of white-hot agony. Still, he didn't let go, not even when he couldn't hold back his own screams anymore.

With a last gut-wrenching tug, the bolt came free. Crin dropped to the ground in a heap, biting back a sob. Time stretched and compressed as he teetered on the brink of unconsciousness. His hands were ruined, their skin stinging and blistered, but it didn't matter. Liviu would heal. He would live.

After a while, he felt a soft hand on his naked shoulder, and he looked up. His red-rimmed eyes met Liviu's green-bronze ones, which were still narrowed in pain.

When Liviu spoke, his voice was strained and raspy. "You good?"

"Will be," Crin said. "I just, just need..."

"Take a few, but then—" Liviu cut himself off with a hiss, clutching at his shoulder. Blood blossomed underneath his fingers, trickling down in sluggish rivulets. "Then, we gotta get going. Before they come back."

Crin straightened up, wincing when he felt rough brambles scrape against his much softer human skin. "I killed one. The other one tried to..." He had to stop to draw a breath. Tears came, whether of pain or just shame, he didn't know anymore. "I hurt him, but he got away."

"Your hands," Liviu rasped. "Let me see."

He didn't wait for an invitation but reached out and took

Crin's right hand into his own. His touch was careful, almost gentle, as he turned it palm up so he could look at it.

Crin averted his eyes. He knew the skin would be raw and bleeding. He didn't need to see.

Liviu whistled through his front teeth. "That looks fuckin' terrible."

Crin dug deep and found it in him to flash a pale grin. "Thanks. I know."

Liviu's fingers closed over Crin's just a little, mindful of the burns. Quietly, he said, "Thanks."

Crin felt something warm bloom across his face and trickle down his neck. It occurred to him that they were both very much naked and, while nudity wasn't a problem for a werewolf, a naked *human* body was another thing altogether. He looked away, suddenly self-conscious, and mumbled, "We should get going. Can you walk?"

Liviu touched his ravaged thigh gingerly. "Don't think so. Not yet anyway."

Crin had guessed as much. The bolt had embedded itself deep, tearing through muscle and sinew along the way. That the hunters hadn't hit a major artery was just dumb luck. Shifting couldn't have helped either.

Crin pushed to his feet and tried not to think about how exposed he felt. "We don't have time to wait, they could come back. I'll carry you."

Liviu managed the remarkable feat of scowling and laughing at the same time. "Fuck that, I'm not some kind of damsel in—"

"We don't have *time*." Crin started shifting back without waiting for another objection. He hoped their clothes were still where they'd left them, at least.

*

"Carmen," József said, slurring her name just a little. It was a good thing he'd had something to drink. It made it easier to be civil, at least.

He had an inkling Carmen would inflict herself upon them even before she pulled out an empty chair and sat down primly, her hands folded above the table. They were the same age or thereabout, though she'd never told him exactly how old she was. She nearly matched him in height and her shoulders were broad and strong, though her back was starting to hunch with age. Her long, sandy hair was pulled back in a stern bun, but József knew what she looked like with her hair loose and spilling around her head like a halo. She wore a layered necklace made of fangs, each one too big to belong to a wolf.

"You look like death warmed over," Carmen said. "I'm glad the boys went up to the lake tonight, else you'd give them a *fright*." She pivoted to Ileana, who'd recoiled slightly in her seat and added, still talking to József, "Well? Are you going to introduce us?"

"Uh." József cleared his throat. "Carmen, this is Ileana. She's, uh. In the business. Ileana, Carmen." He couldn't bring himself to say anything more than that.

Carmen smiled, broad and toothy. Her thin lips were smeared with lipstick the color of blood. "Always a pleasure to see a new face. If you're here to hunt with us, though, I'm afraid you're too late. The boys and I already have what we came here to get."

"And what," Ileana said slowly, "was it you came here to get?"

Still smiling, Carmen reached into one of the many pockets adorning her cropped utility jacket. József tensed, but the only thing she produced was a small lump wrapped in pink-stained tissue paper. She set it on the table with slow, theatrical movements and unwrapped it.

Amidst the irreverent packaging, three ruby-colored scales glistened in the tavern light, refracting it in a halo of bloodlike scintillas.

József felt cold fury twisting just behind his eye sockets. It was almost like a physical sensation, clouding his mind, his vision. *Careful,* he told himself, but he might as well have tried to leash a Cerberus with a piece of twine.

"What are those?" Ileana asked, her nose wrinkling.

She must have smelled the blood; Carmen hadn't even bothered to clean the scales properly.

József thought he was going to be sick.

"Mer scales," Carmen said, her voice so cheerful it bordered on the obscene. "Witches and warlocks pay very well for these. We had a good haul this time." Her eyes shifted to him, her long lashes fluttering, "And it's all thanks to Jóska here. A pity you missed the hunt, my darling. You should come next time."

József couldn't look at either of them, so his eyes fell on the scales again as broken memories of a drunken conversation from weeks ago played in his mind on repeat. They'd swapped stories, he and Carmen and her sons, over a generous amount of home-made wine laced with stronger stuff. Before he knew it, he'd gone and told Carmen and her brood how he'd almost died up at Bear Lake this one time. He'd only sobered up to the realization of what he'd done after the others had already gone.

Through the static rising in his ears, he heard Ileana say, "Thanks to him? What do you mean?"

"Because I was the one who told 'em about the lake," he said before Carmen could. "I didn't think they'd come up here and straight-up start murdering people. And for what? A few trinkets?"

Carmen laughed again. He wanted nothing more than to

wring her neck so he'd make it stop. "Come now," she said. "*People get murdered, that's true, but we both know these were nothing more than flesh-eating beasts.*"

"They *are* people, damn it! They—"

They saved my life.

He couldn't say it. Not after what had been done to them because of him.

Ileana stood, flinging her chair backward so hard it clattered against the table behind her. "I've heard enough," she said. "I'm done."

"Look, now you scared her," Carmen said, chuckling like the whole scene amused her greatly.

József stood as well, clutching the back of his chair for a moment to let the sudden vertigo pass. The floor swayed gently under his feet as he followed Ileana outside.

She'd stopped under a streetlamp on the other side of the street, so he hobbled to catch up.

"Don't talk," she snapped even before he'd reached her.

He sighed. "Listen, I just—"

"Quiet, damn it." She sniffed the air, then turned to him, still frowning. "There's blood. Human. Fresh." Glancing to the tavern across the street, she said, "Did that woman say something about her boys?"

"Yeah," József said, looking around. He couldn't see anything out of the ordinary, but apprehension wormed its way into his gut either way. "There's two of 'em, birds of a feather. They all hunt together."

Ileana pushed past him and into the guesthouse courtyard. József followed, fingering the grip of his revolver over his coat. The courtyard was big enough to fit two cars parked side by side, but right now it was empty save for a kennel which he knew was occupied by an aging sheepdog. They crossed the courtyard single file, her leading, him following. The dog boofed softly, but it didn't stir from its kennel.

When they reached the stairs leading up to the porch, Ileana stopped and bent down to examine a blotted footprint on the bottom step. A trickle of droplets led up and into the house. Ileana bent down to touch one of the bigger ones with the tip of her finger, then rubbed her fingers together. The blood was red and oily. Still fresh.

József's addled mind finally put two and two together. A bleeding hunter. "The boys went up to the lake," Carmen had said. Merfolk couldn't have done this. They hunted in the deeps, never on dry land.

Quietly, he said, "Where's your friends?"

She turned to him, her face pale in the solitary glare of the naked bulb lighting the porch. Her eyes had an amber sheen to them now. When she spoke, her voice was low, guttural. "The fuck do you care? You said you'd changed, but that was bullshit, wasn't it. Carmen said you led them here, and I bet you were so damn drunk you don't even remember doing it. Smells like the same old asshole to me."

"If you think I'm a piece of shit, that's fair enough," József said, "but on this, you gotta listen to me. Go get your friends, then get the hell out of here. If one of 'em went after Carmen's boys, they'll come for all of you."

Her eyes rested on him for a long moment. Then, she nodded and flashed him a tight-lipped smile. "I'll see you on the road, Jóska."

She disappeared inside before he could find anything else to say. He didn't follow.

*

Ileana slammed the door shut and leaned against it, catching her breath in ragged gulps. She wasn't about to waste any time crying, but the urge was still there, suffocating her. The room they'd taken for the night, with its mismatched beds and wobbly armoire, had been somewhat charming the first time they'd all piled inside to shed their belongings. Now, the walls were closing in with each breath, and worn furniture felt like it was crowding her from all sides.

To think she'd believed him. She should have *known*.

She couldn't leave without Liviu and the stray they'd picked up. She also couldn't stay here until they came back. If they came back.

She couldn't wait.

Ileana wiped her eyes with three fingers, then wiped the moisture on her jeans. She swept through the room, shoving their things back into their luggage. Then, she plundered each pocket of Liviu's backpack, looking for his car keys. A door opened out in the hallway, then closed with enough force to reverberate through the thin walls. She flinched at the sound but kept going, the rasp of each zipper opening and closing punctuating her mounting exasperation.

When tires crunched onto the asphalt out in the street, Ileana stole a glance through the window and saw József's truck moving. A tight fist clenched around her heart, but she pushed the feeling down and went back to her search.

It took another minute before she finally admitted defeat. She'd break into Liviu's car and hotwire it if she had to. No way in *hell* was she going out there to look for them on foot.

Ileana slung Crin's rucksack over her shoulders and, gripping Liviu's smaller backpack in one hand and her duffel bag in the other, she rushed out of the room, kicking the door shut behind her. She'd taken a few steps toward the exit when a woman's wail pierced the stillness, coming from behind a different door.

Spurred by a foreboding, Ileana quickened her step. She burst outside and jogged across the courtyard, then out into the street. She nearly stumbled into József's truck, parked awkwardly just off the sidewalk. The woman's sobs drifted through an open window behind her, chasing her as she went.

Ileana's eyes met József's over the truck bed, where he'd been fastening a small trunk behind the wheel arch. He started to say something, but she looked deliberately past him, first left, then right, scanning for Liviu's car.

Instead, she saw both Crin and Liviu turn a corner and lumber toward her, stumbling into each other. Her first thought was that they'd been off drinking somewhere, but her relief was short-lived when she saw the blood soaking through their clothes. Liviu was leaning heavily on his companion, clutching the fabric of his shirt like a lifeline. He was limping too. As the wind shifted, their scent hit her head-on: blood and fear and *humans*.

Time stood still for a heartbeat as their eyes met, and then she dropped everything she was carrying and ran up to meet them.

"What the hell happened?" The question tore from her lips in one hasty breath, every one of her senses keyed into overdrive.

It was Crin who answered, his voice winded and tinged with hysteria at the edges. "Hunters. In the forest, they—I... I killed one, then—"

He cut himself off abruptly when Liviu elbowed him in the ribs and rasped, "Shut *up*."

"We're leaving," Ileana said, her voice much steadier than the erratic beating of her heart. That their little tableau hadn't drawn a gaping crowd yet was a goddamn miracle, one that wouldn't last. "Liviu, where the hell did you park the c—"

In that sliver of a moment, chaos erupted all at once.

"Watch out!" József yelled.

Glass shattered as Ileana started to turn around. Still holding on to Crin, Liviu suddenly lunged at her, his arm slamming into her side and sending all three of them to the ground. A silver-coated bolt skidded on the asphalt next to Ileana, missing her head by an inch. Liviu groaned, a sound chillingly close to a death rattle. She turned her head and saw that his face had paled even further, his eyes starting to drift upward. Gunfire crackled in the air, followed by the tinkle of more broken glass.

József's shout cut through the din. "Get in the truck!"

Gathering her strength, Ileana seized Liviu's arm, ignoring the agonized sound it tore out of him. "Help me," she told Crin, who'd frozen where he'd fallen, "and keep your head down!"

Crin swallowed hard, then bent to loop Liviu's other arm over his shoulder. Together, they lifted him, using the truck as cover as two more shots fractured the air and József bellowed a string of curses.

Ileana wrenched open the truck's back door and shoved Liviu onto the bench, gesturing for Crin to follow. She stooped to gather their strewn luggage and hurled it into the truck bed. Out of the corner of her eye, she saw József vaulting into the driver's seat as she scrambled to get in on the other side.

József threw the truck into gear and stomped on the gas. The truck rocketed forward, grinding against the side of a parked Dacia SUV with a metallic screech that set Ileana's teeth on edge, then tore into the night, leaving Three Rivers behind.

*

József didn't ease up on the gas until the village lights had long since faded behind them, his world reduced to the narrow strip of asphalt in front of the headlights. These mountain roads were treacherous with sudden twists and bends, loose boulders hanging overhead, and thin curtains of trees that gave way to perilous drops. His hands were cold and clammy on the wheel. His thoughts were painfully sober.

He'd finally done it then. He'd set his life on fire.

His mind was a fractured reel playing the confrontation on repeat. He'd moved as soon as he'd spotted Carmen hefting her crossbow over the windowsill, ready to take aim. It didn't even matter which one of the three she'd been aiming at. *I won't let you kill again*, he'd thought, and so he didn't.

He was under no illusion that Carmen would keep this shitshow on the down low. Hunters didn't forgive, much less forget. There would be a reckoning. It was just a matter of time.

His eyes closed briefly as he eased up on the gas. Maybe he deserved what was coming. That didn't mean he wouldn't fight.

The cabin was quiet save for the steady rumble of the Amarok's diesel engine and the labored breathing coming from the back seat. To József's right, Ileana sat ramrod straight, staring out the window. Neither she nor the other two had said a word to him since they'd left Three Rivers, which was just as well. He knew he wasn't welcome in their pack; hell, Ileana had made it abundantly clear. He'd take them to where they needed to go, and then he'd see himself out of their lives.

When they rounded a sharp bend, a deep groan sounded from the back, followed by a guttural, "Fuck."

József cleared his throat. "I know you guys heal fast, but, uh. There's a med kit under my seat if you need it."

There was some shuffling in the back, followed by a shaky "Thank you." Different voice, so that must have been the other one.

József felt something bump into the back of his seat. Rummaging noises followed.

After another minute, the same voice, hobbled by a tell-tale stutter, said, "Could we s-stop for a second? We're moving too much, I c-can't—"

"I'll do it," Ileana cut in, stirring at last. Turning to József, she said, "Can you pull over?"

"Yeah," József grunted, his grip on the steering wheel tightening a little.

Quietly, she said, "Thank you."

He had a feeling she wasn't thanking him just for letting her change seats, but he didn't push it.

József pulled over as soon as he found a spot that let him still see the road in both directions. He left the engine running as Ileana traded seats with her uninjured companion. As soon as the switch was done, he eased back on the road, then sped away.

The kid now occupying the passenger seat took a while to fasten his seat belt. Part of it was because his hands were shaking too much, which József pretended not to notice. The seat belt had been broken for a long time, too—you had to really push to jam it in there—but József had never bothered fixing it. It wasn't like that seat was habitually occupied anyway.

The thought brought a quirk to the corner of his mouth. He'd been roaming all of Eastern Europe alone for years, and suddenly he was traveling with not one, not two, but *three* werewolves who had all, apparently, decided to trust him with their lives. If that wasn't some cosmic fucking irony, he didn't know what was.

"Shirt," he heard Ileana say from the back.

The injured werewolf made a token noise of protest, and then there was more shuffling, punctuated by cursing and groaning. József glanced in the rearview mirror, then immediately looked away. They didn't need him prying into their business out of some misguided sense of concern. They'd be fine.

The kid up front, though, was clearly not fine. He looked young, about twenty-five or so. Too young to be caught up in this kind of bullshit. His fists were clenched tightly in his lap, and his breaths came short and shallow. When he realized he was being watched, he swallowed with an audible sound.

"If you're gonna puke," József said, not unkindly, "lemme know so I can pull over."

The kid turned to him, his eyes dark and wild, and said, "I killed someone today."

József took a moment to process the non sequitur. Then, surprising himself with how gentle he sounded, he said, "First time?"

"Yes." The answer was barely audible.

"Hunter?"

"Yes. They ambushed us in the woods, I..." He let out a shuddering breath. "I didn't know what else to do."

"Well, you did the right thing," József said with a lightness he wasn't feeling, "'cause otherwise he woulda killed you both. Hunters don't fuck around."

The kid fidgeted with the cuff of his sleeve, which bore a dark, reddish stain stretching up toward his elbow. He didn't say anything else, so József let him be.

It was a full minute before he piped up again. "There's a wooden stake under your seat."

"Yeah," József said, drawing out the word.

"But...you're helping us." It sounded almost like a question.

"Well, you're not a fuckin' vampire now, are you?" Seeing him flinch, József took pity. "Look," he said, "Leana and I go back a long time. I'd never let anything bad happen to her. Or her friends."

The kid gave a small nod and turned his head toward the window. József waited, but there was no acknowledgement from the back.

The Amarok tore down the road, swallowing kilometer after kilometer. The sky was starting to bleed pink into the gray when they came to a crossroads.

"Where am I taking you lot?" József asked. It was as good a time as any, he thought.

That got him the name of a town he'd never heard of. He turned the car onto the next road and sped up again, knowing they were headed toward the vampire lair Ileana had told him about. Ravenswatch.

Chapter Eleven

Between Equals

It was well past midnight when Darius looked up from the note he'd been reading to find that he was no longer alone. If the unwelcome guest had walked in, the thrumming bass ringing through the floor from the Bulb's mosh pit below had covered their steps. Knowing them, though, Darius very much doubted that Evdochia had simply strolled into the place.

The vampire lord didn't bother with a greeting. Fixing him with a dead, unblinking stare, they said, "You burned down Nightshade Lodge."

Darius ignored the tingle at the back of his head. He stood and squared his shoulders, swiping the note away with such force he sent it flying to the floor. "This is my club. My office. You are not welcome—"

The pressure in his skull intensified tenfold, and suddenly he froze as though he'd been throttled by an invisible hand. There wasn't anything there, but his limbs failed to obey him no matter how hard he strained against the unseen force pinning him in place.

Evdochia circled the desk, step after unhurried step. The clicking of their heels on the bare wooden floor was like thunder to his ears. "Tell me, Darius. What did you think you would accomplish by drawing more attention to the lodge?"

"I don't answer to you, witch." Darius's voice was a deep rumble as his wolf blood stirred.

Evdochia came to a stop in front of him. They were shorter in stature and had to look up to meet his eyes, but somehow, Darius was the one who felt small. He couldn't bite or claw his way out of their blood magick; all he could do in his half-changed state was to glare down and snarl.

"Did it ever occur to you," Evdochia said, "that some of them might have survived?"

"No one survived. I went there myself. I only found bodies." Exsanguinated bodies already starting to reek and, yes, faint stirrings of the scent of living things. He couldn't tell whether they were human or something else, but he'd assumed it to be of no consequence.

"I see your diligence hasn't improved," Evdochia mused, trailing a pale hand down the side of his face. Their touch was light but cold, like a corpse.

Darius held back a shiver, though it wasn't entirely rage that made his heart quicken. "What are you saying?"

"I found one of them hiding in the woods. Crippled and delirious with blood loss, but he was alive." As they spoke, the magic holding Darius in place relented enough to allow him to move again, though he still felt that there-not-there presence lurking beneath his thoughts, ready to cage him again.

He turned his now fully human eyes back to his uninvited guest. "What'd you do to him?"

Evdochia bent down in a fluid, graceful motion and retrieved something from the floor. When they straightened up, Darius saw they were holding the note he'd been reading. As they smoothed the crumpled paper, they said, without looking up, "He will not be found."

Darius bit back a curse. He dropped back down into his chair and crossed his arms with a scowl, waiting for Evdochia to comment on the note. He knew what they'd find in there, though he scarcely believed it himself.

After a moment, Evdochia deposited the small piece of paper on a desk corner and returned their piercing stare to him. "You engineered a spectacle where caution would have better served us all. What have you to say about that?"

Darius met the question with a shrug, relieved he wouldn't have to endure any questioning about his wayward brother, at least. "Without the bodies, there's no proof. Without proof, who's to say what happened?"

"Had I not found the boy, the truth would have outed regardless. But then, being thorough has never been a strong suit of your kind." Their voice was low, close to a murmur. "It's my fault, I suppose, to have expected any different."

He felt the wolf thrashing at the insult, but he kept it in check. "If that's everything you came here to say, the door's right there."

"My brother's coven has fled to Ravenswatch," Evdochia said with the same infuriating calm as before. "Whether to prepare for a war or to run away from one, I do not know. If it's the former, he must be stopped, lest he bring ruin to *all* of us. You understand that, right?"

Darius had no choice but to nod. The last war over Deva had claimed both his parents and left him saddled with a younger brother, barely two years of age, when he was just a teen. He'd never let himself forget.

"How, exactly, does Iancu intend to wage war from all the way up north?" he asked.

"I cannot fathom, but I intend to find out. At dusk tomorrow, I leave for Ravenswatch." Speaking, Evdochia ran their spidery fingers along the desk until their hand came to rest next to his. "I am one against many, and those who follow him are just as militant. I need allies, Darius. No other coven answers to me."

He didn't move his hand from where he drummed his fingers lightly on the worn mahogany surface. Their eyes met and held, burnt umber against obsidian black. Despite his misgivings, Darius felt an inexplicable draw toward the vampire. It wasn't often he found himself in the presence of an equal, much less someone stronger than he was.

Yet Evdochia, for all of their power, was asking for *his* help. He wanted to savor it.

The silence stretched, thickening as the seconds trickled by. The drumming quickened.

Evdochia was the first to look away, their eyes drifting back to the note that sat, forgotten, among the other papers strewn across the desk. A pale smirk curled their lips upward. "I see your little brother has fled."

Annoyance surged through him like the aftermath of a sickly kill. "It doesn't matter. Either he'll come sniveling back to me, or I will get him back." *And then he'll be sorry he ever thought about running away.* His fingers curled into a fist.

"What if I told you," the vampire said, "that I know where he went?"

"You think I'm that gullible?"

Rather than words, an image came to him, unbidden: Crin, throwing a weathered rucksack into the open trunk of a worn-down sedan. The vision was colorless, but the gray light spoke of either dusk or dawn.

He shook his head like a bull, blinking furiously, and the image faded. A dull ache pounded behind his eyes.

Evdochia leaned back, crossing their arms. There was a glint of satisfaction in their eyes, and Darius realized they knew they'd already won.

"Gather your pack, then wait for me to send word," they said.

Darius paused long enough to pretend he was considering it, then said, "How will I know?"

Evdochia produced a small crystal orb from their pocket. On the surface, it looked perfectly ordinary. It was no bigger than their palm, smooth and opaque. "You know what this is?"

"A sending stone," Darius said.

Evdochia nodded. "Keep it with you and wait for me to send word. Come to me when I beckon. Then, you will have your brother back."

Chapter Twelve

To Catch a God by the Foot

Liviu slept for most of the journey north while his body worked to repair the damage that had been done to it. His thoughts were fleeting, there one second and gone the next, like fractured images from a broken kaleidoscope. As the pain receded, replaced by a sickening numbness, he wondered if he might be dying.

They stopped once—Liviu felt the absence of movement—and then there was some shuffling before he found himself leaning against a soft, warm body. He nestled closer, feeling himself drift away. This time, he didn't fight it.

When he woke again, daylight stabbed at his eyes, his throat was parched, and his skull felt soft as butter. He tried to shield his face with his hand and felt something in his shoulder pull the wrong way at the movement. Groaning, he let his arm drop, taking deep, slow breaths until the pain ebbed away.

After a while, he opened his eyes just enough to see what was going on around him. When his sight adjusted to the light, he found he was alone in the truck's cabin. His panic was short-lived; as he turned his head, he realized they'd pulled over at a rest stop along the road. Not far from him, the old man and Ileana were sitting at one of those weird cement tables, talking over what must have been lunch. His stomach rumbled at the sight, the copious meal he'd had at Bear Lake nothing but a distant memory.

Thinking of Bear Lake kicked him out of any lingering stupor. He bolted upright, ignoring the soreness of his freshly mended flesh, and nearly hit his head on the car roof. Where was—

Something moved at the corner of his eye, and then a scraping sound made him turn his head just as the door on his side opened. He squinted against the sudden rush of light and saw Crin, his silhouette limned in a bright halo, bending in to check on him. For a moment, he almost looked like an angel, but no. It was just the sun.

"You're awake," Crin said, and Liviu heard the smile in his voice. "How are you feeling?"

"Like ass," Liviu said, pairing the quip with a cocky grin even though his voice was hoarse enough to come from a wight. "Ain't dead, though, so that's—*ngh*—progress. How's your hands?"

Crin turned his hands palms up and gave them a critical look. Their skin was scaly and uneven with patches of mottled pink here and there. "I think they might scar."

Liviu winced in sympathy. "Shit. I'm sorry."

"I'm not," Crin said, though his smile was a little watery. "There's more food if you're hungry," he added, looking resolutely away from the pitiful state of his hands. "I'll go get some for you." With that, he beat a hasty retreat, leaving the car door wide open.

Liviu scratched at his stubble as he stared after him, several questions percolating through his mind. He closed his eyes and breathed deeply, letting the breeze from outside wash over his face as he tried to marshal his thoughts into order. It felt nice. Soothing. It also carried the smell of whatever Ileana and the old man were eating, which he refused to parse in any greater detail unless he wanted to start slobbering all over his shirt. The air was cold, even with the sun, so they must have already left behind the rolling hills of central Transylvania for the outer slopes of the Eastern Carpathians. It wouldn't be long before they reached their destination, and then...

And then what? He'd seen a faint blush creep up Crin's face, but maybe it was a trick of the light. Crin had no reason to think of him as anything but the idiot who'd insisted it was safe to go frolicking in the woods back at the lake.

It wasn't like last night had been all bad, though. Sure, he'd almost been killed and all, but he hadn't been too stricken with pain not to remember what had come after. Crin had looked so beautiful as he'd leaned over him to check his wounds, his pale skin painted with the blood of a fresh kill. Not only was he gorgeous, but he had a badass streak too. How about that?

Well, said the sensible part of his mind, *he is Darius's brother.* Killing ran in their family. It shouldn't have come as a surprise.

Liviu sighed, running his good hand through his sweat-matted hair. They hadn't heard the last of Darius. Crin had made it abundantly clear last night, at the tavern, that his brother didn't see him as family but more like something he *owned.* It wouldn't be like the bastard to let go of a prize.

At least I got him out, Liviu told himself, and that lifted his spirits a little. The rest, they could figure out as they went. *If* there was anything to be figured at all.

*

A hauler roared past, its ten wheels spitting out gravel behind them. The after current whipped Ileana's hair in her face. She smoothed it behind her ears and took another bite of her cold pita wrap, thinking, *We've been here before.*

They'd lived on the road for years, she and József, eating at cheap joints and all-night diners, going where the whispers told them to go, killing in the name of. She'd often told herself she didn't miss those days, but being here, now, was bringing it all back. Even the air smelled the same.

She could finally get a good look at József in proper daylight, and it shook her to the core, seeing how unkind the years had been. He was already graying when they'd first met, but now his hair was silver throughout, longer than she remembered, and thinning in places. Deep wrinkles were etched into his face, and his eyes were red-rimmed and puffy. He'd always been a big man, but now he had a beer gut to match his thick arms and broad chest. His movements, too, had slowed.

József fidgeted under her stare. "If you got somethin' on your mind, spit it out."

"I was just thinking," Ileana said, putting her food down. "You and I used to travel together. Just like this."

József huffed a small laugh, but she could tell it was bitter. "You never brought any friends along."

Lightly, she said, "I didn't have any friends."

József turned his head to watch another hauler drive by. This one was an older Dac model with a square front and a bed full of lumber from higher up the mountain. Sawdust trailed after it. Ileana felt it tickle her nostrils when she breathed in.

"Thank you for helping us," she said after another beat. "You didn't have to do that."

"She woulda' killed one of you if I didn't. Hell, she might've killed all three of you, and me." His eyes softened, and for the first time since last night, he smiled with something akin to genuine warmth. "This was a long time coming, Leana. I'm glad I did it, and I'm glad I did it for you."

Crin chose that moment to come and ask for some food to bring back to the truck, which meant Liviu was awake too. Ileana was silently grateful for it. She'd changed out of her soiled shirt and jacket, but she could still smell his blood on her. Last night, when she was patching up his wounds in the dark, she hadn't been sure he'd make it at times. He'd passed out in the back seat, and she could see the whites of his eyes as they'd rolled back into his head. She couldn't get that image out of her mind.

Damn it. This is why I travel alone.

"Can I ask you a thing?" József said. He sounded quiet. Sheepish, almost.

She hummed and nodded.

"After Bratislava, where...?" He made a nondescript movement with one hand, likely meant to indicate the rest of the question. "I know I don't have the right to ask, so feel free to tell me to go fuck myself if you don't wanna talk about it."

With a straight face, Ileana said, "Go fuck yourself, Jóska."

His smile was slow to dawn, so she encouraged it with a cheeky grin of her own.

"I ran," she said. "I hitchhiked out of town, then kept going on foot until I found a forest big enough to hide in. Then, the moon came up. The last thing I remember is stashing my stuff in a cave somewhere. When I came round the next day, I had fur in my teeth." She swallowed thickly, remembering the rancid aftertaste. Her wrap was suddenly far less appetizing. "After that, I did what you taught me. I went where the whispers told me to go. I never stopped to ask myself why I was doing it."

"'Course not," József cut in. His scowl, Ileana guessed, was directed mostly at himself. "I never taught you right from wrong 'cause my own head was too messed up to know which one's which. That's on me."

You're not wrong, Ileana thought, but she didn't say it. "This one time, I found a changeling somewhere around Szeged. The villagers wanted her dead, but I just—couldn't. She was around my age. Lived in the attic of an abandoned house, didn't bother anyone. I mean, you know changelings. Mischievous, yeah, but not the kind of creature that goes out of its way to hurt people."

"I know 'em, yeah." From the rumble of his voice, she knew he'd already guessed how the story ended.

"So I let her be and went on my way," Ileana said. "Later, I ran into the hunter who'd killed her. He told me how he did it, and…"

"Hey," József said, gently. "You don't gotta tell me if you don't—"

"He told me how he'd dragged it out, killing her *slow*, like. Took the whole night, he said. Took his time." Her voice was fraying at the edges. "I let him get through all of it, and then I put him in the ground. I never regretted it. I still don't."

József hummed, his gaze growing distant. "I see."

Ileana waited, breathing slowly. József was no stranger to killing, and neither was she. But spilling human blood was a threshold rarely crossed.

"Did you make him suffer for it?" József asked finally, his pale blue eyes returning to hers with a lucid clarity that pierced through to the soul.

"No," Ileana said, and it was the truth. "I killed him quickly."

With a slow shake of his head, he said, "Better than he deserved."

Something wound tightly in her chest uncoiled at the words. "What about you?" she asked. "Did you ever—"

"No," he said, a little too quickly.

To her, it sounded like he'd meant to say, "Not yet."

*

It was late in the afternoon when they finally drove past a rusted metal sign announcing they'd entered the town of Gorun. The truck was dusty from the road, its front and windshield laden with splattered bugs. Liviu felt a little like that too. After spending the better part of the day languishing in the back seat, he had pangs and aches in places he didn't even know could hurt.

He soldiered through the lingering nausea of the trip to guide Ileana, who'd switched places with József some fifty kilometers back, toward their destination. The way was just as he remembered, only there were more cars these days, and fewer people walking on foot. The Amarok drew a few curious glances, but Liviu didn't mind them. New arrivals were bound to stick out in a town where interesting things happened once every never. *If only they knew.*

They drove past a sleepy street market, then turned right at the town hall with its statue of Ștefan cel Mare—Ștefan the Great—out front, flanked by towering pines. After another right turn, they entered a dusty, narrow street that doubled back behind the first row of houses, hemmed in by courtyards peeking through fences made of wood or metal. At the end of this street was a short ascent toward an unassuming house.

The house loomed from behind a tall fence painted a somber shade of ochre. Its walls were naked red brick with no eccentricity or embellishment. The locals crossed themselves when they walked past the red house. If someone were to ask why, they'd probably say it was because you could just about make out the spire of the town square church with its metal crucifix on top. Most of them believed it too.

In truth, the house had belonged to Evdochia and their coven since the day its foundations had been laid some hundred-odd years ago. Liviu had only been here twice before—once to pick up some books, and another time to reinforce the wards when Evdochia had been away too long. There wasn't a magickal bone in his body, but anyone with a drop of nightwalker blood in their veins could learn how to recite a simple cantrip or wield a scroll. There were words to speak power into the wards Evdochia had set around the house, and then there were other words to sap their strength. These were the ones Liviu spoke now, his left palm spread flat against the wrought iron gate. After a breath, he felt the magick recede, much like a stretched rubber band suddenly released.

As honorary host, it fell to him to usher everyone inside, hobbling ahead of them to unlock the door. He paused in the threshold, sniffing the air. There was dust, of course, and a faint odor of mold underneath. Something else, too, dead and withered. Not ashen like a vampire, so maybe a rat or a mouse.

The house had a parlor with a divan that could easily seat four or five people, a square dining table surrounded by high-back mahogany chairs, and a grandfather clock in a corner. There were two bedrooms, one facing the street, the other opening toward the inner courtyard. At the back of the courtyard was a wine cellar and a separate chamber where Evdochia slept.

There was no kitchen to speak of, and no kitchen meant no food. As Ileana and the old man started bickering over who got to sleep in a bed tonight, Liviu's mind turned to practical matters. The half-eaten pita wrap Crin had pilfered for him on the road could only do so much to sate his appetite.

And, speaking of appetite...

He turned to where Crin was rummaging through his rucksack, and the quip he was about to make flew from his mind like seeds from a dandelion clock. Crin's hair was mussed from the road. His pale cheeks were flushed, a small frown tugging at his brow. He had a mole on his cheek, just above that little dimple that popped up when he smiled.

"Lost something?" Liviu asked, limping over.

Crin muttered an answer to the affirmative, biting his lower lip. After some more rummaging, he finally pulled out a small container made of white plastic. He propped his rucksack against the wall, then peeled open a corner of the lid. The pungent aroma of marinated beef cubes immediately wafted out, making Liviu's mouth water.

"I managed to grab these before I left," Crin said, holding up the container with a slightly crooked smile. "It's Rubia Gallega."

"Ruby Gallagher?" Liviu echoed, his eyebrows scrunching up.

The smile widened. "It's a famous kind of beef. From Spain. Darius likes—"

Crin caught himself a second too late. His face wilted, gaze falling to the floor.

Liviu felt a stone drop into the pit of his stomach. There it was, again: the ghost of Crin's asshole brother, always ready to ruin a good thing. Except Liviu wasn't ready to let things end like that. He wasn't versed in the art of saying the right thing, and saying things usually made everything worse, but fuck if he wasn't going to at least try.

"Do *you* like it?" Liviu asked, his own voice pitched slightly higher in a piss-poor imitation of casual curiosity.

Crin gave a small, disinterested shrug. "It's just beef."

"Don't give me that crap. Just now, you were smiling like you'd caught a god by the foot, and that means my expectations for this Rudy Gallbladder beef are now way up there. You can't hit me with 'it's just beef' and expect me to believe it."

He held his breath, wondering if he'd maybe gone too far. Then, slowly, like moonlight rising over a still pond, a smile began to spread across Crin's face. He looked up, and something mischievous danced in his eyes.

"You've caught me," he said. "It's not just beef. It's *the* best beef in the world."

"Bullshit."

"The Rubia Gallega," Crin enunciated, holding the container aloft like a prized trophy, "has a deep, nutty flavor and a distinct marbling with its characteristic yellow fat. That's because it comes from older cows, typically between eight to ten years of age. The aging process—"

"Okay, okay. Jesus!" Liviu cut in, holding his hands up in mock surrender. "Old cows, good meat. Got it. There's a grill here somewhere. Let's go find it before I starve to death while you talk about it."

Speaking, Liviu turned around, but a cold hand snaked around his wrist, stopping him. He looked over his shoulder, mouth opening to ask if there was something else—

And froze when Crin bent to plant a chaste kiss on his lips. It was more of a peck, really, there and gone between one heartbeat and the next, and then Crin pulled back and looked away, a delicious flush creeping up the side of his neck.

"Let's go find that grill," Crin muttered. He brushed past Liviu and jogged through the door that led to the courtyard, like vampire spawn fleeing for their coven at the break of dawn.

Liviu raised a hand to touch his mouth, blowing out a breath.

Well, that just happened. Under his fingertips, he felt his lips pull up in a stupid grin.

*

Ileana watched the embers glowing under the grill and felt somewhat at peace for the first time since she'd come back to Deva. Maybe she was just tired after the long drive, or maybe the exhaustion of the past few days had finally caught up with her. Whatever the reason, her heart beat slow and steady, and her breathing was easier than it had been the night before.

Her gaze traveled over her assembled companions. József was regaling Crin and Liviu with a bawdy tale from his younger days, the rise and fall of his voice soothing to her ears as she listened. She knew he was embellishing—she'd been there to see it happen, after all—but she gave him a pass this time. József was almost sober, and that alone warranted leniency when it was long past the hour when he'd usually be raving drunk in a watering hole somewhere.

They'd scrounged together a meal from some beef cubes Crin had brought along and a bagful of veggies József had gotten from the market. Liviu had also dug up a dusty bottle of wine from the cellar (Fetească Neagră, a spicy red from the turn of the century), which went nicely with the meat. József had found some tiny plastic cups in the back of his truck for the wine. They'd gathered around the firepit on an assortment of improvised seating and eaten using nothing but their hands.

József wrapped up his tale with a flourish and reached for the bottle to pour more wine into his cup. He caught Ileana's eye and whatever he saw there made him pause. After a moment, he drew back, a shadow passing over his face. "Think I'm done for the night, lads," he rumbled, standing.

He was steady on his feet, Ileana saw. It made her feel some sort of way after last night and the night before that, but then she remembered he liked to keep a flask in his room. Still, she gave him a smile that was as cheerful as she could make it and bade him good night.

Crin was the next to go. He'd been strangely quiet for most of the evening, but she hadn't missed how he and Liviu always kept close to each other, nor how he blushed when Liviu's hand touched his, very much on purpose. *Good for them.* Not that she'd ever indulge in that kind of comfort on the road.

Rather than go after him, Liviu came to sit next to her on a log stool and lit up a cigarette. They stared at the embers together for a while, wrapped in an easy silence.

At length, he flicked the cigarette butt into the ashes. "You used to be a hunter, yeah? So tell me," he said, "what's the best way to kill a werewolf?"

She turned to look at him, but he was still gazing into the fire-pit.

"He'll come for him. Darius." Liviu reached for his cigarette pack again. "Assholes like that don't just let you walk away. And I…" He paused with an unlit cigarette dangling from his lips, then plucked it out and stuffed it back in the pack. "I challenged him once, you know. After the war. He almost killed me, so I know I can't beat him that way."

Ileana chose her words carefully. "If talking isn't an option, then you'll want something quick, precise. A crossbow would be easier to get; a revolver works best. You need to use silver. Poison, too, if you can find something strong enough."

"Whole science to it, isn't there," he said. "Killing us."

"That's because we don't die easy." She tried to sound

cheerful, but there was a bitter edge to her words. "Why'd you challenge Darius?"

"Didn't see any other way to keep living after the war. No pack would take me in, so I figured I'd look for the biggest, meanest bastard I could find and either take his place or go down fighting." He let out a long breath, folding his arms tightly across his body. "I didn't know how much it hurts to die."

He took a deep breath, then stood to retrieve the wine bottle from where József had abandoned it on the other side of the fire-pit. He drank straight from it on his way back, then sat back down, curling in on himself. Ileana grabbed the bottle and took a swig too.

"D'you know why the war started?" His voice was quieter than before.

Ileana shook her head. "We only heard whispers on the road. József didn't want me to know, I think." She still used to cry when she thought of home back then.

"A boy was killed," Liviu said, running a hand down his face. "Hunter's son. You know that part."

The memory of that night throbbed with a dull kind of ache, like a phantom limb or a wound that had never healed quite right. "Yeah," she said.

"There weren't that many of us living in town back then, and we were careful, so hunters had no idea. I grew up used to seeing my folks leaving before a full moon and coming back after, but they didn't say why until I was old enough to swear I wouldn't tell anyone else."

Werewolves in Deva. Another night, Ileana might have had questions. Her family had always thought their hometown to be free of nightwalkers of any kind.

"One time," Liviu continued, "both of them left, but only my old man came back. 'Ma's gone,' he said. Never told me how, but I figured it must've been hunters. Then it was just Pops and I, and he worked out of town, so he was gone most of the time anyway." His shoulders rose and fell in an aborted shrug. "It was a year later, I think. He took too long to come back after a full moon, and then...well, then, I knew he wasn't coming back."

Ileana felt a pang of guilt, heavy and thick. For all she knew, either her family or Luca's had been responsible for orphaning Liviu. And for what?

Quietly, she said, "How old were you?"

"Twelve, thirteen, I think. A neighbor took me in. Human. Didn't know what I was. 'Course...that meant I had to figure out this whole werewolf thing all by myself." He chuckled wryly. "The first time I felt the change coming, I wasn't even sure *it* was happening, only that I needed to get the fuck away before I hurt someone." He buried his face in his hands. "I woke up naked in the woods with a bullet hole in my side and someone's blood all over me, and I realized what I..."

For a long moment, Ileana forgot how to breathe. A ghost wound throbbed where the werewolf's teeth had sunk into her wrist all those years ago.

Liviu turned to face her at last. His eyes were haunted in the dim light of the embers, and his voice was hoarse. "I'm the one who started it, Ileana. I didn't mean to, but it doesn't fucking matter. Everything that happened after that night happened because of me."

"You," Ileana said. Her voice was small and brittle. "You're the one who turned me."

"Yeah." He drew a shaky breath. "For what it's worth, I'm sorry."

"You took my whole life away from me!"

"I didn't know what I was doing, okay?" His voice was rising too. "That's why I fucked off to the woods, so I'd be alone. The fuck were you even doing out there, huh? Following me? Or," he drawled, eyes narrowing, "maybe you were on a hunt, 'cause that's what they taught you to be. A hunter. A killer."

She opened her mouth to answer, then closed it again because, yeah, he had her dead to rights. "I'm going to kill a wolf," Luca had told her, and he would have done it too.

Liviu was right. And yet. *And yet.*

"Look," he said, "all I'm saying is neither one of us was blameless that night, all right? It happened, it's done. I just…" The fight seemed to drain out of him one breath to the next. "I wanted you to know."

"Why tell me now? Why tell me at all?"

"'Cause, if we're going to stop another war from happening, we gotta trust each other first. Last time, we fought in the shadows. If this spills over where humans can see, and I think that's what Evdochia's asshole brother wants, then it'll be more than just hunters coming for us. There's no—"

He cut himself off, leapt to his feet, and sniffed the air deeply. With a low growl, he shot forward and vaulted over the fence, leaving her stunned in place. She heard his pained grunt when he landed and hurried after him. Rather than jump the fence, she took the gate.

She found Liviu out in the street, still sniffing the air. "One of them was here," he said, his eyes trying to pierce the darkness. "I can still smell them."

"I know," Ileana said. The scent was faint but unmistakable, a blend of corpse dust and rich sanguine undertones.

They know we're here.

Chapter Thirteen

Ravenswatch

After nearly dying at Bear Lake and spending the next day on the road, Liviu slept through the whole night and much of the following day. He jolted awake late in the afternoon, plagued by the shadows of a half-congealed nightmare. His wounds had mended enough that he could walk without limping, though his shoulder still hurt if he stretched his arm too far. He could live with that.

The mild crick in his neck from sleeping in an awkward position at the foot of the bed was far more of a nuisance, but that was fine too. He'd come back to the bedroom he shared with Crin to find his companion sprawled across the bed, fast asleep. Even if there had been room for Liviu to squeeze in a corner, they hadn't talked about anything more than kissing yet, and Liviu wasn't about to assume consent. He hadn't had the heart to wake Crin, either, so he'd curled up on the carpet and closed his eyes. Sleep had claimed him quickly, at least.

There was a blanket on the floor, which Liviu vaguely remembered kicking away at some point. He hadn't bothered with any bedding before going to sleep, so Crin must have thrown it over him at some point. Crin was gone now, but he'd made the bed before leaving. Seeing that brought a soft smile to his lips.

Then, Liviu remembered the rest of the previous night, and his mood promptly took a dive.

He'd told Ileana the truth, all of it, and now he had to live with what he'd done. Although, if he was honest, he'd thought she'd tear him a new one, and she'd just...*not*. That was weird, wasn't it?

"Are we, y'know, *good*?" he asked Ileana some ten minutes later, talking over cold sandwiches and steaming coffee. The old man had gone foraging, she'd told him, and Liviu wasn't about to look a gift breakfast in the— *Okay, that one didn't quite work.*

They were out in the courtyard, sitting by the remains of the firepit from the previous night. The sun was already dipping toward the west, tinting the patchy clouds in shades of orange and red.

"We're good," Ileana said. Her voice was shrouded in the kind of ennui that could hide a little or a lot.

He chewed his bottom lip for a second. "Thought you'd be angrier, now you know."

"I had twenty years to get over it. Besides," she said, looking past him, "if you hadn't turned me, I'd be dead with the rest of them, and I'd probably deserve it too." She sighed, running a hand through her short, choppy hair. "There was enough red in my family's ledger to drown a small village. I'm surprised nobody came for them until now, truce or not."

"Why do they kill us?" It was a stupid, bitter question, but Liviu had to ask.

She gave him a sideways look, then went back to studying the sky. "They'll tell you it's just a trade, like tanning or butchering. They go where they're called, kill who—*what* they're paid to kill. They don't think we're people."

He swallowed thickly. "How do they even know—?"

"The whispers. That's..." Her face scrunched up. "Sometimes, there's things in the papers. Other times, you catch something in a tavern. On the road. Hell, you can listen to the walls."

"The walls," he said.

"Walls talk if you know how to listen. There's signs. Shadow-marks, I think they're called. *This is a safe place. There be monsters.* That's all we are to them, really. Monsters. Animals. Mercy's for people, and we're not—"

"Okay, I get it. Jesus, sorry I asked." He rubbed his eyes, feeling a headache building behind them. To change the subject, more than anything, he said, "Where's the old man gone?" *And Crin*, he thought, but he didn't ask.

He heard the rasp of soles on gravel as she leaned toward him. When he looked at her from between his fingers, she was frowning.

"He went out to drink," she said. "He didn't want to have to deal with Evdochia when they get here."

"I don't have to worry about him burning down the place, do I?" As he said it, Liviu realized he was only half joking.

"No. At least, I don't think so." She turned to glare at the fire-pit. "He knows Evdochia's helping me, and he said he'll keep out of the way. That's all I need. If he has a problem with any of it, that's between him and the bottle. Ask me if I give a shit."

She clearly did, but Liviu decided to leave her be.

*

Evdochia arrived in a wisp of red mist that swirled until it coalesced into their corporeal form, just as the grandfather clock struck ten at night. Between the three of them—Liviu, Ileana, and the vampire lord—it was quickly decided that only Ileana would accompany Evdochia to Ravenswatch. Liviu lodged a token protest, but he backed down easily enough. Crin, who'd spent the better part of the afternoon exploring the contents of the wine cellar, had opted to remove himself entirely from the conversation. Evdochia unnerved him; Ileana could smell his fear.

They left for Ravenswatch without further distractions. A narrow path, almost hidden by dead grass, started behind the red house and went up the mountain. It meandered into a forest before long, snaking between pines and chestnuts with long, gnarled limbs. Here and there, a lonely oak stood sentinel, surrounded by sproutlings rising from fallen acorns. Disturbed by their passing, an owl burst from a branch, scattering the night with its wings. Ileana startled at the bird, then cursed under her breath and kept going. The deeper they went, the thicker the trees became. Evdochia's steps never slowed.

It was strange for Ravenswatch to exist so close to a human settlement. Even if the entrance was hidden deep within the forest, anyone who came up here to chop wood or look for game could stumble upon it during the day. Besides, in a town as small as this, any untoward disappearances would have surely found their way into the whispers by now. For as long as she'd been wandering the country, she'd never heard of anything out of the ordinary happening around this region. Was it because Ravenswatch had been deserted until recently, or did the vampires just keep themselves in check?

After a while, the trees parted ahead of them to reveal a

smooth cliff wall barring the way. There was something in the air, though, making the backs of Ileana's hands prickle. Magick. Powerful. *Old.*

Evdochia ran their hands over the stone, murmuring words of power under their breath. Scattered runes materialized in the wake of their touch, ignited by a flickering crimson light that grew brighter with every passing moment. The runes assembled themselves into an archway. Underneath, the rock shimmered like a pond in the rain. When the ripples cleared, Ileana saw a stone keep at the end of a wide courtyard paved with slabs of dark rock. Her breath caught. This was it, then: Ravenswatch.

Evdochia walked into the arcane doorway without looking back. Ileana took another moment to gather herself, then moved as well. Her heart pounded as the world held its breath. There was no time to be afraid.

It was like walking through a curtain made of ice-cold water, chilling her to the marrow. Her surroundings warped momentarily, then resettled into earthly shapes and planes as she emerged, gasping, into the courtyard she'd glimpsed. She turned around and saw the arch's runes scatter into glowing dust, then vanish, and then she found herself looking at a perfectly ordinary section of an outer wall.

The keep was smaller than she'd thought at first, with stone-hewn walls and narrow windows whose soft glow illuminated the surrounding mist. Some of the windows were open, oozing voices and laughter into the night. A string melody blended with the revelry. It might have been a lute.

Ileana sensed movement at her side and looked down into Evdochia's dark eyes. She read apprehension in the way their arms were crossed tightly, fingers digging into the flesh hard enough to crease the fabric of their black cardigan.

"My brother is quick to anger, and quicker still to violence," Evdochia said, speaking softly. "Do not tempt his wrath."

Ileana nodded mutely. She had no intention of leaving her bones here.

Together, they crossed the courtyard and walked up to the keep entrance. The twin doors were carved with rich bas-reliefs depicting an elaborate hunt. A *zmeu*—a two-headed, snake-like dragon—surrounded the outer edges of the scene, its twin heads meeting where the doors joined. When Evdochia raised their hand, they swung wide open of their own accord, and Ileana's senses were immediately assaulted by a cacophony of scents: pressed flowers, incense, roasted meat, pomade—and blood. *So much blood.*

She didn't need to look far to find where the coppery scent came from. Inside the foyer, a dead human lay limp on a red velvet couch. His throat was torn open, blood still oozing from the wound. Two pale women with reddened lips sat next to the corpse, both wearing matching gowns made of crimson brocade. It was clear enough what they'd been doing before the interruption.

One of the women straightened at their approach. "Your Highness," she said, her tone somewhere between surprise and deference.

The other woman hissed under her breath, much like a viper.

Evdochia walked past the tableau without acknowledging them. Ileana followed, taking small, shallow breaths. She could smell the poor bastard's lingering terror and hoped his death had been quick.

From the foyer, they crossed into a great hall lit by wrought iron chandeliers hanging from a vaulted ceiling. The walls were adorned with banners in red and blue, depicting a two-headed raven with a sword in each of its talons and wearing a three-pronged crown. At the other end of the hall, a throne stood raised on a dais, currently vacant.

They'd stumbled upon a celebration of sorts. Food-laden tables had been laid out along two of the walls, which meant that at least some of the guests were warm-blooded; she doubted the vampires would go through the trouble of laying out a feast just for their thralls. The performer she'd heard from the courtyard was standing on a small platform below the throne. His instrument was a black acoustic guitar, not a lute like she'd assumed. As to what the coven was celebrating, Ileana had a stinging suspicion it had to do with the deaths of her erstwhile family.

There were dozens of revelers in attendance, some breathing, some not. Vampires were by far the most prominent demographic. A few were dressed in modern clothes, but most wore outdated finery: long, flowing gowns for the women and elaborate shirts and tights for the men. Ileana caught neither sight nor scent of Tamara, but she saw other humans, scarred men and women clad in practical clothes, leathers and denims and the odd linen shirt or ammo sash here and there. They weren't armed, but Ileana had no doubt that they killed and maimed for a living. Their presence here made little and less sense.

A shorter vampire broke off from a larger group and came up to meet Ileana and her companion. He walked with the unhurried gait of a man who knew he was in charge. Although he looked to be younger than Evdochia, Ileana saw the family resemblance straight away. He had the same smooth skin and sharp black eyes as his sibling, and his pale blond hair fell down to his shoulders in loose waves.

"My brother, Iancu," Evdochia whispered, never taking their eyes off the other vampire. "Remember what I said."

Iancu came to a smooth stop in front of them and gave Ileana a brief, uninterested glance before he turned his attention entirely to his sibling. "You came."

Evdochia gave the smallest of nods. "No crown tonight, brother?"

"They need no crown to know me. Whereas yourself…" Iancu's eyes returned to Ileana for a moment. "I see you insist on keeping the insipid company of humans and beasts over your own kind."

Ileana raised an eyebrow at that, but she didn't comment on it. There were plenty of humans in attendance. Not all of them were thralls.

"We always called upon those of the wolf blood to stand with us," Evdochia said. "You can hardly fault me for keeping the allegiance of a few."

Iancu scoffed at the words. "Prattle all you want about history. I'm going to seize the future."

"You will seize nothing if all you do is repeat father's mistakes." Evdochia spoke quietly, but their words were rimmed with frost. "Your coven broke the blood truce in Deva. To what end?"

Ileana's heart quickened as she listened to the exchange. Challenging a vampire lord under his own roof felt like a prime shortcut to a quick, ugly death.

"These are matters that are best discussed privately," Iancu said, his tone clipped. "Your beast companion can stay here and— feast, I suppose." His bottom lip curled as he looked at her again. "She won't be hurt."

"She stays with me," Evdochia said, and Ileana heard the words twice: once out loud, the second time in her mind. As Evdochia kept talking, she realized they were only speaking to her now. "*It's best that we stay together. Do not trust his word.*"

"In that case," Iancu said smoothly, "I trust you won't begrudge me a witness of my own."

Evdochia inclined their head in acknowledgement. "Of course."

Iancu led them through the gathered vampires and their humans. Ileana closed her mind to the scents and sounds as much as she could, but she couldn't close her eyes, so her attention was still drawn to the grotesque sights around her: the crimson sheen of an inhuman eye here, a trickle of blood there, a pair of fangs sinking into a supple neck as the human screamed. She bit down hard to keep herself from snarling. There was nowhere to look that didn't remind her this was a banquet of bloodletters and murderers.

They crossed the hall and emerged by a grand staircase spiraling toward the upper levels. Here, too, banners hung over the walls. They weren't nearly as glamorous up close; Ileana saw that their colors were faded and they were fraying at the seams. With the spectacle of the great hall now behind them, scents and all, she caught a whiff of mold. The great vampire lord's castle, it seemed, was rotting out from under him.

At the top of the stairs was a long, carpeted hallway guarded by fierce-looking suits of armor holding spears or halberds. Iron braziers lined the walls. Their flames gave no heat, and the light was more prismatic than orange. Ileana felt the tingle of magick on her skin. The air up here had been disturbed by a vampire's passing recently, but there was something else underneath, a sharp, sterile odor that felt utterly out of place. A bead of sweat trickled down the side of her neck.

Iancu threw the door open with a flourish and smiled, though it didn't quite reach his eyes. "After you."

Evdochia went first, then Ileana. On the other side of the door, a small receiving room basked in the faceted glow of a Moroccan lamp lit not by flames, but by magick. A velvet-covered divan laden with furs and pillows of various shapes and sizes stood in the middle of the room, surrounded by smaller ottomans. Flowing silk in all kinds of colors draped the walls. The air was dry and smelled faintly of decay.

A short, wispy woman rose quickly from the divan as Iancu entered. She wore simple clothes—a black shirt, jeans, and hiking boots— and had pale skin and brown hair gathered in a long braid. In life, she'd given birth to three children, two of whom had survived past infancy. Most people had known her as Arghira, matriarch of Nightshade Lodge. Ileana simply knew her as Mother.

*

József was quick to find the nearest watering hole and quicker still to race past tipsy on the way to drunk. When the familiar haze started to creep over him, he deliberately slowed his pace. Gods knew when the vampire would finish their business with Ileana. He could be stuck here all night.

Besides, taverns were good for catching whispers, especially this close to a coven. Tonight didn't have to be a *total* waste.

This tavern was small and unpretentious, with a clientele to match: a few regulars nursing their drinks, a gaggle of travelers in cleaner clothes congregating over a whole roast chicken. The table was sticky under his fingers, but József didn't mind it all that much. This tavern, and a dozen more like it, were as close to feeling like home as he was ever going to get.

He still felt shitty for wandering off when Ileana needed him, but at least he'd been upfront this time. He couldn't trust himself around a vampire. The bite wounds on the side of his neck hadn't even scarred yet. He'd sooner stick a fork in his eye than make nice with a bloodsucker, even a friendly one. Not yet. Maybe never.

He swirled the moonshine in its tumbler and watched the little vortex knock some bubbles around. There was a plate of cold stew in front of him, but he'd barely touched it. It was standard tavern fare, just this side of edible. It probably wouldn't kill him. Before, he wouldn't have had a problem with eating something like that; "Grub's grub," he might have said. Now, it reminded him of the slops they'd fed him in the dungeons.

He hadn't slept right since he'd fled Deva in the night like the gods damned coward he was, and what little rest he'd managed to get had been inevitably tainted by the kinds of dreams he drank to forget.

The white-haired woman had never told him her name. She only came to his cell after the others had drunk their fill. It wasn't blood she wanted but József's body, for reasons he still couldn't fathom. She'd tempted him with food, water, even freedom. He'd turned her down every time, but he was shackled, and she was hungry. He remembered her rancid kisses, her long fangs scraping against his dried, peeling lips. He remembered the metallic after-taste as her fangs cut him just enough to bleed. She'd never gone farther than that. His hatred for her wasn't any less for it.

He downed his tumbler in one go and asked for another. "Make it a double this time," he told the girl.

He was five drinks deep when the tavern doors opened to ad-mit a gust of wind and a man who looked familiar enough to pique József's interest. The man was younger than him and pale as a specter, and, *yeah*, there was a pink, jagged scar that ran across the bridge of his fleshy nose and disappeared into his stubble. He dragged a leg when he walked—a remnant, József knew, from a scuffle with a *strigă*. He was named, rather pompously, Ferdinand.

What are the fuckin' odds, József thought, and then he startled as he realized that the fuckin' odds *were* pretty damn slim. If Ferdinand was here, he must have known there was something here to hunt. His thoughts flashed to the red house, and his back broke into a cold sweat.

He was a big man in a small tavern, so Ferdinand clocked him right away. József gave a half-hearted wave and braced himself for the kind of conversation that would leave him feeling like his brain was covered in lice. Sure enough, Ferdinand fastened to his table like a fat tick on a dog, sitting close enough that József could see the spidery veins crisscrossing his puffy cheeks. After half a glass of red, he was already slurring his words.

"I'm telling you, old boy," Ferdinand said. "These days, it's all about keeping connected."

"Mm-hmm," József said, thinking, *'Old boy'? Fuck you.*

"Padre's got a phone, see? That's how the boys and I caught wind that there's money to be made in this here town."

József slid an empty tumbler across the table, from one hand to the other. He felt tempted to chuck it at Ferdinand's bulbous forehead. "Who's Padre?"

"He's in charge," Ferdinand said, grinning from ear to ear. "Shit's been so much better with him around. Don't nobody tries to shortchange a priest."

So, the name was literal. József rolled his eyes, just a little. A monster-hunting priest was two clichés removed from the ultimate caricature of what people thought about when they imagined a hunter. If Padre had a wooden stake and an oversized crucifix, too, then that would be the whole package.

"What's this about a job, then?" József asked as Ferdinand slurped the remaining contents of his glass. "I ain't heard about anything happening here."

"Really? Why's you in town, then?"

Shit. Just passin' through."

József wasn't the best of liars even when he was sober. He

crossed his toes and hoped he'd sold this one, at least.

Ferdinand squinted at him over the empty glass. "Funny, I thought you was here for the same thing as us. In fact, knowing you, heh—" He paused long enough to raise the glass in a mock toast. "—I'm surprised you ain't heard of this one."

"Let's say I'm interested," József deadpanned. "Who do I talk to?"

Ferdinand hummed and pursed his lips. "I could take you to Padre, on account of old times. But, just between you an' me, I don't think the boys are gonna split the money four ways.

József's eyebrows drew together. Ferdinand was here with two more hunters, then: this Padre guy and someone else. He chanced a guess. "If it's a vampire you're huntin', I'll do it for free."

Ferdinand scratched his stubble and grinned like the idiot he was. "We're staying just across the road. Innkeeper's a beaut'. Tits an' ass like that." He cupped his hands to demonstrate. "Padre don't want us looking at her, mind. Or drinking, for that matter." Speaking, he waved the tavern girl over and asked for another glass of red. József declined a refill of his tumbler. He needed to stay sober enough to think.

The girl had just returned with Ferdinand's drink when the tavern's low murmur dipped into a brief hush prompted by the arrival of another man. József studied him, his body tensing instinctively. This one was short and had a long, braided beard dangling down to his sizable gut. He was clad all in black and wore an enormous wooden crucifix around his neck.

"Lemme guess," József said. "That's Padre."

Ferdinand gave a small nod, then got up and walked over to Padre without a word. His steps were slow, almost sheepish, or maybe the asshole really was drunk. While the two had a whispered conversation by the door, József ate some bits of cold stew just to give his hands something to do. If that was the end of it, then good fucking riddance.

Ferdinand didn't come back to József's table but scurried out the door like an oversized rat. Rather than follow, the priest ambled over and sat across from him like he owned the damn place. His cassock reeked of tobacco and frankincense. His face reminded József of someone, but he couldn't quite place it in the dim light. He tried to picture him without the beard.

"Ferdinand tells me you wish to speak with me." The priest's voice was deep, honeyed. *Dangerous.*

Without any particular effort to sound friendly in return, József said, "I hear you're in town for a job."

"That's right, but it is *you* I want to talk about first." Padre's eyes narrowed, but his voice kept its unctuous cadence. "The whispers are screaming your name, József. What happened at Bear Lake?"

Chapter Fourteen

Mother

"Mother?" Ileana said.

She'd long since thought her mother to be dead, and she saw now that she'd been half right. Arghira looked like she'd been taken young. Vampires were forever cursed to look like they did when they were turned.

"Mother," Iancu repeated, his voice lilting with amusement. "Is this true?"

Arghira's eyes turned to her, suspicious at first, then widening as recognition settled in. Her lips parted, but the words didn't come. She nodded once.

"What a strange little family. Well, far be it from me to keep the two of you from reminiscing." Iancu turned to his sibling. "I'm sure you wouldn't be so callous as to deny a mother and her daughter some time together after all these years either. Right?"

Evdochia gave an infinitesimal nod. In her mind, Ileana heard them say, "*You may go.*" A trickle of annoyance seeped through the link before they severed it.

Arghira looked from one vampire lord to the other, then finally found her voice. To Ileana, she said, "Come with me."

Ileana followed her out into the hallway, her body moving almost of its own accord. She scented that chemical tang again, brighter now, and realized it was coming from her mother's clothes. A dozen different questions crashed through her mind like jagged marbles, but she held her tongue for now. The walls always had ears in a place like this.

Arghira led them through a different door that opened into a small library shrouded in shadows. Rather than linger between the towering shelves, she kept going, her eyes just as keen in the darkness as Ileana's. They crossed the library and reached a smaller door at the far end, hidden behind a brocade curtain. Arghira glanced over her shoulder, then produced a key and turned it in the lock. With a rattle of metal, the latch sprang free, and the door opened.

The first thing Ileana saw was the sky, dark and sprinkled with stars. The second was the blackened chasm gaping from beyond a stone banister, a deadly drop that stood between the keep and a path carved into the mountain on the other side. A cold wind whipped at her clothes as she followed her mother into a small alcove that overlooked the abyss.

"You've grown," Arghira said. Her eyes were a pale shade of blue, not the deep brown they'd been in life.

Ileana's lips pressed together to cage a sarcastic retort. *No shit, Mother. It's been how many years?*

"Tamara said you'd be coming," Arghira spoke on. "She also told me what happened to you. How you were turned." She finally smiled, though it looked uncanny in a face so pale the lines were starting to blur. "I'm glad."

Ileana's gaze lingered on her mother's canines. They were pointed and longer than a human's, and they made her look wrong. "A werewolf bit me, yeah," she said. "I was thirteen."

"And you lived. Of course you did," Arghira said with a quiet laugh. "You're strong. Always were."

Ileana hadn't come here to reminisce. "Is Tam—?"

"Tamara is here, yes. You don't have to worry about her. She's safe."

Here.

Ileana's chest swelled—with what, she wasn't sure. It might have been relief. "I want to see her."

"Your sister isn't ready to see you. Or, rather, she isn't ready to *be* seen," Arghira said, and then she sighed. "She was very frail when I turned her, and I'm not nearly as powerful as my sire."

Ileana heard the words. Their meaning crashed into her a second later. "You turned her?"

"She was dying, Ileana. Human medicine had done all it could, and her father didn't care to look elsewhere. It was luck that—"

"Did she want it?" Ileana said, her voice dropping low as the wolf stirred.

Arghira held back a flinch, but just barely. "She didn't want to die. This was the only way."

Was it really? Ileana wanted to shout. Memories of Tamara as she'd known her flashed through her mind, all thick braids and dimpled cheeks and gap-toothed smiles. She tried to reconcile that with the horror of dying while your family was being slaughtered all around you, then rising again as a fiend. Of being a thrall to the blood hunger for the rest of your undying days. Of never walking in the sun again.

Arghira was still talking. "I did what any mother would have done to save her child. I only wish I'd been there for you when—"

"Don't. Just..." Ileana drew a shuddering breath. She'd told herself she didn't care, that the past had scarred over and didn't hurt anymore. She'd been wrong. "What happened to you?" she whispered, searching the vampire in front of her for a glimpse of the woman who had been her mother.

"What did your father tell you?" Arghira said.

That's not what I asked, Ileana wanted to say. "Only that you were gone. Tamara kept asking when you were coming back. He told her never to speak your name under his roof ever again."

"He didn't tell you," Arghira said with a small, bitter laugh. "That doesn't surprise me. Sebastian always was a coward."

"So, tell me now."

Arghira looked away, a shadow passing over her face at last, but her voice was steady when she spoke. "It happened on a hunt. We were looking for a small coven of vampires down in the southern plains. They found us first." Her face contorted with the weight of the memory, a deepening hatred seeping into the words. "They took me, made me serve as a thrall. And, foolish girl that I was, I kept waiting, hoping, praying that someone would come for me. No one did. My family, my kin, my blood. They left me to my fate." She took a deep, unneeded breath. "That's when I knew the truth. That we were no better than the so-called monsters we killed. That we turned on our own just the same."

"Mother, that's not—"

"Tell me, Ileana. What happened to *you*?" Arghira's voice was rising. "When the change came, what did your father do?"

Ileana didn't look away, much as she wanted to. "He locked

me away. Tethered me to a bed with a silver chain."

"And he would have killed you, too, once the full moon came. My poor, poor child." She brought up a hand to caress Ileana's cheek, a chilling numbness trailing in the wake of her touch. "Nightshade Lodge is no more, and those who hurt you are dead and gone. I hope that gives you comfort, at least."

"It was you?" Ileana whispered, flinching away from the touch.

"It had to be done. For Tamara to live, and for the coven to see me as more than just a spawn. Nightshade Lodge was my offering, the first strike of war that we can only win."

The horror was slow to dawn, devastating when it did. "You want this war. You started it."

"Of course," Arghira said, her eyebrows rising like it was the most obvious thing in the world. "We may not be many, but we are powerful, and we have lived in the shadows long enough. It has taken me years to make the others see, but now—"

Another voice cut through Ileana's thoughts like a red-hot nail through a sheet of ice, drowning all else:

"*RETURN TO ME.*"

The command was absolute. Ileana's body jerked toward its source before she even knew what she was doing. "Take me back," she said, her voice strained. "Evdochia is—calling me." She could still feel the echoes of their will pounding inside her skull.

Arghira nodded, her earlier words lost to the wind. "There will always be a place for you here, should you choose to take it." She turned back toward the darkened passage of the library. "You are my daughter, Ileana. My blood. Come what may."

Ileana said nothing. She'd thought she'd be at peace once she learned what had become of Tamara. Instead, she felt only a crushing numbness in her chest where her heart should have been.

*

"We ain't in a church," József said, "and I don't care much for your god. You have no right to question me." A chill was creeping down his spine. He'd thought he'd have more time.

"I'm not after a confession," Padre said. "Just the truth."

The tavern girl came to hover at the priest's elbow for a second. He swatted her away like a fly.

"Oh yeah? Here's your truth, then," József said, fighting to keep his voice light. "My ex-wife went batshit and tried to nail my ass with a crossbow. I had to protect myself. Wouldn't you?"

As far as excuses went, this one was close enough to the truth to buy him some time to think, at least. He and Carmen had been married once, in the eyes of the old gods. They'd said the words and everything. Hell, József had even believed them.

Padre's eyes bore into his with sudden intensity. That, and something else. Something raw. "One of her sons died up there. Torn to shreds by a pack of werewolves. Have some respect."

József grunted an apology and crossed his arms, feeling the outline of his revolver under his closed fist. It would be poor form to hold a priest at gunpoint in the middle of a tavern, but he had even less interest in ending up on the wrong side of a bolt. His truck was parked just outside; he could probably get to it before Padre had the time to rally his posse, phone and all.

"The whispers have it," Padre said, "that Carmen had one of the beasts clean in her sights. That you shot at her to protect it."

"That beast Carmen claims she was aiming at was my kid, and she ain't a werewolf any more than you or me." József leaned forward across the table and grabbed a fistful of the priest's cassock, dragging him close. "I know what it's like to lose a child, Padre. That's the whole reason I do what I do. If someone threatens one of mine, they ain't walking away from it, and I don't give a shit who they are. Get me?"

Padre gave a jerky nod. His fingers were locked around the edge of the table in a white-knuckled grip.

"Good." József let him go, then sat back in his chair, glowering. "Now. Either you tell me about this job of yours, or I get up and walk."

"Hm," Padre said after a beat, smoothing down his wrinkled cassock. He squinted across the table, but the tension seemed to have drained out of him somewhat. "We're here to hunt a vampire. An old one."

"Shit," József said before he could catch himself. "I mean—old vampires are serious fuckin' business. How the hell do you plan to take it out?"

Padre wrinkled his nose at the swearing, but at least he had the decency to shut the fuck up about it. "Ferdinand tells me you're something of an expert when it comes to the undead," he said, neatly sidestepping the question. "There's fire in your heart, however misguided you may be in other things. If you want to join our hunt, I will allow it. Your cut would be smaller, of course."

"Of course," József said, forcing himself to sound far more chummy than this asshole deserved. "I already told Ferdinand, if it's a vampire, I'll do it for free." He tented his fingers above the table and leaned forward once more, his eyes searching Padre's. "An ancient though? That's *dangerous*. You sure your boys are up to it?"

"We'll strike during the day, when the vampire sleeps."

"This one's bound to have thralls," József pointed out. "Human thralls. They got no problem with daylight."

"Anyone who dwells with the unholy will receive no mercy when the judgment comes. In the name of the Father, the Son, and the Holy Ghost." Padre crossed himself slowly as he spoke: forehead, then down, then the right shoulder, then the left.

József had met his share of the Christian faithful over the years. *Thou shalt not kill*, Christ the Lord had said, and most of them were decent folks who stuck to that tenet, more or less. This one struck him as the kind of zealot who needed a bunch of footnotes after that. He decided that this was his cue to get the hell out of there. He had no intention of joining the actual hunt, and he'd gotten as much as he was going to get out of the priest.

"All right," he said, starting to get up. "I got places to go tonight, so why don't we just—"

Padre pushed to his feet abruptly. His sizable gut collided with the table on the way up, sending a shockwave through the gathered tumblers. "There's something I need to show you," he said, "before you go. As someone who knows how to kill these fiends, I think you might appreciate it."

József steadied himself with a palm spread flat on the grimy table. His vision lagged a little when he turned his head. Maybe skipping straight to the moonshine hadn't been the brightest fucking idea. Padre was already walking ahead, so he shuffled to catch up, thinking, *I gotta get back to the red house.* He had to get Ileana out of there. If the other two wanted to come as well, he'd have nothing against it. The vampire could go to hell. It and the hunters could off each other, for all he cared.

The night air hit him like a punch to the lungs, colder than he'd expected and thick with the smell of burning firewood. His foot caught on a loose chunk of asphalt and he stumbled forward with a curse. His body felt sluggish, bloated, even though he'd barely touched his food.

Never knew when to stop, came a wry thought. It was true for his drinking, and it was true for other things too.

"This way," Padre said as he rounded the tavern.

Whatever he wanted to show József must have been back there. Stashed in a parked car, maybe. József gave his truck a wistful look before he followed.

Behind the tavern was a narrow alley ending in a fence made of thick, wooden planks. A few metal dumpsters were lined up against the tavern's back wall. The reek of days-old garbage made him gag. He started to turn and ask what the hell was going on here when he saw movement by the dumpsters. Before he could reach for his revolver, a sudden *thwack* shattered the night.

It felt like a blow at first, more force than pain. Looking down, he saw a silver shaft sticking out of his chest. His hand was halfway up to the bolt when the agony struck. He didn't know when he'd started falling, only that the shock of his knees hitting the asphalt rattled through his entire body, wrenching a cry from his lips. Somewhere behind the fence, a dog let out a mournful howl.

When the crossbow thwacked again, he almost didn't feel it. He thought he heard Padre's voice drifting from somewhere above him, but he couldn't turn his head to see. A creeping haze, blacker than the blackest night, was gathering at the edges of his mind, pressing inward. Something cold and hard cracked against the back of his skull, and that was the last thing József ever knew.

*

Evdochia waited in the hallway, shadowed by a suit of armor whose gauntlets rested on the pommel of a great bastard sword thrust into its wooden pedestal. Where a human might have worn grooves into the floor, the vampire lord stood so still they might as well have been a statue themselves. There was no sign of Iancu.

"What happened?" Ileana asked.

Evdochia's head turned her way just a fraction. In her

thoughts, Ileana heard them say, *"We will speak elsewhere."*

They descended into the banquet hall, which had grown more raucous in their absence. Smells that had been just this side of bearable when they'd arrived now mingled into a revolting ensemble, blood and incense, mouth-watering roasts and the pungent smell of sweat and fear. Everywhere Ileana turned, something flowed freely, whether it was wine or blood. No one challenged their passing, but she saw more than a few pairs of inhuman eyes follow them. The stillness of the courtyard was a welcome respite after all that debauchery. They only lingered long enough for Evdochia to conjure a portal to take them back.

Ileana went first this time. She stumbled out of the portal and kept going for a few more steps, trying to walk off the chill. Moonlight trickled in from above and caught in the branches on its way down. The air was clean, but she could still smell the nauseating reek of the vampires' keep whenever she breathed in. She sniffed and wiped her nose with the back of her hand. That didn't help any. The stench clung to her clothes, her skin.

Evdochia, for their part, hadn't moved from beside the cliff. Their chest didn't rise and fall with any labored breaths, but fury still radiated from their unmoving body, a thick, oppressive force that made Ileana's hair stand on end. The wolf in her sensed that a greater predator was nearby. It urged her to flee.

"Did you find what you were looking for?" Evdochia asked, out loud this time. Ileana was almost grateful for the banality of it.

"I think I did," she said, thinking, *I wish I didn't.*

"Good," Evdochia said without inflection. "Let us return."

Ileana fell into step beside them despite her unease. "I'm guessing that didn't go as planned?" she asked, to fill the silence more than anything.

Evdochia shook their head, the silver fall of their hair flaring behind them. "I should have killed him."

"Why didn't you?"

The pointed look Evdochia gave her was answer enough. They could have easily turned to mist and fled the keep. Ileana, being what she was, had no such magick at her disposal. The thought of how close she'd come to a gruesome, untimely death brought a renewed chill to her marrow.

"My brother talks about the future but acts like we're still in the days of our father's court," Evdochia spoke on. "He thinks the banners of old will rally to him when they see his strength. He's a fool's fool."

Ileana said nothing. Their steps crunched on the dead leaves.

"And what of you?" Evdochia asked.

Ileana glanced at the vampire. It was hard to tell where their question was meant to lead. "There's nothing more for me here," she said. "Tomorrow, I'll go."

"I still have need of your strength," Evdochia said, an almost question.

Ileana shook her head. "I don't—"

"You are a mercenary, are you not? Name your price."

"No. Not to sound ungrateful," Ileana added quickly, "but I've had my fill of this place."

"I see," Evdochia said, and Ileana thought she felt a cold reverberation of disappointment through the remnants of their earlier link. "In that case, you had best leave quickly. My brother's war will be upon us before long."

It wasn't her war, Ileana told herself, even as she felt a pang of regret. She'd never traveled in a group, much less with other werewolves she might have called her pack. Finding József had been an unhoped-for miracle, and the fact that he'd changed enough to accept her, beast blood and all, was something she'd never thought she'd live to see. Maybe they'd go together, she and József, try to salvage something out of their reconciliation. They'd live, war or no war. The rest they could figure out along the way.

Evdochia didn't speak again until they reached the red house. Ileana stopped by the gate and sniffed the air. She smelled blood, not stale and putrid but freshly spilled, singing red into the night. The sight of József's truck parked at an angle by the fence was hardly reassuring. He'd gone out to drink, and she was under no illusion he'd come back sober. She burst through the gate and into the courtyard, her mind already going through the likeliest scenarios. *He picked a fight with the locals. He got into a fight at the tavern. He ran into a fiend.* The pit in her stomach grew and grew.

There was no merry gathering to greet her this time. The parlor windows were lit up, but the curtains were tightly drawn. The short walk to the front door seemed to grow longer with every step. The handle was slippery underneath her sweaty fingers.

She found Crin and Liviu seated on either end of the divan in the parlor. They'd been talking in hushed voices, but their heads snapped up in unison when she entered. The sudden silence was deafening.

"What's going on?" Ileana asked. "Where's József?"

Crin shrank in on himself, looking away. Liviu's expression hardened, but there was something else in there, too, a cant of the brow, a look that almost held pity. Behind her, Evdochia called out to Liviu, and he went, touching Ileana's arm in passing. She thought she heard him whisper, "I'm sorry," before the door closed behind him and the vampire lord.

"Where's József?" Ileana said again, hating how her voice shook. He was probably nursing a hangover, maybe a black eye. She didn't have to be so, *so—*

"He's gone."

"His truck's out front," Ileana said, a reflex, and then her mind caught up with the words.

Crin didn't look up from where he was wringing his hands in his lap. "That's not—he's *gone,*" he said, and then a tear rolled down the side of his face.

She went to sit on the divan next to him, and then she listened, numb, as Crin told her how he and Liviu had gone out for a pint and found a tavern. They'd caught József's scent, mingled with the scent of blood.

"We found him behind the tavern with a vampire on top of him. We chased her off, but..." Crin shook his head, his eyes squeezing shut. Another tear fell after the first. "Liviu thought we should bring him back here. We didn't want humans to find him like that."

Ileana clenched her fists, feeling her nails dig into her palms. "A vampire." She almost choked on the words. "A fucking vampire, are you kidding me?"

Crin flinched at her tone, but he kept talking. "That's not everything. Somebody shot him with a crossbow, but I don't think vampires..." He swallowed, an audible sound. "When I touched the bolts, they burned me."

It made no sense—until it did.

Word of Bear Lake must have spread, and this was the reckoning. Only a hunter would have used silver bolts.

She wiped her sweaty palms on the front of her jacket and said, "Where is he?"

"Are you sure you want to see him? We didn't have time to clean him, there's still—"

"Where?" It sounded like her voice, and yet it didn't. Her heart was a dead weight in her chest, pushing her down.

Crin looked like he wanted to touch her arm, but then he

seemed to think better of it. "Bedroom on the right," he said. "I'll be out here if you need anything."

She stood and walked, her breath hitching on a sob that wouldn't come out. Four steps. Three. Two.

She stopped at the threshold and took as deep a breath as her constricting throat would allow.

She entered.

*

József would have looked peaceful in death if not for the blood. The bite marks on his neck stood in stark contrast to his pallid skin, and trickles of the crimson liquid had left long trails that disappeared into the hair at his nape. There was blood all around his mouth, too, crusted over his gray stubble. They'd laid him down on the bed and crossed his hands over his chest underneath the bolts sticking out from his flesh.

Ileana stared down at József's body without understanding. Her legs were suddenly too weak to support her. She fell to her knees next to the bed, her lips parted in a soundless entreaty. When she touched the back of his hand, she found that the skin was already cold. Her fingers wrapped around his much bigger ones. The flesh, too, was rigid to the touch, with less give than a living man's.

She bowed her head and stayed like that for some time, neither crying nor moving, until her vision blurred, and her knees started to hurt.

I'm sorry, she would have told him if she could. *I thought we had more time.* There were so many other things she wanted him to know, but it would forever be too late now that he'd gone where she couldn't follow.

There was, however, something else she could do.

She straightened, wincing as the blood in her legs started flowing again, and went to her duffel bag, which lay discarded in a corner. She rummaged around until she found a handkerchief; then, wrapping it around her hand, she went back to his side. With her skin protected by the thin cotton cloth, she wrapped her hand around one of the bolts and pulled.

She had to wiggle it to get it loose, steeling her mind against the squelching, sickening sounds it made. When it was finally out, she held it up and examined it. It was about as long as her forearm, wrist to elbow, with a barbed tip and smaller striations all along the shaft. The tail ended in dark fletching made of black feathers, likely from a raven or a crow. To think that something so small could fell a man.

The second bolt wouldn't come out no matter how hard she pulled. She went at it until the handkerchief tore and silver singed her palm, then used the hem of her shirt and tried again. Tears finally came, searing long trails down her face. With no one there to see, she let them fall.

You said you'd come back to me, she thought, or maybe she whispered it to the man that had been her József. *You said you weren't going to leave me again.*

Chapter Fifteen

Blood Omen

Ileana slept. For how long, she couldn't tell; her body felt leaden, and her thoughts, too, moved at a sluggish pace. She woke slowly, her mind still sifting through half-remembered nightmares. It took her another moment to realize that the pounding she was hearing was very much real.

The crack of splintering wood woke her the rest of the way in an instant. She pushed to her feet, her head whipping this way and that as she pieced together her surroundings. She'd fallen asleep on the divan, daylight trickled in through the cracks in the curtains, and someone was trying to break down the front door with an axe.

There was no time to think. As the axe bit into the wood again, Ileana bolted for the nearest bedroom. She pulled the door shut behind her, looking around frantically. This was the room Crin and Liviu shared, but it was empty. The window was open, curtains billowing in the wind. The street beyond promised safety and a chance to regroup.

She took a step back, preparing to vault over the windowsill, then thought of József, cold and lifeless in the other room.

He's dead, she told herself, but her steps still faltered.

The front door, or what was left of it, slammed open. She heard someone yank the curtains open with a rattle of metal against metal. Daylight suddenly flooded through the crack under the bedroom door.

A man's voice came from the parlor. "Spread out. Find the vampire."

Ileana tensed. A few steps away, the window beckoned.

Footsteps were drawing near; two distinct sets, she thought. Another man said, "I'll check here. You go that way."

She remembered the cold give of József's hand. The silver bolts.

She flattened herself against the wall by the door and held her breath, waiting.

The hunter crashed through the door, crossbow at the ready, just as she'd expected. In that split second when both his weapon and his attention were still trained ahead, Ileana lunged.

The man made no sound as she punched him in the side of the neck, halfway between the ear and the collarbone. The crossbow slipped from his fingers and clattered to the floor, sending the bolt thwacking into the wood. His body followed a second later, either out cold or dead. Ileana didn't take any chances. She aimed a kick down at his neck and felt the snap of bone under her heel.

One down.

The other hunter had been about to breach the second

bedroom. His hand was still on the door handle, but now he looked straight at her, eyes wide in alarm. In his other hand, he hefted a woodsman's axe. He started to shout a warning when the door behind him exploded in a shower of splinters, and something flew at him from the darkened room beyond.

Ileana jumped out of the way as both hunter and assailant crashed past her, disturbing the body of her first kill. They grappled and rolled, each one trying to get ahold of the axe between them. At first, Ileana thought it was either Crin or Liviu, who'd somehow circled back while the hunters were still trying to break down the door. Then, she recognized the man, and time fractured.

József, his hair wild and his lips pulled back in a snarl, wrenched the axe from the hunter's grip and flung it aside like it weighed nothing. Gray wisps of smoke rose up from his pale flesh wherever the sun touched it.

But—he's dead, she thought, despite what her eyes were telling her.

József let out a guttural cry and ducked his head, trying to shield it from the sun with his arms. Light flooded the room. Ileana ran to the window and pulled the curtains shut. *Dear God. He's alive. He's turned.*

Hearing a curse behind her, she whirled around to see that József now stood over the dazed hunter, holding a bloodied bolt in one hand. A silver bolt, she knew, which he'd pulled from his own chest.

Snarling, József drove the bolt through the hunter's left eye socket, as deep as it could go. The man shuddered once, then went still.

In another life, Ileana might have stopped him.

József didn't look up from the dead man. He was breathing heavily, even though his body was long past the point of needing it. "Leana?" he said, his voice brittle and dry. "What the fuck happened to me?"

A feral growl sounded from the parlor before Ileana could think of a response, twinned with another voice raised in a frantic prayer, all "God" this and "Jesus" that.

Right. She'd heard three men before. That must have been the one giving the orders.

József clambered to his feet. Ileana struggled not to turn away at the wrongness of it all. She'd done her best to clean him the night before, but blood still clung to his ashen skin, crusty patches the color of rust mingling with the bright red of his latest kill. When he turned to her, though, his eyes were still as she remembered them, steel-blue and wide with apprehension.

"We need to deal with that first," Ileana said, jerking her chin toward the parlor.

József gave a sluggish nod. He didn't move from where he stooped over the bodies.

She sighed and stepped past him, her nose wrinkling at the whiff of dead flesh. The third hunter was in the middle of the parlor, pinned down under Liviu's much larger werewolf form. Crin, who had also shifted, stood in the ruined door frame, leaving the human no hope for escape. A cut on his left forearm was bleeding into his dirty white fur. A bloodied survival knife lay on the floor a short distance from him.

Liviu's maw was wide open and inching downward toward the hunter's exposed throat. He was already slobbering. For a moment, Ileana let herself imagine she was the one looming over the human. She pictured the crunch of bones in her teeth, the taste of marrow sliding down her throat.

The priest's baleful eyes locked with hers. He was a large, middle-aged man wearing the black cassock of Orthodox clergy. His praying never wavered, but the reek of his sweat cut thick through the air. He was afraid. The wolf found that intoxicating.

"Liviu," she said, not caring if her voice betrayed any of her nature. "I need to talk to him. Let him go."

Liviu turned to snap his fangs at her, and she blanched, taken back to a dark forest in the dead of night. For an endless moment, it was her, not the priest, struggling to break free from the werewolf's grasp.

With a last defiant snarl, Liviu drew back. He started shifting to his human form, a spectacle even for those who knew what to expect. The popping of bones shifting and shortening as the muscles and sinews rearranged themselves to fit a smaller, human frame were enough to make Ileana wince, even knowing what was happening and why.

When it was over, Liviu stood in the middle of the parlor, wearing the tattered remains of the clothes he'd slept in. His scowl was no less feral for being worn by a human face.

"I'm gonna ask the questions," he said. "You broke into this house, tried to kill us. What the hell for?"

The human, who had grown noticeably paler, rolled up into a sitting position. His lips pressed in an obstinate line. He didn't try to stand or flee.

"They were looking for a vampire. I heard them talk." Speaking, Ileana went to close the curtains. The last thing they needed was an audience.

Liviu crossed his arms, glaring down at the priest. "Here's how this goes, asshole. You talk, you live. If you don't? You don't."

"I'm not afraid of death," the priest shot back, though his voice cracked around the words. "God will preserve—"

"God won't preserve jack shit if I have anything to say about it."

The priest froze, mouth agape. His lips quivered, sending a tremor down his beard, but the words didn't come. He crossed himself with a trembling hand, slowly.

József strode forward with deliberately unhurried steps. "What's the matter, Padre?" he drawled. "You look like you've seen a ghost."

*

"You." Padre stood quickly, his face twisting into a scowl. "I knew you'd strayed from the path, but to debase yourself? To become this?"

József faced the outburst with a calm that frightened him. He felt nothing; not the pain of the gaping wounds in his chest, nor the horror of what he'd done to that poor bastard back in the other room.

"You had me killed in that alley," he said. "I wanna know why." His voice was a gravelly rasp. His throat felt parched with a different kind of thirst, one he refused to acknowledge.

"Look at yourself," Padre said, sneering. "Was I wrong?"

"It wasn't about that and you damn well know it. Who put you up to it? Carmen?"

"Does it matter? What's done is done. You stand here now, and I," the priest said, fingering his wooden crucifix, "am going to meet my God."

József bared his fangs before he even knew he was doing it. "Not if your soul's stuck here with me."

"You wouldn't."

"Wouldn't I? I didn't ask for any of this, and yet here we all are. So, tell me, Padre," he said, savoring the horror dawning on the other man's face. "Why not?" He didn't know if he was strong enough to raise a fledgling and didn't care to find out, but the priest didn't need to know that.

Padre's eyes flicked from him to Ileana. She glared at him; her own eyes were red-tinged and not entirely human. The priest recoiled at the sight.

"She won't help you," József said, and something inside him uncoiled in malicious glee. "The choice is yours."

Padre hung his head. He stayed like that for a moment, hands clasped around the crucifix, and then he straightened and looked József in the eye. "If this is to be my punishment, then I repent. I'll tell you everything. All I ask is that you give me a clean death once it's done, then let me rest."

"That depends," József said. "Talk."

Padre wrapped a hand around the crucifix. József had always found them tacky, a garish display of faith that was a far cry from the teachings of Christ. Something about tassels and phylacteries, he remembered.

"You turned on us, József. You knew our ways, yet you still did what you did." Padre's voice hardened. "What did you expect?"

That touched a nerve at last, though where there once would have been rage, only a flicker of anger managed to stir. "I didn't kill anybody at Bear Lake. That was the *point*. Carmen's boys went up there to slaughter peaceful mer. Y'know who they went after? Elders. Children."

"God made man alone in His image," Padre intoned. "Everything else is facsimile. Abomination."

Liviu surged forward, grabbing the priest by the front of his cassock. "Why? Just because some bearded cunt in a monastery said so? Or is it because you're scared, huh? That it?" He pushed his face closer to the priest's. "Do I scare you, you fuckin'—"

With a sudden twist of his wrist, Padre yanked the bottom part of the crucifix open, revealing a thin, needle-like blade. He'd underestimated Liviu's reflexes though. Before the silver could touch him, Liviu grabbed his wrist, then snapped the fragile bones in one quick motion.

Padre let out a blood-curdling yell and dropped the shiv, staggering backward when Liviu shoved him away. He managed to keep upright, but only just.

"Now," Liviu said, clearly savoring this turn of events, "I'm gonna ask you some questions. You're gonna answer, or I start breaking more bones. Who told you about the vampire?"

"I don't know," Padre said. Tears trickled into his matted beard. "The whispers—"

"Ferdinand said there's money in it," József cut in. "How were you gonna get paid?"

"Dead drop. In the forest." Padre closed his eyes tightly and swallowed. His face was paper white. "We were meant to leave proof of the deed there, then come back for the money. Three days."

"What proof?" Liviu asked.

"A signet ring. Two-headed bird. A crown. Something..." He opened his eyes, breathing heavily now. Beads of sweat rolled down his sloping forehead. "Something like that."

Ileana, who'd been quiet until now, suddenly said, "I know who he's talking about."

József shot her a glance. "You do?"

"Yeah. I saw the same symbol at Ravenswatch. It's the family crest of the House of Drăculeşti."

A slow grin dawned on József's face. He didn't care that his fangs were out for everyone to see. "Y'hear that, Padre? Workin' for a vampire? And not just any vampire, but the one they all answer to. How about that?"

The priest said nothing.

"What do you want to do with him?" Ileana asked, nodding toward the motionless human.

József sighed, tired and world-weary. He'd already killed a man today. The prospect of doing so again left him completely disinterested. "Why don't you give him to your vampire buddy?" he told Ileana. "Let 'em sort him out."

"Y-you wouldn't!" Padre stammered. "You promised!"

"I'll see you in hell, Padre." József said, and then he turned and walked back to the room he'd awoken in, his mind empty save for the thirst.

*

József sat on the edge of the bed, staring at the blank slate of wall in front of him. A thin ray of sunlight cut through the gap in the curtains, suffusing the room in a pleasant glow. Here and there, motes of dust danced in the light like fruit flies. Noises drifted in from the rest of the house—voices rising and falling, the raspy drag and occasional thuds of bodies being removed. Someone laughed, high-pitched and strident, the kind of laugh someone let out so they wouldn't start screaming instead.

There was only one thing left for him to do: go outside and let the sun burn him to a crisp. He'd get to it soon enough.

A bottle from last night lay forgotten on the nightstand, and on the bottom of it were the dregs of whatever it had been filled with. He brought it to his lips and drank. There was no fiery heat rolling down into his belly, no relief from the thirst.

Again, he looked to the light.

He stood up slowly, shrugging his coat off as he went. There were two, maybe three steps from the bed to the window. He should have been terrified, but his body felt lighter than it had any right to be. For the first time in an untold number of years, nothing hurt. Not the old wounds he'd picked up on his many hunts, nor his guts, taxed by decades of terrible food and enough booze to drown Atlantis all over again. His thoughts were quiet, smothered by a leaden kind of numbness. There was the thirst, of course, but soon it wouldn't trouble him anymore. Nothing would.

He reached out and touched one of the curtains, rubbing the fabric between his fingers. It was velvet, thick and a little scratchy to the touch. The color was a faded brown, but he could see echoes of its original russet in the creases here and there. He held up his fingers and saw they were coated in a fine sheen of dust. Soon, he, too, would be little more than that, burned away by the sun, and all would be right with the world.

Well, no, that wasn't quite right. The world would be just as fucked up as it had always been. But his part in it would be done.

The thought brought him no peace.

He brought up his hand and thrust it into the light. His skin started smoking right away, small whorls that dissipated into the air almost immediately. He pulled back with a hiss. *Fuck*, that hurt.

He couldn't half ass it, then. He'd have to be quick, decisive. It'd hurt like a mother, but all he had to do was bear it until his legs crumbled from under him.

He swayed on his feet, cradling his blistered hand.

I want to die.

And then he thought, *I'm already dead.*

In the untold number of hours between his death and his resurrection, there had been nothing: no heavenly light, no fair maiden on a pale horse, not even a lick of hellfire to roast him for his many sins. József worshiped the old gods, but the gist of it was supposed to be the same no matter whose holy sign they carved into your tombstone. If he let the sun take him, there would be pain, and then there would be nothing. Funny how he'd never thought about it all those times he'd jammed the muzzle of his loaded revolver into his temple and spun the cylinder.

A faint rustle by the door made him startle and turn. Crin looked back at him from the doorstep, eyes wide in a face so pale he looked almost like a ghost. József felt a faint twinge of shame. Crin was a smart kid; he must have realized what he was about to do. Or, maybe—fuck, maybe he was actually scared of him now, after seeing and hearing him earlier with Padre.

"Hey," József said, again in that dry, gravelly voice. "What, uh. Whaddya need?"

"Ileana sent me to…" Crin floundered, then rallied with a pale attempt at a smile. "I just wanted to…"

"She sent you to keep an eye on me. I get it. Well, I ain't going anywhere." József crossed his arms and nodded to the window to emphasize his point. "I'm sure you got better things to do."

Rather than take the hint, Crin walked into the room. "How are you feeling?"

"Like a dead man walking." József said it with a straight face, and Crin huffed the smallest laugh, which he supposed was an improvement. "What about you? You look like you've seen some shit."

Crin's shoulders sagged at that, his eyes shifting to the side. There *was* something bothering him, clear as day. Something other than his condition, József suspected.

He nodded to the bed. "If you wanna talk about it, I got time."

Crin walked up to the bed, but he didn't sit down just yet. He frowned, rubbing at his forearms like he wanted to warm himself, then said, "I don't think this life is for me. All this killing. This isn't who I want to be."

"Sometimes, you got no choice," József said, as gently as he managed. "Doesn't mean you gotta like it. If some asshole's got you over a barrel, one of two things is gonna happen: you kill, or you die. Like that bastard at the lake. D'you think he would've let you go if you asked him nice?"

Crin made a small, defeated sound and plopped down on the bed.

"Look," József said, "this kinda shit's going to find you no matter where you go. You are what you are, and some people will always have a problem with it."

"That's what my brother says. The only way for us to live is to be stronger, faster, more resilient. I must've heard that a thousand times when I was young." Crin shook his head. He was talking to the sheets now. "Of course, he also thinks I'm none of those things."

József scoffed. "Disagree."

That earned him a half-hearted shrug.

"I mean it. Carmen's boys were seasoned hunters, and you beat 'em two to one. When push comes to shove, you *know* how to fight. It's in your blood."

"What if I don't want it to be?"

József sighed, feeling old and brittle. "You don't get to choose what you are. Best you can do is choose what you wanna do about it. If this ain't the kinda life for you, then find something else. You're young. You got time."

He felt like the world's biggest hypocrite saying it. "Best you can do is choose what you wanna do about it," and here he was, dragging his feet, when the only thing left for him to do was end himself. He'd have to dig deep and find the strength to see this through. *Soon.* The thirst was getting harder to ignore.

"What about you?" Crin said. "You are—you were human. Why be a hunter? You could have chosen anything else."

"I didn't choose." József ran a hand through his hair. It was greasy with blood, and crusty dirt still clung to his skull. "I was a constable down south. I had a kid. A family. I didn't care about the underworld and honestly thought it wouldn't care about me either."

"What happened?" Crin sounded almost like he was apologizing for the question.

József dropped down on the other side of the bed. His lungs made a sound much like a tire deflating. "Vampires happened, whole nest of 'em. One day, my little girl vanished. By the time I figured out where she was, they'd already..." He swallowed hard, pinching the bridge of his nose. He'd never told the whole story to anyone else, not even Ileana. "Before I buried her, I went back there and burned down their coven on top of them. And then, I kept going. Plenty of other vampires to kill." He looked at his hands. The skin was chalk-white and taut over his knuckles, so thin he could see the blue-green web of spidery veins underneath. "Didn't think I'd end up one of 'em too."

Crin made a small sound—it was hard to tell whether it was sympathy or muted horror—and József felt like a piece of shit all over again. He had no right to dump any of this on the poor kid.

He felt the mattress shift, and then a smaller hand landed on top of his. He'd always thought Crin ran cold, but now his skin was surprisingly warm to the touch.

"You are one of us," Crin said, speaking softly. "Not because of what you are, but because of what you did. The way you stood up for us. Even if it cost you everything."

József grunted, but he didn't shuffle away. *Why do you care anyway?* He wanted to say. *I'm not some saint. A week ago, I would've killed you at the lake just the same.* Instead, he closed his eyes and forgave himself this one last kindness before he went into the light.

*

Out in the parlor, Ileana let her forehead drop against the wall and closed her eyes.

Now that Padre had been handled and the bodies of the other two were stiffening in the cellar, she was out of excuses. She'd have to go talk to József. Last night, she'd hoped they would leave Gorun together. Now, she wondered if he would ever leave here at all. József had spent most of his life harboring a deep hatred for vampires. She was under no illusion he'd just accept what he'd become and move on with his unlife.

How the hell, she wondered for the hundredth time.

Hunters had killed József. That, she could understand; there was a code, and he'd broken it. Him being a vampire made no sense at all.

She steeled herself, then crossed the parlor, stepping around the bloodstains and scuff marks on the floor. She slowed as she got closer to the ruined door, hearing voices coming from inside: József's gravelly baritone, which sounded even raspier than when he'd been alive, and Crin's gentle voice with its melodic rising and falling.

Before her nerves failed her, Ileana knocked on the door frame to announce her presence.

Crin stood up quickly and scurried out, his hand brushing against Ileana's arm in passing. She swallowed a pang of miserable envy. They'd known each other for all of two days, and already József was closer to Crin than she and he had ever been.

When József looked up and their eyes met, his expression hardened. "Why the hell am I turned?"

Ileana lingered by the door, trying to make sense of the question. "I don't—"

"Did your vampire do this to me? Did *you* put 'em up to it?"

She shook her head weakly, words failing her for a breath. When she gathered herself enough to speak, her voice was shaking. "I would *never*. Why would you even ask me that?"

"Yeah, you're right, you're—*fuck*, I know you wouldn't." He muttered something too faint for her to catch, then patted the bed next to him. "Sit down. I gotta talk to you."

She did as she'd been told, trying to shake off the wrongness of it all. His eyes were pale and sunken underneath the tangled mess of his hair. The front of his shirt was still torn and bloody, barely covering the wounds that had felled him. Those were nothing to a vampire, of course; a minor inconvenience that would melt away after he'd fed enough.

Christ, he'd need to feed sooner or later, wouldn't he? Vampires couldn't survive without blood, and newly turned fledglings were said to be particularly ravenous.

"So, you don't know how this happened either," Ileana said.

József ran a hand down his face, scratching at his stubble. The stench of blood lingered around him, cloaking his once familiar scent of moonshine and sweat. "Can't say I remember much. Bastard hit me in the head with a brick. I won't be around long enough for it to matter anyway."

Her breathing stuttered. "What do you mean?"

"I can't live like this, Leana. Well, *live*." He scoffed at the word. "I'm glad I got to see Padre squirm, but it's not like I asked for it, and I sure as hell ain't gonna start going around biting people's necks."

"There's other ways—"

He cut her off with a gesture. "You know how I feel about vampires."

She grabbed a fistful of the covers so she wouldn't fly at him. "I know how you used to feel about werewolves."

"It ain't the same."

"Bullshit."

"I killed that guy, Leana. Didn't think twice, just drove a bolt straight into his skull. And then I wanted to tear out his throat so I could get at the blood. That's all I could think about. The hell does that say about me?"

"It says you're thirsty," she said without thinking, and then she wished she could take the words back when his gaze wilted.

"Like I said." He stood, then turned to look at the window, where sunlight still warmed a portion of the room, fainter now. "Not for long."

"So, what?" she said. "Is this goodbye?"

His shoulders rose and fell. "Nothin' more to it, right?"

Ileana stood and circled the bed, feeling time quicken around her. She couldn't let him leave. Not like this.

József didn't react when she wrapped her arms around him and buried her face in his shirt. She held onto him tightly, like she could piece his shattered heart back together, if only she were strong enough. It occurred to her that they'd only been this close once before, when he'd carried her through the forest on the night they'd met. Two neat bookends to their story. A beginning and an end.

She thought she heard him say, "I'm sorry."

A great pressure was building in her chest, and she knew she'd scream if she tried to say anything. *Don't go*, she thought, but it was selfish, so she didn't say it. The words pounded in her skull in time with her hammering heart. *Don't go. Don't go. Don't go.*

And then she was crying, great, ragged sobs that shook her body and choked the breath out of her lungs. For József and Tamara, for the father she'd lost and the mother she would never have. For the life that could have been and the one she'd let herself believe she could have. She cried for the first time in longer than she could remember. She cried until her body had no more tears left to give.

At length, her sobs subsided into whimpers, then shaky breaths. Her face was wet with tears and snot and gods knew what else. She felt József rub his large hand up and down her back, soothing her, and her heart broke all over again. She knew what would happen when she let go.

"I'm sorry, Leana," József murmured into her hair. "You deserved so much better than the shit I put you through. I'm sorry."

Her voice rough, she whispered, "I forgive you."

A long breath left him, and she realized his chest was shuddering too. Maybe he'd been crying with her. She didn't look up to see.

"I can't be here when you go," she said.

He smoothed back her hair, and she stood on tiptoe so she could push into his touch.

"That's okay," he said. "Do what you gotta do."

Ileana disentangled herself from his arms at last, then wiped her face with the back of her sleeve. There was blood on it, either József's or the hunter's. Now that they were standing apart again, she saw that József's eyes were red-rimmed, too.

Lingering felt like a transgression, but she still couldn't bring herself to turn away. There were so many things she'd wanted to tell him, but when she tried to grasp them, all she came up with was a chorus of *Don't go. Don't go. Don't go.*

"Go," he whispered, flashing her a crooked smile.

She sniffed and tried to smile back. "I'll see you on the road, Jóska."

The light was fading when she turned away, or maybe it was just her vision that was misting again. She left the room, then the parlor, and then she was outside and she was running, running, running.

Chapter Sixteen

Grim Reprieve

A fine rain began to mist as Ileana raced up the path behind the red house. She flew past the first trees, her heels kicking up splatters of mud. As the forest thickened, she veered off the path with no destination in mind other than *away*. Her sides hurt with a dull, stabbing ache. Was she far enough yet? Would she still hear József's screams when he burned?

Her steps faltered after a while. She doubled over with her hands on her knees, gasping in breath after breath. Every mouthful of air burned in her lungs, in her throat.

Slowly, she sank to her knees.

She almost didn't notice when the rain turned into a deluge. Fat droplets filtered through the leafless canopy in cold, thick ribbons, soaking through her clothes. The tears were warm and heavy on her face. Her thoughts felt like shards of broken glass swirling in a tempest; they clinked against each other in their turmoil, and they hurt.

Don't go, she'd meant to tell him, but she'd bitten back the words, over and over. She should have said it, for whatever it was worth.

She stayed like that, with her head bowed and the rain pelting her back and shoulders, until her body started shivering. When she tried to take a deeper breath, a sudden cough wracked her body.

Christ. Sickness was the last thing she needed right now.

That finally pushed her to stand, wincing as pins and needles took hold of her calves. When she looked up, shielding her eyes from the rain, she saw a patchwork of gray and purple clouds stretching like bruises across the sky. Somewhere beyond the treetops, the sun was setting. She wiped her hand across her face, then shook her head to displace some of the moisture in her hair. Would József have gone out with the weather like this? Was there even enough sunlight to do the deed? She'd only ever hunted vampires in bright daylight and under clear skies, but she knew they could move around during the day, so long as they kept out of the sun. Was there a chance that maybe—

No. Hope was poison. József wanted to go; she had to respect that, no matter how much she disagreed with his choice. Besides, the man was already dead. She hugged herself, sniffling miserably. How selfish was she to think he'd stick around the way he was just because she was loath to let him go?

Something foreign caught in the spinning wheels of her mind. She sniffed the air again, trying to tease out the one scent that didn't belong from the other things crisscrossing the moist, fragrant air. Dead leaves, pines, tree bark, lichen—*there*!

Nestled among the other scents was an ashen undercurrent that gave way to the thick, rusty odor of stale blood. A flash of hatred electrified her from head to toe. A vampire had wandered nearby.

She crouched low and followed the scent. The patter of rain would hide her footsteps. As long as she saw them first, she'd get the drop on them. *And then…*

She'd never been one to kill just for the sake of killing, but the vampires at Ravenswatch had taken too much from her: mother, sister, József. She would give them no mercy in return.

Color was quickly draining from the world as the night descended. The vampire's scent meandered through the trees, teasingly close one second, almost entirely gone the next. She moved quickly and quietly, pushing low branches out of the way. The bark was cold and rough against her human skin, but the discomfort barely registered.

Ileana was hunting.

When she found the path again, her heart quickened. Footprints were etched into the soft soil, leading back towards Gorun, all of them belonging to the same person. Their feet were smaller than she would have expected, but that didn't have to mean anything. She remembered Radu's attempt to dominate her mind. Child vampires were no less dangerous if they'd been raised by a powerful lord.

She picked up the pace, her gaze darting to the side every few steps in case her prey had realized they were being followed and tried to get a drop on her. It wasn't long before she saw a flash of movement farther ahead. Her lips curled up to reveal teeth that were growing sharper. *There you are.*

Ileana slipped between the trees, putting a thick trunk between herself and her prey. Their scent was easier to tell apart now, trailing behind them like a comet's tail. Too, there was the slightest hint of a bitter, chemical tang, like the aftertaste of medicine on the tongue. It was so faint she wondered if she was imagining it.

She crept forward, careful not to make any noise. The rain was petering out now, but the smell of churned earth and petrichor lingered, and the cold wind carried the promise of a reprise. She now had a better view of the vampire. They slipped and fell as she watched, flailed around in the mud for a few seconds, then staggered back up and kept going. They were dressed in a simple shirt and loose, baggy pants, both sporting a pattern of faded browns and greens that blended with the terrain. Hunter clothes. Vampires lured their thralls with promises of eternal life. Maybe that was how they'd turned this poor wretch to their cause.

She pulled out her hunting knife from the sheath in her boot, then picked up the pace, weaving in and out of the shadows. She felt more than heard the dull snap of a branch under her foot and froze, but the vampire kept going, seemingly none the wiser. Ileana counted to five, then moved again.

They were coming up on a bend where the path narrowed and tall rocks jutted up from the earth, squeezing out the trees. This was as good a spot as any. As the vampire disappeared around the bend, Ileana broke into a run. She didn't care about the noise anymore. Even if the vampire heard her coming, it would be too late.

What Ileana hadn't expected when she rounded the bend at full speed was to catch a blow right in the middle of her chest, underneath her sternum. The vampire must have been waiting for her, hidden in the shadow of the inner wall. If she didn't feel like she'd been hit by a truck, Ileana would have chided herself for letting her bloodlust overrule her common sense. Had she run into a knife rather than a fist, she'd have been dead by now, werewolf or not.

Rather than stay and fight, the vampire bolted, but not before Ileana caught a glimpse of them: a woman, she thought, skewing young, with a heart-shaped face and short, wispy hair plastered to her skull. Her faded camos hung loosely on her gaunt frame. She certainly looked like a corpse.

Ileana fought the instinctive panic and deliberately slowed her breathing: in through the nose, out through the mouth, relaxing the muscles in her abdomen as she went. When she could get in a lungful of air without coughing, she retrieved the knife from where she'd dropped it, then resumed her pursuit.

The vampire hadn't gone too far. Ileana was on them again almost immediately, and this time, she was prepared. She tackled them from behind, using her superior strength to pin them down. They managed to free one of their arms and struck back with their elbow. Again, Ileana couldn't shimmy out of the way fast enough. It was a glancing blow this time, but it still made her lose focus for a second or two, enough for the vampire to crawl forward and twist, aiming a kick at her midsection.

Ileana drew back just before the vampire's boot made contact. Freed from the weight holding them down, the vampire whirled around on the ground and sprung like a coiled snake, aiming a blow at Ileana's throat this time. She saw it coming and snatched their wrist, then twisted it and pushed down, pinning their arm to the ground. She planted a knee on the vampire's chest for good measure and raised her knife with the other hand.

Up close, the vampire was so pale their—*her* skin was almost translucent. Her eyes were wide with blown-out pupils, black on black. Her cheeks were covered in a dusting of freckles, and two small moles dotted the skin just above the corner of her mouth.

Ileana's heart stuttered. *She almost looks like—*

"Leana! Wait!"

Ileana froze, her knife still hanging over the vampire's throat. She knew the voice.

*

When the summons came, József had made up his mind. He had no right to subject anyone to the spectacle of his final moments. And then, what were the others supposed to do once the sun finished him off? Gather his ashes with a broom and a dustpan? No, he had to get the hell out of there first of all. He'd get in his truck and drive out of Gorun, then pick a road he didn't know and take it as far as it went. At the break of dawn, he'd ditch the truck and keep going on foot. The sun would take care of the rest.

Besides, it had started to rain.

If anyone asked where he was going, he'd bullshit some excuse. He didn't have any more soppy goodbyes in him, and they didn't need to know anyway. Ileana might tell them. He'd be long gone by then.

"All right, you old bastard, get a move on," he muttered to himself.

He patted his pockets to make sure the car keys were still there, then pulled out his revolver and put it on the nightstand, next to the empty bottle. He took a moment to run his fingers down the worn grip as a wistful smile played on his lips. It had always fit into the palm of his hand like it was made for him, but he wouldn't be needing it where he was going.

Rain pattered a steady cadence against the window. It was time to go.

He made it two steps into the parlor before Liviu stood from the divan to bar his way, his bushy eyebrows drawn together in a frown. Two beer bottles stood aligned at his feet, one empty, one full.

"Evdochia said they wanted to talk to you when you're ready," Liviu said. "They're waiting for you in the cellar."

It took a second for the name to track, then József said, "Nah." He wasn't about to make nice with a vampire on his last day on the gods' green earth.

Liviu's frown deepened. "You're a guest in their house. Least you can do is give them the time of day."

"I got nothin' to say to—"

"It's about the night you died. The night you got *turned*."

József shut his mouth with a click.

"Yeah," he said. "Okay."

He followed Liviu outside without grumbling, wishing he still had his revolver. If he'd been worried about bursting into flames the second he crossed the threshold, that concern was quickly dispelled when he saw that the sky was plastered with gray clouds. Rain pummeled the packed-earth courtyard with abandon.

The door that led to the cellar was down a flight of stone steps on the other side of the courtyard. It was made of wood and looked flimsy enough that a child could have kicked their way through. As he entered the cellar, József didn't feel the telltale tingle of wards either. This was just a door. Was this oh-so-powerful ancient really that careless?

Nah, that couldn't have been it. This was easy on purpose. *Come into my parlor, said the spider to the fly.*

The cellar, too, was an unremarkable affair of red brick walls lined with wooden wine racks. Old glass bottles peeked from under a thick layer of dust here and there. József wondered what those were for. The wine he'd drank earlier had tasted like mud. He tried not to look at the two dead hunters piled unceremoniously in a corner.

"Well?" József asked. There were no other doors that he could see. No trapdoors, either; the stone floor rang solid under his boots.

"Give them a minute." Liviu's eyes were nowhere near him as he said it.

József thought he understood. Battered and bloodied as he was, not to mention pale and shambling, he must have made for one hell of a sight. No wonder Liviu refused to look at him. Maybe he wanted to remember him like he'd known him. *Alive.*

"Your, uh." Liviu cleared his throat. "Your smell."

József blinked at him. "What about it?"

"It's"—Liviu waved a hand in a vague gesture, saying—"a lot. For me, I mean, I know you don't— Look, I'll draw some water from the well so you can wash off when you're done here, yeah?"

Oh. "I'm not—"

"Change of clothes wouldn't hurt either," Liviu said, his nose wrinkling.

Before József could find it in his heart to tell him he didn't have to bother, a shimmer ran through the far wall, like an old screen when you took a magnet to it. The wine racks twisted and dissolved into strings of silvery runes, and the bottles went with them. A chuckle rumbled from deep inside his chest when he realized the runes were skittering around to form the outline of a door. How Padre and the others had hoped to even find this fucker, he had no idea. Deluded, the lot of them. Deluded, and now they were dead.

"You comin' too?" he asked Liviu.

"They only said you," the werewolf answered, already turning on his heel. "Don't worry. They don't, uh..." He left the sentence dangling as he headed back up the stairs.

József found himself chuckling again. Had Liviu been about to say, "They don't bite"?

"Fuckin' hell," he muttered under his breath, and then he reached for the door.

The handle felt solid as you please when he turned it. The skin on his palm prickled like he'd burned himself with a cigarette, but only for a second. *Wards.* The roots of his hair tingled as he opened the door and entered.

The space he'd emerged into was so different from the rest of the cellar his battered mind took a moment to recalibrate. Gilded sconces adorned the walls, casting a warm, inviting glow across a room that was some three meters wide and three across. Dark wooden panels framed sections of wallpaper with ornate, floral patterns. The furniture—two chairs and a settee, a low table, a bookcase, and a four-poster bed half obscured by a hanging velvet canopy—was stately and elaborate, each piece meticulously carved with bas-reliefs and inlaid with gold foil. A thick, soft carpet covered the floor. József could feel his feet sinking into it even through the thick soles of his boots.

Evdochia waited in the middle of the room, their arms folded in front of them, fingers laced together. They were an ancient, all right. Their skin was marble-smooth with the slightest rosy sheen to it, so they must have fed recently. József felt a pang of thirst, stronger than before. He did his best to ignore it.

In a voice as lifeless as their chiseled face, Evdochia said, "You must be József." They didn't smile, nor did they offer their hand in greeting.

József didn't move from his spot by the door. "And you must be the vampire."

"You are observant," Evdochia said. It was hard to tell whether they had taken offense. The flickering lights were the only thing moving in the stillness of the room, making strange shadows dance across their face.

"You wanted to talk to me," József said, "so talk. I ain't got all day."

Evdochia studied him for a few moments longer. They made him feel like a fly trapped in amber: small, powerless, *insignificant*. He knew it was just a trick of the mind. Still, they *could* probably crush him, if not with a thought, then with a gesture, at least.

"How did you become this?" the vampire said finally.

József did his best impression of a careless shrug. "Beats me."

"You do not remember?"

"Look, uh." He'd been about to say *lady*, but he had an inkling that wouldn't be well received. "I remember dyin'. Beyond that, I couldn't tell you."

"No," Evdochia said, gliding forward with silent steps, "but I could tell you. If you want." They came to a stop in front of him, seemingly unbothered by their height difference. József had to force himself to hold their gaze.

"If you were there, come out and say it." József was itching to lunge forward, grab the vampire by the neck, and twist.

"I wasn't," Evdochia said, "but the human mind is a curious thing, you see. You may think you have no memory of what happened. That does not make it true."

"Speak plainly, damn you." He didn't know whether it was anger or exhaustion that throttled his voice, but he winced at the way it cracked either way. Maybe it was the damn thirst. His tongue felt like sandpaper in his mouth.

The vampire didn't seem fazed by the outburst. He doubted there were many things that could faze them, all told. "Like I said, József. Your mind remembers things, even though you, yourself, may not. I can help you unlock those memories, if you let me."

He skipped the part where he asked them how they even knew his name. "What's in it for you? Don't tell me you're helping me out of the kindness of your wretched little heart."

"Knowing helps me as much as it helps you," Evdochia said, their voice smooth as silk. "Open your mind to me. Let me see."

"Huh?" he snapped, somewhere between derisive and incredulous. "You want me to—"

He clamped his mouth shut. Something weird was happening inside his head. It almost felt like an itch, except it was on the brain, right under his skull.

Images started flashing before his eyes. He could still see what was in front of him, but he was also back in the alley, staring down the tip of a bolt. The scene was frozen, the bolt suspended mid-flight. He flinched out of the way instinctively and bumped into an ornate chest, rattling its wooden drawers.

Evdochia's voice echoed inside his mind. *It's just a memory. You won't feel any pain.*

With that as his only warning, things inside the vision began to move.

True to the vampire's words, he felt nothing when the bolt sank into his chest. Now that he was free from the abject terror of knowing he was going to die, he saw it hadn't been Ferdinand who'd shot him but the other guy, who was now reloading his crossbow with quick, efficient movements. His hands were swift and steady. Suddenly, József didn't feel all that bad for having killed him earlier.

The world tilted, then righted itself again, and József remembered he'd gone down on his knees. When the second bolt struck, he *heard* the sound of silver hitting flesh. His hand flew to his chest before he could stop himself. His shirt was still torn and stained with caked blood. His wounds were still there too. They wouldn't mend so long as he didn't feed.

In the memory, a deep voice rumbled, close to his ea. "This one's for my mother, heathen."

József felt a trickle of curiosity from Evdochia, whose mind was now twinned with his. His own shock was a deluge. Now, he remembered why Padre had looked familiar. He had his mother's eyes and the same delicate brow. Even the way he scowled at him reminded him of Carmen.

With a deafening *crack*, the vision twisted and blurred. Sparkles danced in front of his eyes.

He didn't remember anything past this point and, judging by the curtain of blackness he was staring at now, this was probably the end of it. There were still sounds, faint and muffled: the low voices of Padre and the other guy, the rasp of something being dragged (his body, he assumed, bristling at the indignity). He tried to listen in on the conversation, but either they'd been whispering or his own mind had already been too far gone. He only caught the odd word here and there: Carmen, and then vampire, and tomorrow.

Then someone screamed.

It wasn't either one of his killers but a woman, her voice shrill like a banshee's. József felt a phantom jolt as his body was dropped in the memory. He thought he heard a scuffle, the two men cursing, the scratch of boots on gravel. The sounds drifted in and out of his awareness. His own breathing was loud and uneven, gurgling with the blood filling up his lungs. He was thankful, at least, that he didn't remember what that had felt like.

"Curious," he heard Evdochia say in the present, though he wasn't sure if they'd spoken out loud or if their voice was still in his mind.

He waited as the echo of his breath grew weaker and all other sounds faded. He'd been dying. The enormity of it was somewhat diminished by the fact that he was still around to remember it.

"*Worry not. Your life is over, but this isn't the end for you,*" a woman's voice said at last. It wasn't Evdochia but someone who had spoken to him as he lay dying. Someone he recognized.

József's eyes flew open.

"No," he said.

*

Ileana jumped back to her feet, breathing heavily. She didn't trust herself with the knife. If this was a trick—

"Mother said you came to Ravenswatch," the vampire spoke again, the words tumbling out one after another. And, yes, it *was* her, it had to be her. "I wanted to talk to you, but you were already gone. I didn't know—"

"Wait," Ileana said, her voice cracking on the word. "How—?"

"I followed them out," Tamara said. "They wouldn't let me come, but...but the way was still open, and—"

"Wait. Wait." Ileana took a breath. "What are you talking about?"

"The coven. All of them." Tamara stood up slowly, trying to sluice the mud from her clothes. "They gathered out in the courtyard and left before the sun came down. I don't know where." She was talking in short, frantic bursts as her eyes kept darting to the trees around them.

"Where were you going, then?" Ileana couldn't smell any other vampires around, but that could change quickly if the whole damn coven was on the move.

"I was running away. I thought, if they're all gone, there wouldn't be anyone left to stop me." Tamara hugged herself tightly. "I never wanted to be one of them. Not like this."

Ileana pinched the bridge of her nose, thinking, *Of course you didn't.* "Mother said this was the only way—"

"But I didn't want it, okay? Becoming this"—Tamara gestured to herself—"was one thing. Becoming a *vampire*. I never thought I'd have to be a part of...of what you saw last night. The blood, the killing, the—" She shook her head, her short hair flying everywhere. "Our family is dead, did you know? They killed them all. Father, everyone. Yes, I wanted to live, but I never, never—"

Ileana closed the distance between them and grabbed Tamara's arms to steady her. "I know," she said quietly. "It wasn't your fault."

"But it was!" Tamara wailed. "I just—I was so sick and scared, and I—I didn't want to die. And then Mum came back and, and..."

"And she brought the others," Ileana said when Tamara's sobbing became too thick for the words to slip through. She held her sister close, gently guiding Tamara's head to rest on her shoulder. "It's all right. I know."

It took a long time for Tamara's crying to subside. Ileana held her through it, but her heart was numb. Arghira had done something terrible in the name of saving her child, and that could never be undone. There were no words of comfort for that.

Eventually, Tamara looked up. Her eyes were red-rimmed and glistening, and her tears had a faint, rosy sheen to them. Ileana tried not to think about what that meant.

"You," Tamara said. "You knew? What I did?"

"Yeah. I went up to meet you, but you never came, so I went to the lodge." She took a small breath. "You wanted me to see, didn't you?"

Tamara swallowed a whimper. "I thought, maybe, someone else might have..."

"No," Ileana said. "I'm sorry."

"Gods," Tamara whispered, burying her face in her hands.

"That's not on you." Ileana cast a quick glance around them. There was no telling what lurked in these woods at night, and she didn't feel like sticking around long enough to find out. They'd already lingered here enough.

"C'mon," she said, "Let's go. We can talk more on the way."

Tamara sniffed once, but other than that she seemed to have come back to her senses enough to listen. "Go?" she said. "Go where?"

"I know a safe place in town. A house." Ileana took her sister's arm and gently turned her around. The cold had seeped into her bones while she'd stood still.

Tamara went easily at least. Her wet clothes stuck to her body and were so big for her that the fabric bunched up in odd places and the hem of her pants dragged through the mud. They'd need to find her something else to wear, something that fit a little better. Ileana wondered if she could ask Crin for some of his clothes, since they were closer in size, but then she quickly banished the thought. She didn't even know if Tamara wanted to live past tonight. Maybe, she—like József—

She slipped her right hand under the left cuff of her jacket and pinched the soft skin above her wrist hard enough to feel the pain. She couldn't think about József, not now. Not when the mere ghost of a name still made her heart feel like it was breaking into a million jagged pieces all over again.

"Why did you come to Ravenswatch?" Tamara said after a few minutes. Her voice was small but steady now.

"I was looking for you."

"How did you know where to go?"

"I found a vampire who told me," Ileana said. "And a werewolf. Two werewolves, actually."

Tamara hummed. "Was there a changeling, too? And a far-seer, maybe?"

Ileana let out a startled laugh. "A farseer would have made things easy. Besides, I don't think there's any of them left this side of the Danube." Farseers—or just seers as most people called them—had the power to scry into the many different pathways time could take, but the last one she'd known of had died in a monastery south of the Carpathians some fifteen years ago.

"I envy you, you know," Tamara said. "You got to see the world. Meet all those people."

"What about you?" Ileana asked. The trees were getting thinner ahead of them.

Tamara made a dismissive sound, something between a sigh and a snort. "I hunted with them, that's *all* I did. Sure, I wanted to go to university, but Father wouldn't let me. This isn't the kind of life you walk away from, he said." She paused for a breath. "I'm glad you did."

"Did he ever talk about me?"

"No. If anyone asked, he said you were dead, too, like Luca."

"Fucking figures," Ileana muttered, and then she felt a cold stab of longing in her chest when she heard herself. It sounded like something József would have said.

They walked for another minute before Tamara stopped abruptly. "Do you hear—?"

"I do," Ileana said. A shiver ran through her.

From the flickering lights of Gorun stretching down below, the deep toll of church bells drifted on the wind.

*

József felt a cold shock of anger wash over him. It wasn't *his* anger though; it came from Evdochia. Their presence had been a quiet, skittering thing until now, sticking to the outer layers of his mind. Without warning, they dove in, rifling through his memories with careless abandon. He saw what they saw, fractured vignettes of the past few days: Ileana smiling by the fire, a stretch of darkened road illuminated by the headlights of his truck, a greasy table at the tavern in Three Rivers. The images came after one-another in a dizzying kaleidoscope, spinning faster and faster. He saw the still expanse of Bear Lake under the stars, the road leading up to the Carpathians, sunrise bleeding red into the skies over Deva. Crisp linen sheets covering a low, rickety bed. An inn whose name he'd already forgotten.

Then, suddenly, he was trapped in a cell back at the coven, and a dead woman's rancid lips were pressed against his own.

With a small noise of disgust, Evdochia withdrew from his mind, and the vision winked off like a candle snuffed by the wind. József wiped his mouth with the back of his hand. He could still smell the woman, *taste* her. There wasn't enough booze in the world to cleanse the memory of that.

"I see," Evdochia said. Their brows had drawn together in a frown, upsetting the stillness of their face.

József cleared his throat. "I take it you know her?"

"Madeleine. They call her the Maneater." Evdochia looked past him for a moment. "I would have seen her banished, but my brother always liked to humor her."

Madeleine the Maneater. It was too on the nose, like something from one of those kitschy vaudeville renaissance shows they peddled in the cities.

"I saw in your mind what you intend to do," Evdochia said, their expression easing into something that might have been kindness. "I neither can nor will prevent you from seeking your death, if that is your wish. But, if you stand with me against Ravenswatch, you could avenge yourself before you depart and also cleanse the world of some of the vampires you so despise."

"You're a vampire too," József pointed out.

Lightly, they said, "As are you."

As if he could forget. "You wanna make a move against Ravenswatch, then?"

"Soon. I've already started gathering my allies, but there is one more thing I must do before we are ready. I depart tonight. If fate holds out a little longer, I shall be back before I am needed."

József didn't say anything. He felt the thirst burning him from inside and wondered which was worse: that or the sun.

If he died now, he wouldn't be at peace, that much he knew. He was no stranger to the siren song of vengeance, and this time the object of it was almost within reach. He'd laid waste to the coven that had taken his Stefánia from him. Surely, he could afford another day of this accursed existence to avenge his own death.

"All right," he said. "I'll fight."

"Good." Evdochia turned and glided toward the back wall, where a brocade curtain hung over one corner. "In the meantime," they said, "you need to drink. You are too weak to be of use otherwise." They pulled the curtain aside to reveal a plain-looking wooden door.

József tried to swallow. His throat felt like it was lined with razor blades.

Evdochia's mind brushed against his, more tender than inquisitive. The ghost of an image flashed before his eyes, and then he knew whom he'd find beyond that door.

"It is your choice," the vampire said.

József cleared his throat again, for all the good that did. "He still alive in there?"

"For the moment, yes."

The thirst was agony. His vision swam. His hands and knees felt weak. The promise of relief was a tempest, an avalanche, burying all else.

It's only for another day. One day, one more soul, and then he would gladly go.

Hoarsely, he whispered, "Yeah. Okay."

Evdochia nodded, the corners of their lips curling slightly upward, and motioned with their hand. The door handle began to turn, untouched.

Chapter Seventeen

Song of the Prey

Sensing his presence might not be needed for some time, Liviu had wandered into town in search of food. He already knew Evdochia was leaving tonight—in search of a boon, they'd said, because gods forbid they talk like a normal person for once. That they'd leave now with the threat of Ravenswatch hanging over all of their heads was bad enough, but the last thing they'd said to him was "Watch over Crin." Did they know something he didn't? It wouldn't have surprised him. It definitely pissed him off.

The mouthwatering smell of grilled meat was suddenly more important than Evdochia being a cryptic asshole. He followed the heavenly aroma to a food stall tucked at the mouth of an alley. With the few coins he had in his pocket, he bought a sandwich consisting of a beef patty pressed between two greasy buns. As soon as he rounded the next corner, he ditched the buns, scraped off the few sorry bits of lettuce that clung to the meat, and wolfed down the patty in a few hungry bites, groaning in satisfaction. It was a touch more cooked than he would have liked, but it was still warm and juicy, so he couldn't complain.

He wiped his hands on his jeans; then, rather than head back, he kept walking. The red house held more people than he was used to being around. He thought he liked all of them, but their lingering presence was starting to crowd him. He needed some distance to put his own thoughts in order, and wandering around for a bit would have to be good enough for now. Later, he'd maybe go hunting in the woods. There was bound to be good game up here.

With no hunger to distract him, his thoughts began to churn again. "Watch over Crin," Evdochia had said. The hell did that even mean? Crin was fine. Sure, they hadn't had a chance to talk much after the kiss, and they'd slept without touching the night before with most of the bed between them. But they were fine.

They *were* fine, weren't they?

He kicked at an empty can in passing. Yeah, they were fine for now. But what about next week? Next month? They couldn't stay here forever, not with a war about to fuck shit up for everyone. Liviu might have been keen to fight, but Crin wasn't like that. This wasn't his world. He deserved better. Better than Darius. Better than him.

He caught up with the can and kicked it again. *Fucking shit.*

Without knowing it, his legs had carried him toward the heart of Gorun. The town had been built in concentric circles around an old Orthodox church in the middle of a cobbled square. The houses around the square were stately, neoclassical affairs, two or three stories tall, with elongated windows and sculpted colonnades adorning their façades. Their courtyards were on the inside, which meant that alleys of various proportions had sprung up between them, stacked high with dumpsters and household refuse. Some of those also housed rusted cars hoisted up on cinder blocks.

The air was suddenly thick with the smell of vampire—blood, dust, and a hint of sickly sweet cologne that told him this wasn't anyone he knew. He turned to look and, sure enough, there he was: a tall, slender man who looked to be about fifty, wearing a black, fitted coat over a ruffled white undershirt. Dark tights and a pair of polished boots completed the ensemble. He couldn't have been more conspicuous if he tried.

Their eyes met for less than a second, then Liviu turned his head again, ostensibly scanning a shop display on the other side of the street. He kept his ears alert for any sounds of pursuit, but he didn't hear anything aside from his own footsteps on the cobblestones.

It was late, but not late enough for the streets to be completely deserted. If that vampire was out to feed, he'd find prey soon enough. A week ago, Liviu wouldn't have cared. Tonight, knowing what he knew, he decided it was long past time for someone to take one of those pretentious assholes down a peg.

He slipped into the shadow of a store awning and stopped, pretending to check a watch he didn't have. The street behind him was empty save for a short human clad in black from head to toe. Squinting, he saw they were a teenager, one of those kids stuck firmly in their "no, Mom, this isn't just a phase!" phase. The teen stopped suddenly, their head snapping up as though they'd heard something. After a moment, they turned and marched into a darkened alley, close to where Liviu had seen the vampire earlier.

Liviu moved, too, walking toward the alley at a brisk pace but careful to keep his steps light. He didn't have a plan beyond whatever his body could reasonably do under the circumstances, but then again, he hardly ever had a plan. He wasn't worried about the vampire's magick either. Only the old, powerful ones could ever hope to bend the mind of a werewolf.

The alley looked empty at first, but that was just because a tall, metal container filled with branch clippings and bits of dead shrubbery blocked the far end from view. Underneath the heavy smell of compost wafting from the rotten greenery were lighter notes of blood, warm and red. Liviu's mouth twisted in a snarl. *Fucker's already feeding.*

The scene that greeted him when he rounded the container was far more gruesome than he'd expected. For one thing, there were not one, but two vampires. The second one was a woman who would have looked old but for the unnatural smoothness of her pale, round face. Her hair was long and white, falling over her shoulders in loose ringlets that reminded him of coiled snakes. She had latched on to the teenager's neck and lapped away at the blood flowing freely from an open wound. The other vampire was nibbling on their wrist, his fangs glinting in the shadows.

The woman's eyes shifted his way. Liviu felt another presence touch his mind, then retreat. A whisper, if that.

"This doesn't concern you, mutt," she said, shifting so she was facing him. "You can have the carcass when we're done."

"No, thanks," Liviu said, "and also, you're not killing anyone today. Get the fuck away from them."

The teen stood placid throughout the exchange, oblivious to the fact that the other vampire's fangs had sunk into their neck once again. Their eyes were brown and wide, like Crin's.

"Fuck it," Liviu said. He'd never been a man of too many words.

He moved with all the speed his human form could muster, going for the vampire who was still feeding first. Liviu pried him loose and tossed him against the nearest wall, which the vampire hit with a satisfying crunch of bone. He rounded on the woman, who'd flung herself backward with a hiss, only to feel the tendrils of her mind begin to wrap around his own, not a whisper, but a deluge.

He didn't give her a chance to take hold of his mind fully but moved again, striking out with suddenly sharp, wicked claws. The woman jerked back, but she wasn't nearly fast enough. His claws raked across her face, sending her reeling. Her mind slid away from his like melting snow off a branch. Vampires were vain, fussy creatures. This would take her out of the fight for a while.

Liviu started to turn back to the man, and that was the only thing that saved him from having his neck pierced by a jeweled dagger. He took the blow in the shoulder and felt the skin part, but the cut didn't go any deeper than that and the knife pulled away easily. The burn came a second later. Silver, *again*. Why did everything have to be made of fucking *silver*?

He struck out blindly, biting back a curse. His attack was slower this time, and the vampire side-stepped it easily. Still brandishing the dagger, he flashed Liviu an unhinged smile, made all the more terrifying by the blood staining his long, sharp fangs.

Something collided with the side of Liviu's head.

He blacked out for a few seconds and came back round when the ground had already reacquainted itself with his bones. His shaken mind wasn't the quickest on the best of days, but it did make one crucial connection: ground, rock, *danger*. He rolled away a second before a brick came crashing down where his head had been, so close he tasted the reddish dust when he took a breath. He looked back up just in time to see a silver blur materialize out of nowhere and slam into the vampire who'd been about to stomp his boot down on his neck.

Liviu blinked, then rolled over and out of the way. The sounds of a fight erupted all around him: growling, hissing, the wet squelching of parting flesh. A whiff of vampire blood, stale and acrid, caught in the back of his throat and nearly made him gag. His vision darkened—not because of some trick of the light or the concussion he'd likely have to deal with once this was over—but because the vampires had turned into black mist and were now fleeing with their metaphorical tails tucked between their legs.

"Are you okay? Are you hurt?" said a voice Liviu had briefly thought he'd never hear again.

He felt a slender hand on his shoulder—a human hand—and looked up to find Crin looming over him.

"I'll be fine," Liviu said while his heart did a little somersault.

His ears were still ringing, and there was an ugly bump at the back of his skull that hurt when he poked it, but he'd had worse. He'd live.

With a grunt (and a whimper he bit back just as quickly because, *Jesus*, his shoulder was on fire), Liviu pushed to his feet. Wobbling a little, he turned around just in time to see the back of the teenager who, having snapped out of the vampire's charm, had wisely chosen to book it. He also realized he'd been wrong to assume that both vampires had made it out of the fight in one piece. One of them, the man, was well and truly dead on the ground, his head nearly torn from his shoulders. Immortal or not, there was no way to heal from something like that.

Good fucking riddance.

Crin hovered next to Liviu, his hand lingering next to his arm but not quite touching. The shirt Crin had worn now hung tattered from his bony shoulders, and the obliterated remains of his pants left slightly less than was strictly decent to the imagination. Both were casualties of his earlier shifting.

"There's blood on you," Crin said.

Liviu snapped out of wherever his mind was trying to limp to and gave him what he hoped was a reassuring smile. "Don't worry about it. And, uh, we got even back at the lake, so I guess this means I owe you now."

Crin watched him, his eyebrows slightly raised.

"Oh, uh. Thanks. Thank you," Liviu said again when the first thanks didn't quite do justice to whatever the hell he was feeling right now.

Crin's face relaxed into a smile, and, yeah, that had definitely been the right thing to say. Seeing that smile, knowing he was the reason for it, would never get old.

"We should head back," Crin said. "Can you walk?"

"Fuck that." Liviu's shoulder stung, but he could already feel the wound starting to mend. His head was clearing even as he spoke. "One of those fuckers got away. I'm going after her."

Quietly, Crin said, "I don't think she was alone."

Liviu glared at the dead vampire. "He's not going anywhere."

"Not him. I saw another one of them when I was following your scent. Another woman. She was younger than the one we fought."

"That makes three. They're bolder than usual too." Liviu tapped his lip with his index finger while his mind worked. "You don't think—"

Whatever else he was going to say was drowned by a deep, mournful toll reverberating through the night. Another one came, and then another, and another. Something had awakened the great bells of the town square church.

*

József stood in front of the red house. The street ahead of him was deserted save for a lone man stumbling his way back to town. A drunk, most likely. József wondered if that was what he'd looked like to people too.

The bells had started tolling some minutes ago, and it didn't sound like they were going to stop any time soon. At first, he'd thought that was odd. It wasn't the top of the hour, and it was too late in the evening for a sermon. It wasn't just one church, either; what had started with the lone call of the town square bells had morphed into a mayhem of at least five different timbres. Another day, he might have wondered why a town as small as Gorun had so many damn churches, but he was starting to understand. Churches were built on hallowed ground. Vampires couldn't go there.

The sky was black and moonless, but the night was bright to József's newly awakened senses. Darkness was no obstacle to a vampire's preternatural sight. Where the world was devoid of color, the shapes of things stood out like black ink on moonlight-gray parchment. That made it easy to spot the vampire who had been watching him from across the street.

As soon as their eyes met, the vampire winked and exploded into a cloud of black mist. József, who'd already drawn his revolver, was left blinking at an empty space. He grit his teeth and returned the revolver to his coat pocket, then started down the street. The drunk had run off, but that vampire could still find him.

Not if I find him first.

The bells reverberated up and down the empty street, covering the sound of his footsteps. He'd find the fucker, put a bullet between his eyes, and then there'd be one less vampire in the world. It was worth holding on for another day or two if it meant he still got to do that, even if he'd had to kill again to buy himself the time.

Thinking of Padre should have turned his stomach. It was wrong that it didn't. Then again, there wasn't anything in his stomach to throw up, other than blood.

Padre had accepted his fate almost peacefully, come to think of it. His lips were still moving in a soundless prayer when József's fangs had sunk into his neck. He remembered feeling ashamed at first. The thirst had been stronger, erasing all else. The blood was sweet ambrosia when it touched his lips. It quenched and soothed, nourished and rejuvenated. It brought him peace.

The thirst was gone for now, replaced by the singing of warm blood in his dead veins. The self-loathing he'd expected was slow to come. For now, all he cared about was the hunt. There were six bullets in his revolver, each one doused in holy water. They were lead instead of silver, but still enough to take down a vampire. József had rarely bothered with silver bullets after he'd lost Ileana. Even years later, nightmares still haunted him—that he'd killed a werewolf, only to learn it had been her.

Six bullets would have to be enough. He'd pop five of them if he could, then save the last one for himself.

Gorun was a ghost town, its streets deserted and the windows dark and barred. As soon as he placed the wrongness of it, József breathed a knowing chuckle to himself. These people understood. They'd locked their doors, shuttered their windows and, if they were smart, they'd huddle together around a censer, grab some holy water, and wait for the night to pass.

The street doubled back, then led him to the main road. There was no sign of the vampire, so József kept walking. The bells were louder the closer he got to the church, and their cadence wasn't slowing. He had to commend whoever was pulling on the ropes.

He'd just crossed the main road, using the church spire as a compass, when he heard someone scream.

József ran toward the sound, one hand closing over the grip of his revolver. His legs moved faster than they ever had in life. He couldn't remember when he'd stopped breathing, but it didn't bother him in the slightest. Where his lungs would have burned with the exertion and his heart would have threatened to burst out of his chest by now, he felt only a growing lightness. He wouldn't have been surprised to look down and find that his feet were hovering above the asphalt.

His elation was as short-lived as the time it took him to reach the source of the scream. An elderly man, dazed rather than dead, was sitting with his back propped up against a wooden fence. Blood trickled from two puncture wounds on the left side of his neck, just above where a thin collarbone threatened to poke through his weathered skin. József scanned his surroundings, but there was nobody else around, undead or otherwise. Just him and the old man, whose lips were parted enough to let out a faint gurgle.

Before he could stop himself, József thought, *Pathetic.*

That startled him into another grim realization: not that long ago, he might have ended up just like the man on the ground, except maybe drunk rather than exsanguinated. The man was older, but not by much. József had been hurtling toward the same kind of fate unless he'd offed himself first.

Droplets of blood had started to congeal down the man's neck, pooling in the hollow just above his collarbone. József's eyes were inexorably drawn to the sight. The thirst began to stir again. It wasn't nearly the same kind of agony he'd grappled with earlier in the day, but this poor wretch's blood would sate it all the same. He was doomed to rot and decay anyway, but it would take months, years. Death would be a mercy.

József shook himself, then turned his head to the side and

spat. He'd die, truly die, before he gave in to the thirst again. With one last look at the gaunt old man, he turned and walked away.

The next time he rounded a corner, he almost tripped over a corpse.

For a man with a gaping wound in the middle of his chest, the lack of blood was conspicuous enough, but the clothes were what really sold it, all crushed velvet, ruffles, and lace. It was a vampire, all right; not the one József had been tracking, but a vampire nevertheless. A lump of flesh lay crushed and discarded a few steps away. It might have been a heart. This was the work of claws, not weapons.

As though answering his thoughts, a howl erupted from nearby.

*

Ileana smelled cinders on the wind long before she saw the blaze. Something was burning. She quickened her pace.

When she and Tamara emerged from the forest, they saw tall flames below them. It was hard to tell from a distance at first, but she thought they came from the edge of town. The red house was there. Ileana's heart leapt to her throat.

"Stay close," she told Tamara.

Her sister nodded once. She was shivering, even though her undead form should have been impervious to the elements by now. From what she'd read about vampires, Ileana knew that cold, hunger, even pain would fade as the magicks working to preserve the body slowly twisted it away from its humanity.

"Are you okay?" she asked Tamara, the cadence of her own words disrupted by a slight chattering of teeth.

Tamara nodded again and kept going. Ileana didn't say anything else.

A little while later, they came to a stop in front of a roaring inferno. The red house was burning, tall flames licking at it from the floorboards to the blackened shingles on the roof. The fire made shadows dance across the courtyard and lit up the street beyond. As they got closer to the fence, Ileana's skin erupted in a sheen of sweat, but a different kind of cold lingered underneath.

"This was them," Tamara whispered.

Ileana couldn't tear her gaze away from the fire. *József, Liviu, Crin...*

Tamara nudged her arm. "The fire. Can you feel it? It's not natural."

Slowly, Ileana turned to look at her sister. A half-formed thought found its way to her lips. "They would have fought."

Tamara's eyes were wide and glistening. "What are you talking about?"

"József. Liviu. Crin." Ileana's voice had taken on a frantic edge. "They wouldn't have let this happen without a fight."

But then, why can't I smell any of it? Why can't I—?

She forced her breaths to slow. There was no blood in the air, and she didn't smell any charred flesh, undead or not. Too, she could feel the crackling of spent magick, now that she knew to look for it.

Ileana turned around, her mind focusing entirely on what her senses were telling her. She took a few steps out into the street. It was hard to pick up a trail this close to the fire, but she thought she sensed a faint undercurrent of moonshine, and blood, and...soap?

József's truck was still parked where they'd left it the night before, far enough from the blaze that the flames didn't touch it.

Ileana heard Tamara call to her. "Just a second," she said, and then she closed her eyes.

She thought she could also smell cigarettes and the diffuse, floral scent of whatever cologne Crin liked to wear. Liviu smoked, and the moonshine could have been József. Maybe they'd gone somewhere together, all three of them, before the fire had broken out. But then, why would the vampires burn down an empty house?

"No one's coming to put out the fire," Tamara said suddenly.

That, too, was strange. The fire must have been burning for some minutes before they'd even gotten here, but there was no telltale flash of red lights, nor the wailing of a firetruck siren coming up the street. All she heard was the bells.

"Come on," she told her sister. "I need to find my pack."

They'd taken about half a dozen steps when the red house's roof collapsed behind them in a shower of sparks.

Chapter Eighteen

The Bells

Liviu quickly discovered that undead blood ran thick. You couldn't just wring it out of your shirt. It stuck, and it reeked.

They'd found more vampires after the first. The last two lay dead across the street. The third had managed to flee to the roof-tops, but not before Crin had gotten in a good hit, right across the stomach. It was as close to evisceration as he could manage at such a bad angle. Liviu was secretly impressed.

At least there were no more humans to worry about. The bells must have served as a warning system of sorts. Humans were smarter than he'd given them credit for if they actually listened.

Liviu pulled what was left of his bloodied shirt over his head and tossed it away, then wiped his face with the back of his hand. The stench was the worst of it. Some of these bastards had been dead for hundreds of years, and their innards sure as hell smelled like it.

"Why are they doing this?" Crin said next to him, in-between pants. He was in just as much of a state as Liviu, and he looked decidedly less happy about it.

"They're sending a message," Liviu said. "Vampires don't hunt out in the open like this, not unless they want to bring every damn hunter in the country down on their heads."

"That makes no sense. Why would they want that?"

Liviu hacked and spat. The taste of rot at the back of his throat lingered. "'Cause they're finally looking to start that war they wanted." He stopped just short of adding: *And I think they just did.*

Ileana's old man chose that particular moment to come running at them from the other end of the street, so Liviu used that distraction to steer the conversation back to their more immediate problems. He didn't want to think about what any of this meant just yet. He'd do it later, and he wouldn't do it sober.

He noticed, as he gave József the rundown of what was happening, that the old man had taken his advice and cleaned himself. He'd even put on a black turtleneck instead of the bloody rags he'd died in. He still wore his ratty old coat, which was tarnished with blood and mud, but Liviu assumed he didn't have another one.

"Church went quiet," József said at the end, tossing his head in the direction of the town square. He sounded more like himself, too, and less like someone who gargled glass on the regular.

The old man was right. Liviu hadn't noticed when the bells had stopped, but he couldn't hear the closest ones anymore. Other churches were still going, but those were farther away.

"We should check it out," Liviu said. A niggling unease burrowed at the back of his mind. There was no way the coven was already calling it a night, not if they'd come here to stir shit up.

The other two fell in line without protest. Walking slightly ahead, Liviu took a moment to marvel at the absurdity of it all. He had a hunter at his back when, not even a week ago, that thought would have been enough to send him into a panicked frenzy. The man next to him, who'd stolen his goddamn heart when he wasn't paying attention, was Darius's brother. *Darius*, who'd nearly fucking ended him once.

Well. How about that?

The town square wasn't far. There was an outdoor café right on the corner, little more than a scattering of white plastic tables, rickety chairs, and patio umbrellas dangling from thin, metal poles. The three of them filtered between the tables, keeping their heads low. This was as good a spot as any to watch from without being seen.

In the middle of the square, a small congregation of vampires had gathered in front of the church. Liviu and the others were upwind so he couldn't catch their scent, but he didn't need to. They stood unnaturally still in the dim glow of the square's lights, where humans would have fidgeted and squirmed. He counted seven of them.

"What are they doing?" Crin whispered.

What were they doing? One of them—Liviu assumed it was their leader, maybe Iancu himself—stood facing the other six on the marble steps leading up to the church proper. At first, Liviu thought he might have been giving a speech, but there were no words on the wind, and the man was as unmoving as the rest of them.

József grunted. "Looks like they're waiting for something. They can't get into the church, and I'm guessin' local folk know that too. Might be some of 'em are holed up in there."

A shuffle of steps behind them made Liviu turn his head. He saw Ileana coming toward their hiding spot from a side alley, her steps purposefully loud. She had a vampire in tow. *The sister*, his brain supplied immediately; the resemblance would have been uncanny if she weren't so thin he could almost see the outline of her skull through her skin. A funny look passed between Ileana and the old man, enough to make him wonder what had happened between them earlier, but the moment passed quickly. Then, it was time for hushed introductions—he'd been right that she was Ileana's sister, Tamara—and for him to catch them up, which he did as they shuffled forward to get a better look at the square.

The sisters listened in silence, and then Tamara leaned in to whisper something to Ileana.

"Do you think she'll see reason?" Ileana asked.

Tamara frowned, looking away. She didn't answer.

"Something's happening," Crin whispered suddenly. His breath was so close it tickled the hairs behind Liviu's ear.

More vampires were pouring in from the shadows, moving with silent, gliding steps. There were close to a dozen now, though it was hard to be sure. Something made their silhouettes shimmer and blur.

"They're going to burn down the church," Tamara said.

Liviu's head whipped back to her. "How do you know?"

"I heard them talking about it. They want to be seen." There was a frantic edge to her voice.

"Can we stop them?" Crin asked. He, too, sounded horrified.

Liviu scoffed before he could stop himself. "I'm not dying for an empty church."

"Ain't empty," József cut in. "Somebody's moving up there. In the tower."

Sure enough, after a moment, Liviu spotted it too—the faint

outline of a person, a different shade of black against the surrounding darkness.

Who gives a shit about some fucking humans? Let them burn, he thought but didn't say it. Looking into Crin's brown eyes was all it took. He wanted to be the man Crin apparently thought he was. Do better. *Be* better.

There were four of them, not counting Tamara. Ten, maybe twelve vampires in the square, and more were coming. They had the element of surprise, but the vampires had magick. Some of them were old too. Iancu was an ancient.

Fuck.

"What do we do?" Crin asked, his fingers seeking Liviu's as he said it.

Liviu chewed on his lower lip. They were fucked either way. Whether the church stood or burned, there was no way to bury this anymore. Once the humans heard about what had happened here tonight, Iancu would have his war, one way or the other.

"Let me go first," József said. "Maybe I can get 'em to trust me, seeing as I'm, y'know" His eyes traveled over the assembled group until they met Liviu's. "When you hear me start shooting, feel free to join in."

"How many bullets you got?" Liviu asked.

"Six," József said. "I doused 'em in holy water."

Six bullets. Best case scenario, that meant two or three vampires dead and the rest of them pissed off. Then again, if József managed to take out Iancu...

"Rock, hard place," Liviu muttered, rubbing his eyes. Then, louder, he said, "Yeah, okay. Fine. You go first, we follow. Try to aim for the vampires, yeah? We're on your side." He tossed in a confident smirk he didn't quite feel.

"Jóska," Ileana said. "I need to talk to you before you go."

The old man sagged visibly but moved next to her anyway. As they started talking in hushed voices, Crin nudged Liviu's shoulder. When Liviu turned to look at him, though, he frowned and looked away.

"Hey," Liviu whispered.

Crin's eyes snapped back to him. His mouth opened, then closed.

"If you don't want to do this, you don't have to," Liviu said, patting his hand. "Just hide and wait. We'll be—"

"No! That's not—I want to fight. With you. I just—"

"That's okay," Liviu said, swallowing the panic starting to churn in his own gut. "Whatever it is, we can talk about it when we're done here. Meantime, just follow my lead, yeah? Keep moving. We're faster than they are, so try to kill them quickly. Don't think about—"

Crin bent down to kiss him. It was quick and sloppy and maybe a touch desperate, but Liviu went with it anyway, stealing a few more seconds for the two of them before the world went to shit.

*

József stepped out into the square with a far more confident swagger than he felt. His revolver bumped against his thigh with every step. He wondered how many vampires he'd get to pop before the rest of them jumped him.

As many as it takes, he thought, patting the revolver under the guise of adjusting his coat.

The sisters had told him about their mother, not as a plea to spare her life, but as a warning. "She was a hunter," his Leana had told him, "and it was an ancient who turned her, so she'll be even stronger." Touching his arm, she'd added, "Be careful."

József had no intention to die for nothing, but he was also under no illusion about his chances of walking away with his life.

Well. *Life.* He still wasn't used to thinking of himself as anything but "alive."

He counted nine—no—ten of them as he approached. Number ten was partly hidden in the shadow of one of the columns supporting the grand portico, so József hadn't clocked them at first. Their face was obscured by a hood, and shadows swirled around them despite the fact that there was a light directly overhead. An old one, then. Dangerous. He made a mental note to take them out quickly.

Most of the vampires were plain-looking men and women wearing an amalgamation of fashions from the last few centuries. Some had swords, rapiers, and other kinds of blades whose names József didn't know. He didn't see any guns, but that didn't mean there weren't any. He assumed at least some of them knew how to use their weapons too.

A slight woman broke away from the rest of the group and sauntered up to meet József. Three parallel gashes marred her face, so he didn't recognize her at first. When he tried to walk around her, the woman's hand snaked out, latching onto his forearm with a strength belying her frail appearance. A broad smile pulled the skin of her face taut, making the gashes stand out all the more.

"I see you found your way back to me," the woman whispered. "Well done, my József."

If József had been human, his skin would have broken into a cold sweat. Her hair was different now, spilling down her shoulders rather than tightly coiffed, and she'd traded the brocade gowns he'd seen her in for a set of hunting leathers. The gashes were new as well. That voice, though—husky and dolorous, temptress and corpse horror all in one—sent a knife of dread straight through his core. It was the last voice he'd heard in life.

Rather than reach for the revolver, József clenched his fist and nodded back to the woman. Madeleine, Evdochia had called her. The Maneater.

Still smiling, Madeleine nudged him forward, falling into step next to him. He tried not to think about how close she was as the circle of vampires parted to let them pass, then immediately closed behind them. She was marching him toward the figure standing under the grand portico, who stepped forward and lowered their hood. They were a man who'd died in the prime of his life, with a head of straw-blond hair and a sharp, angular face. The sloping forehead and a hook nose left little doubt as to his lineage. His black eyes glinted red in the moonlight.

"Is this the one?" the vampire asked.

József didn't give Madeleine a chance to answer. "If you're asking whether I'm the guy she turned, the answer's yes."

The vampire looked him up and down, his gaze lingering, unhurried. József felt like an ant under a magnifying glass when the sun was out. For once, he was almost glad he didn't have to breathe.

A foreign mind touched his for a few moments, then retreated. "You were a hunter in life," the vampire said.

"Was, yeah." József didn't have to try very hard to sound offended at that. "Can't say I liked it, but I was good at killing."

The vampire's eyes narrowed. "What is it you want?"

To put you in the ground. That wasn't an option, though, not yet. There were too many eyes on them. He could maybe get off one shot before the other vampires fell on him, and the leader would see it coming.

"I'm looking for somewhere to be," he said instead. "It's not like I'll ever be able to go back to my own, given the circumstances." He glared toward Madeleine, who still idled placidly at his side, as he said it.

"Don't let him trick you," another voice interjected. "He's armed."

A woman detached herself from the shadow of another column. She was short and slim, with long, black hair woven into a braid. Unlike the others, her face hadn't smoothed out into an ivory mask just yet but retained some of its human imperfections.

"I know he is," Iancu said slowly, almost like he were talking to a child. "And you, dear Arghira, will make sure he keeps out of the way until we're finished here."

József's mind latched on to the name. Ileana's mother was called Arghira—she'd told him as much before she'd let him go—but the woman in front of him was nothing like he'd imagined. For one thing, she looked like *she* could have been Ileana's younger sister.

Madeleine let out a quiet hiss, like a pissed-off alley cat, and dislodged her claws from his arm. She scurried back to the throng of unmoving vampires behind them. József looked from her back to Iancu and Arghira before it clicked. *Vampire magick.* They could talk to each other in their heads.

"Come," Arghira said.

József bowed his head and followed. "What's he gonna do?" he asked her as they took their place on the opposite side of the gathering.

She looked at him, but she didn't answer. He couldn't reach for his revolver without being seen, and someone who'd been a hunter in life wouldn't be as easy to dupe as her haughtier kin either. He had to choose his moment carefully.

The leader had turned his back to the congregation. He was

moving his hands in a wide, rhythmic pattern. The air felt suddenly oppressive, like the prelude to a summer storm. A ripple of excitement passed through the assembly. If he was conjuring up some magickal fuckery, József had to act now; most spells were impossible to stop once summoned.

"Your daughters say hi, by the way," he said to Arghira, keeping his voice low. "Leana and—what's the other one? Mara?"

That goaded her into reacting, just like he'd hoped. "How do *you* know my daughters?"

"Leana and I go way back. I found her on the night she got turned, if you gotta know. Her old man wanted to put one between her eyes there and then." His words were purposefully unhurried despite the urgency prickling under his collar. "Mara, I just met. She's a sweet kid. Don't think either she or Leana would approve of what's happening here."

Arghira glared at him. She didn't dignify the jab with a reply.

"These humans never did anything to you, and your coven came out to murder them," he pressed. "Doesn't that bother you, even a little?"

"They would kill us in a heartbeat if they had the chance," she snapped.

"So that's it, then? Kill 'em first so they don't kill you back? An eye for an eye until the whole damn world goes blind?" Impatience was starting to seep into his words. The leader was chanting now, his voice rising and falling. It sounded like Latin.

"The world was already blind long before I died," Arghira said. "The old order that you and I were a part of needs to die so we can live as we are. There is no other way."

József fidgeted with the cuff of his sleeve. The leader's chanting was reaching a crescendo. There was no more time.

"They're watching us, you know," he said, raising his voice

slightly. "Leana and Mara. They let me go alone 'cause they thought I'd be safer from you lot, but they ain't far."

And there it was: the small start, the way her eyes darted behind him. "Where?"

He raised his hand to indicate the mouth of an alley on the other side of the square. "Right...there."

Arghira turned to look. József's hand slipped inside his coat pocket and found the grip of his revolver. The leader's back was still turned to his congregation. He wouldn't, couldn't miss.

With a deafening *fwoosh*, white and gold flames erupted from the leader's fingertips, coiling around the stone columns of the grand portico. Within seconds, they'd found wood. József remembered to pull the trigger a second too late; Arghira barreled into him, and the bullet hit stone rather than flesh.

He saw the flash of a dagger and twisted away as the blade whistled through the air, a hair's breadth away from his neck. Arghira pressed him with swing after swing. He dodged and weaved but couldn't find an opening to bring his revolver around and fire without leaving himself exposed. She wasn't the kind of opponent he could wait out until she ran out of breath either. And, the longer the fight dragged on, the taller the flames became.

"No! He's mine!"

From somewhere to his right, Madeleine swung into the fray, grasping for the blade. She was a much older vampire than Arghira, but the other woman clearly knew how to fight. For a moment, neither had the upper hand.

József took aim at both of them, the tip of the barrel swinging between the grappling vampires. The towering flames now starting to engulf the church cast long shadows over the square, making lights dance across their sneering faces.

Hands, cold and clawed, reached for him from behind, so

József whirled around and squeezed another shot. The bullet caught the nearest vampire in the chest. Within seconds, a mass of gray was already spreading from the point of impact and peeling away into flakes of dust. The vampire opened his mouth to scream. His body crumbled into nothing before any sound could come out. The others flinched back at the sight.

That's two bullets. He had four left, and there were at least twice as many vampires closing in on him.

A loud, guttural howl sounded from the edge of the square, and then another answered it, higher and clearer, rising above the crackling of burning wood. The werewolves had joined in the fray.

*

Ileana closed her eyes rather than watch József go. She'd already lost him twice. Tonight would be the third time, and the pieces of her heart were too small to break again. She wouldn't turn back from the fight though. Ravenswatch had earned her ire. If she died here, tonight, she'd make sure to take as many of them with her as she could.

"What should I do?" Tamara whispered, pulling her back to the present.

Ileana turned to look at her sister. Part of her still couldn't believe that the gaunt, cadaverous face in front of her belonged to the plump little girl from her memories. There was a whole life lived between the two, a life Ileana knew nothing about. She hoped there would be time for them to reminisce together at the end of this.

Giving Tamara's hand a quick squeeze, she said, "I need you to hide." She jerked her thumb toward the darkened windows of the café. "Get in there and wait. I'll come get you when it's safe."

That might have been the last time they'd ever speak, Ileana thought, watching her go. *What a shitty way to say goodbye.*

Minutes dragged by. József had reached the gathered vampires, but he hadn't given the signal yet. A gust of wind cut through her jacket and shirt, still heavy with rainwater, making her shiver. She shucked off her jacket, then folded it neatly and removed her belt and boots too. The rest of her clothes wouldn't constrain her as much when she turned. She drew the knife from her boot, and tossed it up, end over end, catching it by the tip, then the handle, then the tip again. That made her think of Luca. What would he say if he saw her now?

"Any second now," Liviu whispered.

Another minute, and the shot finally came. There was no time to fear or doubt after that. With fire crackling up the church walls and the square erupting into chaos, she threw herself headfirst into the fray, beckoning the wolf.

The beast answered with fervor. It didn't just fill her; it became her, twisting her flesh, her bones, her mind. Her strides never faltered even as her body changed and her breaths turned to snarls. Clawed hands spread wide, ready to pierce and maim. Her eyes narrowed on the mass of vampires in front of her. She was the hunter. They were soon to be her prey.

She fell upon the nearest vampire. Their face was a blur as her fangs sank into their flesh, and the taste of blood immediately filled her senses: raw, coppery, alive. This one was well fed. That meal would be their last.

Ileana dropped the carcass and leapt to her next target, a pale man wielding a rapier with a golden pommel. She feinted hard to the left, then as the vampire thrust the rapier there to meet her, she banked right and thrust her arm to the side. Her claws raked across his throat, nearly separating his head from his shoulders. She bounded away as the vampire's body crumpled behind her.

A third vampire ran up to meet her, a woman brandishing a dagger that was already bloody. Ileana grabbed her wrist and twisted, then went for her throat before the dagger had even hit the ground. Ileana felt the snap of her fangs closing over empty air reverberate through her skull as the vampire dissolved into a cloud of mist.

A sudden weight closed around her temples, pushing inward. Growling, she shook her head to clear it, but the pressure persisted. Her limbs seized, then moved without her mind having anything to do with it. Before her body was made to turn around, she glimpsed Iancu standing in front of the church, his silhouette haloed by the flames. He was looking straight at her.

Chapter Nineteen

Ashes and Dust

József barely had the time to be grateful for the assist before another vampire was on him. Hissing, she bared her long, yellowed fangs, and tried to gouge out his eyes with her claws. He answered her with a bullet. *That's three.*

Somewhere beyond his immediate field of vision, he heard snarling and the crunching of bones breaking. It sounded like the werewolves were holding their own. He was starting to see that the vampires' decades and centuries didn't matter all that much. He'd only been turned for a day, but he'd been hunting for the last thirty years. If anything, undeath had given him the edge he'd lacked in life. Now, he was ready to pay the fuckers back in kind.

József roared a challenge and charged the nearest vampire, who had a younger face that might have been pretty if it weren't twisted into a mask of pure hatred. The vampire's body turned to mist before József's tackle could land, and he hit the ground hard enough to feel his brain rattle in his skull. The lack of pain took another second to register. By then, he had another vampire on top of him, trying to drive a dagger through his throat. He caught her wrist and moved the barrel of the revolver to her sternum, then pulled the trigger. *Four.*

He turned his head to the side as the vampire's ashes rained down on him. With his eyes half closed, the writhing mass of bodies in the square looked like a *danse macabre* on the cobblestones. He rolled over and stood, spitting to rid himself of the taste of dead vampire on his lips.

Something large moved behind him. Instinct made him duck just as obsidian claws, sharp and wicked, whistled through the air above his head. He whirled around and found himself staring into a snarling muzzle and a pair of eyes that burned like embers.

"Leana?" he blurted out.

It really was her; he recognized what was left of her shirt.

Ileana lowered her head slightly, but she didn't move. Her arm jerked forward, then froze for a second before resuming its arc. József had enough sense left in him to draw back before she could eviscerate him. She shook her head and let out a growl that sounded almost pleading, then her eyes narrowed on him again. Something wasn't right. Whatever it was, she was fighting it, else he would've likely been torn to shreds by now.

"It's okay," he said, lowering his revolver. "It's just me."

Ileana blinked, then snarled and lunged at him again. He barely had time to jump to the side. She kept swiping at him, or lunging, or trying to body him to the ground. He dodged every time. Had he been human, he would have been out of breath by now.

She, on the other hand, was starting to get sluggish. He wondered if the fatigue came from trying to fight whatever had gotten ahold of her. Her movements were too erratic for them to be completely deliberate. Her breath came in long, ragged pants.

"Leana," József tried again. "You gotta fight this. Let me help you."

There was a flicker of—something. Recognition, maybe.

"That's right, kid." He dredged up a smile and held out his hand, palm forward. "Come back to me."

Without warning, she swiped at him again, and he wasn't fast enough this time. Her claws raked across his arm.

József stumbled back. He may have been beyond feeling pain, but his limbs still needed nerves and tendons to work.

Ileana whined, a long, lugubrious sound. Then, suddenly, her head snapped up. Her body jerked toward the burning church, an aborted half step before she froze again.

The church.

A second too late, József understood.

With a plaintive whine, she turned back on him, her maw open wide. His right arm was too mangled to be of any use. The revolver hung heavy in his other hand, but he'd let himself be torn limb from limb before he shot his Leana. If this was how he'd finally go, he could only hope she'd forgive herself when her senses returned.

Ileana charged at him. Before she could reach him, another werewolf tackled her. This one was slightly larger and had dappled white fur. József's revolver snapped up before he recognized Crin. He also remembered, absurdly, that the only reason he'd ever found Ileana in the woods all those years ago had been his hunt for a white werewolf. Turns out they were real, after all.

He looked around, taking in the state of the square. There was no sign of Arghira or Madeleine. A small pile of fiends lay dead and dismembered some twenty paces away and, among them, a larger form lay prone and still, its dark blood seeping through the cracks between the cobblestones. It could have been Liviu. More vampires were gliding toward him as he began to stir.

József looked from him back to where Crin and Ileana were snarling and biting at each other, neither of them gaining the upper hand. The flames lit the night with a hellish glow.

He looked to the church.

Sure enough, the vampire who'd set the place ablaze with his magick was still there, basking in the glow of his handiwork. He hadn't even joined in the fray. As to what had happened to the poor souls inside the church, József could only hope there was a back door somewhere, one that the vampires didn't know about. He had two bullets left. If the stars aligned, that would be one too many.

József took aim. He'd always been a decent shot, even from a distance, but he had to shoot with his left hand, not his right. This time, he didn't hesitate; he fired as soon as the vampire was in his sights.

The revolver kicked. The shot went wide.

Cursing, he fired again. The second shot must have missed as well, because the fiend didn't topple. He looked directly at József and raised a hand in an almost lazy gesture.

A ribbon of flame arched from his open palm and zigzagged toward József. He threw himself to the side, and the flames missed him by a breath. He felt their heat singe the tips of his hair. When he straightened, he spotted a curved sword lying at his feet, next to the severed hand of its former owner. He dropped the empty revolver and picked up the sword, looking around wildly. Another flame roared past him, smaller than the first. Fiends, too, were closing in on him once again.

"Come on, you bastards!" he bellowed, raising his sword in front of him. "I haven't got all day!"

Before he could charge the nearest vampire, a piercing howl answered his challenge from the other end of the square. Dark, enormous shapes charged into the fray, tearing and biting their way through the undead host.

József stared around, bewildered. The battle was turning faster than he could keep track. Here, a vampire fell to the fangs and claws of a werewolf with reddish fur and blazing eyes. There, several of the shaggy behemoths fell upon a group of fledglings whose blood still ran thin and red. It occurred to him, belatedly, that he was just as much of a vampire as the rest of them. He turned and ran, clutching the sword for all the good it would do him against an entire pack.

He'd nearly made it to the relative safety of a nearby alley when a werewolf cut him off. His momentary panic melded away into something much harder to pin down, something warm and shapeless and not a little heavy.

Crin, bleeding from half a dozen wounds that were healing even as he watched, gave his uninjured arm the gentlest of nudges, then moved to put himself between József and the square. He bared his fangs in a snarl towards the rest of his kin. The message was clear: "This one's with me."

József shifted the sword to his right hand and brought up his left to gently touch the werewolf's flank. Crin's fur, where it wasn't bloody and matted with grime, was almost soft under his touch. It wasn't at all how he'd imagined it.

"Thanks, kid," József whispered, aware of a sting at the corners of his eyes he'd never own up to if anyone asked.

*

As the battle turned, Liviu was all too glad to lose himself in the carnage. He thought he recognized one or two of the newly arrived werewolves, but their presence was a smear of fangs and fur on the edges of his awareness. His injuries were like the scratch of fabric or the constricting grasp of city shoes—a pain in the ass, but not nearly enough to stop him.

Whatever vampires were still left were fleeing the square in all directions. Some turned to mist, others tried to run away on foot. The few who'd stuck around to fight were quickly learning the error of their ways. As he pursued a fleeing fiend toward the far edge of the square, Liviu ran past a small clump of humans who lay on the cobblestones behind the church, either dead or dying. He paid them no mind.

The vampire must have been a fledgling, too new or too weak to have learned how to use the mist trick. Still, they were light on their feet. Between his injuries at Bear Lake and the earlier run-in with not one but several vampires, Liviu was slower than usual. His prey weaved in and out of the shadows, turning corners at the drop of a pin. He almost lost them in the maze of streets and alleys beyond the square, but the trail of their scent was easier to follow now that the soot and smoke from the burning church were behind them.

Liviu jumped on top of a car, then to the flat roof of a newspaper kiosk. From there, he vaulted to the roof of the nearest house, ran across as his feet kicked up terracotta shingles, and jumped back down on the other side. He cut the vampire off as they emerged from behind the house he'd just jumped. His claws felled them before they'd even seen him.

He sat back on his haunches, contemplating the kill. The sting of dozens of scrapes and cuts healing all at once washed over him, but he'd gotten off lightly, all in all. He was far enough from the square that the sounds of fighting had faded into the night, or maybe it was already over. The pack's arrival was too convenient for it to be a coincidence. Evdochia must have had a hand in that too.

He had enough time to think, *All's well—*

A shadow darker than the night moved at the other end of the alley.

Liviu immediately knew him by his scent: a dark, oppressive musk, always with an undercurrent of blood, even when there was no fight it could have come from. He remembered a different time, when that scent had pressed all around him, mingling with that of his own blood as he lay dying. Dread twisted in his gut.

Darius stopped and sniffed the air, his amber eyes burning in the gloom. After a moment, he stalked forward, his muscles rippling underneath his fur. He started to shift as he walked, limbs shortening, black fur receding. By the time he came to a stop in front of Liviu, Darius was entirely human, though he still stood almost as tall as him.

I could end him now. Darius's human flesh was no match for a werewolf's fangs and claws. *I could even make it quick.*

Darius, for his part, didn't seem worried about that prospect. He glared up at Liviu and said, in his typical brash manner, "Evdochia didn't say you'd be here. You're lucky you ran."

Liviu couldn't do much more than snarl.

Darius ignored it. "Where is Evdochia? They owe me and my pack for what we just did."

Despite his better judgment, Liviu started to shift back as well. He needed his words for this. He also knew he couldn't go for the bastard's throat without his whole pack jumping him later.

Darius waited in sullen silence, his arms loosely crossed. His biceps bulged from under the tatters of whatever he'd worn before he'd shifted.

Liviu took another moment to crack his neck, making a show of it. "Evdochia's not here," he said. "You can take this up with them back in Deva."

Darius scoffed and widened his stance slightly. The scowl remained. "Not that it concerns you in any way, but Evdochia said my brother was here too. They said they'd take me to him if I dealt with their enemies." With a dark chuckle, he tossed his head toward the square. "I think I've earned my answer."

Watch over Crin, Evdochia had told Liviu before they'd left Gorun. He felt the blood drain from his limbs, leaving him cold and numb.

"You're quiet," Darius observed, his voice dropping low. "Makes a man wonder what's got you so tongue-tied all of a sudden."

Liviu's heart pounded. When he'd last seen him, Crin was still fighting in the square. If Darius had traveled here with his whole pack, someone might have already recognized him. Worse, Liviu couldn't exactly head back to the square to warn Crin without leading this asshole right back to him.

Darius was suddenly in his space, his eyes radiating malice. "I asked you a question, mutt."

"I don't know where your brother is," Liviu said, glaring back. "Town isn't that big. Go look."

He'd expected the punch. What he hadn't been ready for was how fast the fucker still was. He flung himself back and barely dodged it, but the second swing was quicker than he'd anticipated. He blocked with both arms, which saved his face, at least. He felt a bone cracking and couldn't hold back a yell, retreating a few more steps.

Darius sauntered toward him, slowly. From the cant of his

head and the way his lips parted to reveal teeth that were just a little too sharp, the bastard was enjoying this.

"I'm not scared of you, asshole," Liviu spat. "You're strong, so fucking what? End of the day, you're just a sadistic piece of—"

Darius lurched forward, but Liviu was prepared for it this time. He dropped low so the swing went over his head, then uncoiled himself and struck. He'd been aiming for the bastard's nose. He got him in the throat instead.

Darius fell to his knees, one hand flying up to his throat as a strangled wheeze burst from his lips. The blow would have been enough to drop a human, maybe even kill them. A werewolf would recover in a matter of minutes, if that.

Liviu didn't stick around to find out exactly how long. He ran.

The streets were unfamiliar, but any direction was fine as long as he was moving away from the square. He called on his beast blood as he sprinted away, shifting forms without ever breaking stride. Pain enveloped his injured arm once again as the bones stretched and rearranged themselves.

He turned onto a wider street, hoping he'd at least give himself more room to maneuver if Darius came for him again. It was deathly quiet now that the bells had stopped, which made it all the easier to hear the footsteps thundering above him. He looked up just in time to see Darius, fully shifted, leap from a roof ahead of him and land in the middle of the street.

Darius tried to growl, but it came out as a ragged whimper, a sound Liviu had never imagined he'd hear the other werewolf make. That didn't stop him from charging forward, his maw wide open and ready to tear.

A second before their bodies collided, Liviu jumped to the side. Darius barreled past him, carried by his momentum. Liviu whirled around, then exploded forward, sinking his own fangs into

Darius's flank. The bite wasn't deep enough to cripple, but the taste of blood sent a surge of triumph through him all the same. *I can do this. I can make him bleed.*

They circled each other, snarling and growling. Liviu pressed his advantage, feinting to the right, then darting left. His claws raked Darius's arm rather than his torso, which he'd been aiming for, but Darius was still too slow to turn. Liviu didn't waste the opportunity. He leapt and bit into the crook of Darius's neck as his claws found purchase in his fur. There was no spurt of arterial blood, which meant the bite was either too shallow or in the wrong place. He clamped down harder, feeling the strain in his jaws, and held on as Darius shook himself, trying to dislodge him.

With a frustrated whine, another sound Liviu had never thought he'd ever hear from him, Darius flung himself backward into the nearest car. Liviu felt the metal dig into his spine and let out a yelp. His hold loosened, but not enough to save him when Darius smashed him between the car and three hundred kilos of muscle and malice a second time. He was vaguely aware that the car's alarm was blaring. He let go and shimmied away before Darius could actually break his spine, then he half ran, half crawled until he put a fair distance between them.

Okay, dipshit, he thought, a little desperately. *Now what?*

Rather than go for him again, Darius paused, his head snapping up as he inhaled deeply. Another werewolf howled from somewhere nearby.

Liviu's heart sank. He'd barely held his own against Darius. Two against one, he wouldn't stand a chance.

Darius, however, was still sniffing the air, his body rippling with what might have been uncertainty. Liviu heard darting footsteps behind him—soft, almost like a cat's—and a familiar scent enveloped him. As a silver form materialized in his peripheral vision, he didn't know whether to thank the gods or curse them. If there was anyone up there, or down there—he didn't judge—he bet they were having a good laugh at his expense right about now.

Crin kept moving toward his brother, intent written in every taut curve of his body. When Liviu started forward as well, he turned his head enough to snap his teeth at him. Liviu backed off slightly, baring his own teeth on instinct. *What the hell are you doing?*

Darius was favoring his injured side and his back was slightly hunched, but he still towered over his younger brother. He let out a low, rumbling growl that chilled Liviu to the core. This wasn't just a spat between brothers anymore. This was a predator going in for the kill.

Crin answered with a growl of his own, and Liviu finally understood: he wanted to do this alone. Words were beyond his reach, else he would have had some choice ones for Crin right now. He'd be sure to give him an earful tomorrow if they both lived that long. For now, ignoring the pain gnawing at him from too many wounds to count, he moved forward until he was standing next to Crin. *I know this asshole,* he would have said if he could. *I fought him before. Neither of us can take him alone.*

Darius charged.

Crin and Liviu leapt apart, each jumping to a different side as though they'd planned it. Darius went for his brother, leaving his back wide open, and Liviu pounced. He clawed at Darius's back, his arms, his thighs, wherever he could reach. When Darius turned to fend him off, Crin came at him from the other side, biting his leg, then leaping out of the way when Darius swiped at him. At the same time, Liviu renewed his assault. He fought with his fangs, his claws, his *hatred.* The taste of Darius's blood was sweeter than white meat, more intoxicating than red wine.

Darius held his own for a while, but he, too, was injured, and there was only one of him. His movements slowed as wounds blossomed all over his body. His bites had little and less strength.

He went down.

Liviu blinked away the bloodlust. The pains from his many, many wounds had morphed into a throbbing veil of agony that shrouded him from head to toe. He looked up from the aftermath and saw Crin looking at him too. There was barely any silver left in his fur now; the rest was blood black.

Catching his eye, Crin jerked his head toward the mountains looming above Gorun. He let out a questioning whine.

Liviu nodded as he caught his meaning. They couldn't afford to stick around long enough to be found. Neither of them was in any shape to fight again. He mirrored Crin's earlier gesture. *Let's go.*

Crin bounded forward toward the mountains, dragging his right leg a little. With one last glance toward Darius's still form, Liviu followed. He'd thought he'd be ecstatic to finally give the bastard what he deserved, but there was no joy in this, just the grim satisfaction that he and Crin would live to see another day.

Together, they disappeared into the night.

Chapter Twenty

Shadow of the Four

Ileana drifted in and out of a troubled sleep. When she finally came out of the haze, she felt like her entire body had been put through the wringer. She didn't move just yet, shielding her face from the harsh glare of the sun with an arm that was so tender it hurt whenever she took a deeper breath. Her wounds were knitting together, which made her flesh throb and her skin itch. Her clothes stuck to her skin under the heavy covers.

After a long time, she opened her eyes.

In an instant, she was wide awake and struggling to throw off the covers so she could stand. The room was unfamiliar, but it resembled Nightshade Lodge closely enough that she almost expected to feel the burn of a silver cuff around her ankle.

Standing so quickly turned out to be a mistake when her vision darkened and her knees threatened to give out. She grabbed onto the headboard, waiting for it to pass, then lowered herself carefully onto the bed. Pain writhed behind her eyes, from sunlight as well as the sudden wave of vertigo. There was a gaping hole in her mind where last night's memories should have been.

She found a pitcher of water on the nightstand, along with a tin cup like the ones they gave soldiers in the king's army. She sat back down and sniffed at the clear liquid to make sure it was clean, then poured herself a cupful and drank, her gaze roaming around the room. The ceiling was open beam. In the middle of it, a wrought iron chandelier dangled at the end of a thick, metal chain. The walls were bare brick and held several hunting trophies, all of them antlers from deer and chamois. Aside from the bed, there was a battered leather armchair with a matching footrest, an open bookshelf, and a wooden console by the window. The room smelled like it was lived in, but Ileana didn't sense anyone familiar.

She was wearing a nightgown, which she had no memory of putting on. A fresh change of clothes lay folded on the armchair. No shoes though. Clearly, she was among allies, if not friends. They wouldn't have bothered otherwise.

She gathered her legs under her and got up again. When that didn't trigger a repeat of the earlier episode, she walked to the window.

The vista that greeted her was unfamiliar at first. The window was high above ground—second or third story, she guessed. Forested hills stretched out into the distance. She saw clumps of green here and there, but the branches were mostly bare, which told her this was high enough in the mountains that spring hadn't fully arrived yet. Steep, rocky peaks rose not too far off, their tips covered in snow. One of them was oddly shaped, its top flat and uneven rather than pointed like the others. That had to be Mount Retezat, which meant that Deva would be nearby as well.

Another wave of nausea made her lean against the windowsill until it passed. She wanted to remember. She was almost grateful she couldn't.

When the sickness passed, she changed into the clothes that had been left for her—a black cotton shirt and a pair of jeans that were a little loose around the waist—then smoothed down her hair. It was damp, she found, and her skin was moist and warm to the touch.

She crossed the room and tried the door handle, finding it unlocked. Nothing moved on the other side, at least nothing she could hear. Quietly, she pushed through.

When she emerged into the hallway, a young girl with a mane of brown, shaggy hair stood up quickly, snapping the book she'd been reading shut. Her face was round and pockmarked, but her black eyes were just as weathered and world-weary as Ileana felt.

The girl tossed her book on the carpet and turned on her heel. "Come with," she said.

Ileana glanced at the book in passing. The cover had a stylized drawing of two moons in black and gold, a waning crescent and a waxing gibbous. She followed the girl down the hallway and up a flight of wooden stairs. The walls were adorned with more trophies: boars' heads, birds of prey, even a stuffed mountain cat and a pair of enormous bear paws. Her bare footsteps kicked up small puffs of dust. She saw no one else, but their scents lingered. The air had been disturbed by the passing of several people not that long ago; she didn't recognize anyone. Thinking of others made her think of Tam and József and the rest of her pack. She couldn't smell them any more than she could bring herself to hope that they were here too.

Eventually, the girl stopped in front of another door and knocked three times. The raps were quick and confident.

From inside the room, a gruff voice called, "Come in."

"Go," the girl told Ileana.

Ileana took a breath to steady herself, turned the handle, and entered.

This room had a simple bed, a fireplace with two armchairs beside it, and no books. A table by the far wall held the remains of a meal, small game by the looks of it. Like elsewhere in the manor, trophies hung on the walls here too. Among them, she spotted a bleached skull with needle-sharp teeth.

A burly man sat in one of the armchairs by the fireplace, taking up most of it. His height was apparent even seated. A long gash, barely healed, stretched across his face, from the right temple to the opposite corner of his mouth. His eye had, miraculously, survived.

The man jerked his chin toward the other armchair. Ileana complied, watching him out of the corner of her eye as she settled down. Her body was still sore, and the leather-bound cushion was hard as a plank. Despite the heat radiating from the fireplace, she felt a chill raising gooseflesh along her skin. She'd met enough killers in her life to know she was sitting across from one.

Her host was the first to speak. "We found you in the square, unconscious. You looked like you'd been fighting. Question is, on whose side?"

Ileana's mind pieced together the rest of what he was asking. "Not the assholes who burned down the church," she said.

He measured her with an appraising stare. "You're one of Evdochia's, then?"

She couldn't tell what kind of answer he was looking for. This close, she could smell the blood on him, which meant he'd fought too. "Evdochia and I had a common goal," she said. "We parted ways once I had what I wanted, but the vampires attacked before I could leave."

Her breath almost caught on the words. *We. Before we could leave.*

The man shifted in his armchair, grunting as if the movement had pulled at wounds that weren't quite healed yet. "You had my brother's scent on you."

She frowned at him. "Your brother?"

"His name's Crin."

This was Darius, then. The man Liviu had wanted to kill. Her outward expression didn't change even as fresh sweat beaded on her brow.

"We traveled together from Deva," she said, keeping her voice light. "We didn't talk much."

"But you traveled together." His eyes glinted like he'd caught her in a lie.

"I wasn't looking to make friends," Ileana said, shifting so both her feet would touch the floor. "My deal was with Evdochia. No one else."

"What was the deal?"

"A family affair. Personal." He hadn't earned the rest of the story.

"Was there anyone else with him?"

Without hesitating, she answered, "Yeah."

After a moment, he nodded and crossed his arms, and she realized this had been a test. Her tension eased a little.

"So, you don't know where Crin or his companion might have gone," Darius said.

She shrugged with as much nonchalance as she dared. "Like I said, we didn't talk much. Your brother kept mostly to himself.

The other guy was a prick."

That wrung a grin out of him at last. "The other guy's name is Liviu. He's been a thorn in my side for years."

"I see," she said, keeping her tone politely disinterested.

He waited for a second or two, then started picking at a scab on the back of his hand. He didn't break eye contact though. "Where will you go now?"

Back to Gorun, Ileana didn't say. "North, I think. I don't like to stick around in one place for too long. You know how it is."

"Stay here."

She blinked at him, wondering if she'd misheard. "You don't even know me."

"You're one of us. Hunters don't know about this place, and we have strength in numbers if they find out. The roads won't be safe for a long time coming." The fingers picking at his scab stilled. "Stay."

He spoke with the casual authority of someone used to being listened to. She wondered what that meant for anyone who refused him. She also knew they'd brought her here with nothing, not even the clothes on her back.

There wasn't much of a choice, all told.

*

In a small cave in the mountains above Gorun, Liviu let his head fall back against the stone wall with a long exhale. He remembered climbing up here last night, but not much else after that. He'd been pretty beat up, even by his usual standards, and so he'd slipped into a deep, dreamless sleep while his body pulled itself back together. He'd awoken from it sore and ravenous and let Crin browbeat him into starting a fire while his companion went to hunt some food.

Two small rabbits now roasted on makeshift spits above the fire as the flames bit into the darkness, their sizzling meat dripping grease into the flames. The smell made Liviu's mouth water, but the nausea he'd woken up with made the prospect of dinner far less enticing. He was thankful for the warmth, at least. The air was freezing up here, and his human form, although more resilient than an actual human, hadn't been made to withstand exposure for very long. At least they'd had the presence of mind to grab some mismatched garments off a clothesline before they'd left Gorun.

From across the fire, Crin caught his eye and canted his head to one side, his eyebrows falling minutely in a frown. He'd been keeping his distance since last night. They hadn't talked much either. So far, Liviu was trying his damnedest not to think about what that meant.

Crin bent forward to turn the spits so the meat would cook evenly. He favored his right hand, cradling it close to his chest, even though it should have been healed by now. For a moment, he almost looked like he was going to say something, but then he sat back on his haunches, his hands fidgeting in his lap.

Liviu didn't pry. Something about the sudden distance between them felt sickeningly familiar. *Figures*, he couldn't help but think, turning his face away from the fire. Good things never lasted for long, not for him.

"Do you think he's dead?" Crin said suddenly, his voice stirring echoes in the small space.

Liviu's head snapped up. He didn't need to ask who "he" was, but he was in no mood to deal with the ghost of Darius tonight. "He was still breathing," he said with a small shrug. "Doubt he bled out before his pack found him."

"He raised me, you know. After the war." Crin's voice was

small, barely registering above the crackling of the flames. "And it wasn't all bad. I remember…" He closed his eyes. "I remember when being around him used to make me feel safe. I miss that sometimes."

"That don't make it right," Liviu said. "What he did to you."

"And what about what we did?" Crin drew a shaky breath. "Darius—my brother—is the only reason I lived after the war. And we almost, almost—"

"And what about me, huh?" Liviu drew himself up enough to glare at Crin over the fire, ignoring the aftershocks of the previous night. "He had no problem trying to kill me. Was that what you fucking wanted?"

As soon as he said the words, he wanted to take them back. Crin's eyes widened and, fuck, they were moist. He opened his mouth to speak, then closed it again.

Liviu fell back and closed his eyes. "You're the one who wanted to come along," he said, hating himself a little more with every word. "Doubt he'd take you back, even if you asked."

He heard shuffling, then footsteps and a small exhale as Crin sat next to him, keeping a solid distance between them. He peeked out of the corner of his eye and saw that Crin was hugging his knees and gazing into the fire. A tear rolled down the side of his face.

Liviu suddenly felt like the world's biggest asshole. His anger turned inward, tinged with a bitterness he knew all too well. He always did shit like this. Always ruined things.

"I don't want to go back," Crin whispered, "but I wish I could. Not to—not like he is now, just—like I remember him. Before."

"I get it," Liviu said, even though he didn't. He stuck a hand out and touched Crin's shoulder lightly. When Crin didn't flinch away, he rested his hand there, but he didn't try to pull him closer.

The hand felt heavy, as did all of him.

They stayed like that until the rabbits were done cooking, and then they ate quietly, the only sounds between them the crunching of cartilage and small bones. Liviu glanced at him every now and then, but Crin looked away every time, so he let him be.

Some time after their dinner had morphed into a small pile of bones and bits, Crin asked, "What happens now?"

Liviu startled himself awake. Torpor had snuck up on him again almost without noticing. He scratched the back of his head, wincing when his nails found crusty blood. "What do you want to happen?"

"I want," Crin said, and then he stopped, his lips parted slightly.

Gods, he's beautiful.

Quietly, Crin said, "I want to stay with you."

Liviu let out a long breath. Something was squeezing his heart, but it didn't hurt, whatever the fuck it was "'Course," he said, scoffing like that much was a given. "I'm the one who dragged you all the way out here, remember? I'm not gonna just—"

He grunted as Crin flung himself into his arms. The weight aggravated his still-healing wounds all over again, but he didn't care.

"We'll be fine," he whispered into Crin's hair as fresh sobs wracked his body. "Whatever happens. We'll be okay."

He desperately hoped so anyway.

There was no going back after last night, not for the two of them and not for the rest of their kind either. The roads would be swarming with hunters, but they had to leave Gorun while they still could. Deva was the safest place they could be—strength in numbers and all that—and, obviously, they couldn't go back there. Not as long as Darius was still around.

Tomorrow, Liviu told himself, wrapping his arms around Crin and pulling him impossibly closer. Tomorrow, they'd think about all that. For now, they were together, and they were alive. That had to be enough.

*

József's truck chugged along a thin strip of road toward the west. The sun was a small, incandescent ball ahead of him, dipping toward the horizon. Its light seeped bloody into the patchwork of clouds still covering the sky. The evening air was cold, and the old clunker needed several of its parts replaced, an oil change, and maybe some air for the tires, but they were making steady progress. He'd get to the repairs later, now that later was an option at all.

Rather than take the highway, József had turned to the old, pothole-ridden roads crisscrossing the Transylvanian plateau. Highways were busy, and he couldn't trust being around humans after the events of the previous night. Couldn't trust himself to be around humans either, truth be told.

The hunger was still there, waiting at the back of his mind whenever he went looking for it. It wasn't nearly as ravenous as it had been in those first few hours after he'd awoken, but he knew he'd have to feed again eventually. Otherwise, he would either shrivel up and become like the mindless husks he'd seen so often on his hunts, or he would lose himself to the bloodlust and kill until someone put a stake through his heart. Neither option was one he was willing to contemplate. True death wasn't in the cards either, at least for now.

The road meandered up and down, following the terrain. Every now and again, it passed through a village or a small town, its sleepy lights winking off the Amarok's battered hood. Unlike before, there was no need to stop for food or rest. The tank was still half full and would last for a while. Had he been alone, he would have been content to drive through the night and find somewhere to hole up come morning.

József glanced in the rearview mirror. Tamara was looking out the window, her chin resting in her open palm. She hadn't moved since the last time he'd checked on her, and that had been a while ago.

He didn't need any vampire mind reading to know what was gnawing at her. The fact that they'd both fled with their lives was nothing short of a miracle. They owed it all to Crin, who'd kept the other werewolves at bay long enough for them to get the hell out of there. Without him, József's innards would be decorating the Gorun town square. Probably hers too. He didn't know what had happened to any of the others.

"I'm tired," Tamara said suddenly. "I'd like to rest."

Vampires didn't need to sleep at night, but József didn't argue the point. He pulled up at the first motel they came across, threw the truck in park, and motioned for her to follow. He'd ditched his torn, blood-stained coat and turtleneck and now wore a gray hoodie he'd pulled from the go-bag he always kept in his truck. Tamara still wore her mismatched clothes from last night, faded camos and some kind of dress shoes, all of them a size too big. They'd have to find her new clothes later.

Later. His brain kept getting caught on the word.

This motel didn't look like it saw much business on the regular. There was nobody at reception, but an old black-and-white TV droned in a corner, and a plastic cup filled with coffee steamed behind the desk. József crossed his arms and waited, watching Tamara out of the corner of his eye. She looked like she didn't want to be here. Hell, she looked like she didn't want to *be.*

A short, pimply man eventually came from the back and plopped down behind the reception desk. He gave József and Tamara a disinterested glance, then slid a plastic clipboard across the desk with a form clipped to it. A ballpoint pen dangled from the clipboard at the end of a piece of twine. The man picked up his coffee and fished around for a remote, ignoring them completely.

József took the clipboard and skimmed the form. It asked for the usual information, name and contact details and intended stay. With the TV droning in the background, he picked up the pen and scribbled down "Gábor Szabó," the first name that came to mind. He still had a cassette with Gábor's last recordings in his truck somewhere, but this guy didn't look like he dabbled in Hungarian-American folk jazz.

Tamara touched his arm suddenly, then indicated the TV with a jerky nod. "Listen," she whispered. "They're talking about Gorun."

Frowning, József turned to look. The TV had a small screen and the contrast was shit, but he still recognized the square where they'd fought. The camera cut to the church, or what was left of it. It took another second for the words to start registering.

"*—whom frightened residents describe as magick-wielding vampires. Accounts vary as to how many, but one thing is clear: a supernatural attack of this magnitude has never happened in modern times. The king has gathered his ministers at Peleş Castle. So far, there has been no—*"

So, it was all out there now.

Nightwalkers had lived on the fringes of the human world for so long that a balance of sorts had emerged. Most humans were happy to pretend that the monsters in their fairy tales lived somewhere far, far away. Those who spotted one and wanted them gone knew how to put out the word, and sooner or later, a hunter would come and take care of the problem for some coin, a warm meal, and maybe a bed for the night. This wasn't a nosy midwife wanting a hag gone from her turf though. This was war.

"We should go," Tamara whispered, pulling at his sleeve again.

József looked up to see the receptionist gaping at them. The man's face was paler than the whitewashed wall behind him. His hand squeezed the TV remote so hard it was a wonder the plastic didn't splinter.

Magick-wielding vampires. József supposed they looked the part.

For a second, he envisioned vaulting over the reception desk, pinning the man to the wall, and tearing his throat open to get to the blood gurgling within. The thought filled him with a revulsion so deep he couldn't help scowling, which sent the pimply man into a shaking frenzy.

József put his arm around Tamara's shoulders and ushered her ahead of him, keeping an eye on the human until they were out of sight.

*

On the other side of the Carpathians, in a cave overlooking a nameless monastery, Evdochia passed the day in a torpor. While vampires didn't fall into a death slumber when the sun was up like some humans believed, they still became brittle, sluggish. The older the vampire, the weaker they were during the day. And Evdochia was very old.

Evdochia's father had ruled what was now southern Romania—known then as Wallachia, a kingdom of its own—more than six centuries ago. The monastery they'd come to visit was far to the north of the old voievod's domain, in what had once been the principate of Moldova. It was here their father had taken leave of the mortal world after a long and bloody reign.

That was what the nobles of the time told the rest of the world anyway. Evdochia witnessed a different story. Besieged by enemies on all sides, their father made a pact with a devil, offering his immortal soul in return for near-limitless power and eternal life. He then used that power to repel countless attacks on Wallachia's borders and lead incursions into enemy lands as well. He was a cruel but fair ruler, and the nation flourished under his reign.

The voievod's court, however, grew wary of both his power and his renown among the common folk, and conspired to depose him. They eventually succeeded. Rather than burn him or impale him, they sealed him in the crypts below this monastery, under heavy slabs of stone and powerful holy wards. Should the need arise, they reasoned, they could always unleash him upon the world once again.

Since then, Wallachia—and, later, Romania—had seen countless wars, each bloodier than the last. Its provinces had been unified, then divided, then brought back together. Kings and queens had come and gone, from Vladislav II to Ferdinand III, who ruled to this day. Throughout all of it, Evdochia's father had slumbered, guarded by stern stone peaks and a monastic order who had never allowed themselves to forget their charge.

Evdochia had journeyed here to make sure Vlad Ţepeş would stay that way.

At dusk, Evdochia stirred from their rest and stepped back into the world. Outside their temporary refuge, a light but steady rain covered everything in a thin film of water. They looked down to the monastery, raising a hand to shield their face from the droplets. The wooden buildings down below nestled against the rugged slope of a mountain peak, blending almost seamlessly into the rocky terrain. There were no roads wide enough for a car or a truck to make the ascent, so the monks still traveled like their forebears had, on horseback or on foot.

There was something else in the air, apart from the rain. Something *wrong*.

Evdochia spread their arms wide, and their corporeal form dissolved into thick, blood-red mist. They descended and re-formed in front of the gates, shaking their limbs to dispel the lingering numbness that came with the transformation. Yes, they sensed magick, but...it was faint, chaotic, like drifting shards rather than the focused blade of a warding spell. They raised their hand to touch the gates, expecting a warning sting, at least. Instead, they felt nothing but the smoothness of wood polished by the touch of countless hands. The gates swung open with a small push.

The courtyard was deserted, though signs of activity still lingered here and there. A horse was waiting near the gates, a bulging sack still tied to its saddle. An old radio warbled its tinny tunes from the deserted gatehouse, where a cup of tea had gone cold.

The vampire lord hesitated for a second, then stepped into the courtyard. When their foot touched the packed earth, a small tremor coursed up their leg, but the ground out here wasn't consecrated, so they felt no compulsion to turn and flee. They walked past the gatehouse, then the small, wooden church, giving its closed doors a curious glance. If there was anyone in there, they didn't come out to confront them.

Beyond the church was a dormitory, its windows darkened despite the early hour. Next to it, a short fence enclosed the gardens where the monks grew their vegetables. Someone had been spirited away while they were planting saplings. The trough was still there, as was the bundle of plants, their roots clawing at the damp air like small, spidery fingers. The earth nearby was disturbed by many different footprints, as though a scuffle had taken place.

Evdochia walked on. Rain pattered softly on leaves and rooftops. Gravel crunched under their feet.

At the back of the monastery grounds was the entrance to the crypts, a dark square cut directly into the stone. When Evdochia stepped through, they felt the remains of another, more powerful, ward feebly trying to push them back. What was left of it shattered as soon as they reached out with a mind-magick tendril of their own. When they looked down, they saw a bloodied boot discarded not far from the entrance, though there was no sign of its owner anywhere.

Down and down they went, past carved wooden ossuaries and bleached skulls whose empty sockets bore silent witness to their passing. The torches along the walls were extinguished, but Evdochia's eyes were attuned to the darkness. Although fear was something they'd left behind along with the other trappings of the mortal world, their cold heart stirred with something akin to unease. Death was at home here, in more ways than one.

At the bottom of the passage, a heavy metal door barred the way. Words of power had been carved directly into its surface in concentric circles, then painted over with holy blood. To someone attuned to the ebbs and flows of magick, they should have been glowing, a testament to their potency, but the old Latin letters were dark.

Evdochia took a long, unneeded breath, and then, for the first time in centuries, released it on a whispered prayer. Then, they stepped into the chamber that had served as both crypt and sanctuary to their father since the end of his third reign in 1476 A.D.

Here, they finally found the monks.

A pile of exsanguinated bodies lay at the far end of the

sanctuary, where three stone steps led to a raised dais holding a sarcophagus. The heavy slab that had sealed the tomb had been sculpted to resemble the face of the ruler whose immortal body it concealed. It was cleaved clean down the middle, one half resting against the sarcophagus, the other shattered against the far wall.

With slow, halting steps, Evdochia walked past the dead monks and up the steps.

The sarcophagus was empty. On the wall beyond, someone had written three words in flaking red blood:

HE IS RISEN

Glossary

MICLOVAN, Commissioner

Fictional police detective (*comisar*) from a popular series of films by Romanian actor and director Sergiu Nicolaescu. Known for his clever crime-solving and quick wit. Somewhat like America's Lieutenant Columbo.

MIHAI VITEAZUL

lit. Mihai the Brave (1593-1601), the first Romanian *voievod* to unify all three Romanian principates (Wallachia, Moldova and Transylvania) under his rule.

POLITEHNICA TIMIȘOARA

lit. Timișoara Polytechnic, name of a local football team in Timișoara, Timiș County. The university with the same name is one of the best technical universities in the country. Worth noting that the sport Romanians call "football" is generally known as "soccer" in North America.

ȘTEFAN CEL MARE

lit. Ștefan the Great (1457-1504), Moldovan *voievod*, sainted by the Romanian Orthodox Church in 1992.

ȚUICĂ

Romanian moonshine, strong and flavorful, typically home-made.

VLAD ȚEPEȘ

lit. Vlad the Impaler, monicker given to Vlad III (1456-1462), *voievod* of Wallachia who served as the inspiration for Bram Stoker's *Dracula*. Known for being a cruel but just ruler.

VOIEVOD

Title given to Medieval rulers of the Romanian Principates (Moldova, Wallachia, and Transylvania).

Acknowledgements

To my grandmother, Domnica Ciolna, who first introduced me to Romanian folktales and let me raid her many bookshelves every summer. You taught me the joy of storytelling; this book exists because of you. I miss you every day.

To my partner, Andrei, who's been putting up with my bullshit for a whopping *thirteen years* and counting, across four countries and two continents.

To my editors at NineStar Press, thank you for believing in this book and for letting me stay true to my heritage and to the story I wanted to tell.

To my social media manager, Candice Kapp at Kapp Co Digital, thank you for helping me get the word out there. I continue to be in awe of your talent and your speedy work.

To Christie Golden, whose *Warcraft* novels first inspired me to try to write fantasy, and whose grace and resilience have kept inspiring me to be a better person ever since, thank you.

And, finally, to my wonderful LGBTQ+ community:

You are all beautiful, you matter, and I love each and every one of you.

About the Author

Keira North is a queer, nonbinary, Romanian author living in Montreal. They use storytelling as a medium to explore their heritage and identity and strive to be the change they want to see in the (literary) world. When they're not writing, they like to make music, play video games, and read copious amounts of fanfiction and indie works.

Email
author@keiranorth.com

Website
www.keiranorth.com

Instagram
@keiranorthwrites

Bluesky
keiranorth.bsky.social

YouTube
@KeiraNorth

TikTok
@keiranorthwrites

Connect with NineStar Press

Website: NineStarPress.com

Facebook: NineStarPress

X: @ninestarpress

Instagram: NineStarPress

BlueSky: NineStarPress

Threads: @ninestarpress